BLOOD WITCH DRAGON

Dragon Fae Book I

K. Panikian

K. Panikian

The characters and events portrayed in this book are fictitious. Any similarity to real persons, living or dead, is coincidental and not intended by the author.

Cover design by: Etheric Designs
Editor: Jaime Watson, Baker Street Revisions

For my first. Lost but never forgotten.

CONTENTS

PART I

CHAPTER 1

The playground gleamed silver and cold in the foggy fall morning. I glared at the empty parking lot and at the dew-slicked slide, and I sighed.

"You get five minutes, monkeys. We will *not* be late today."

Dara's predictable, "Yes, Mama!" piped from the backseat as I met Finn's solemn dark eyes in the rearview mirror. My glare communicated my unhappiness to my son, and his wide-eyed look reflected his feelings of injured innocence. I snorted.

"I'm serious," I threatened. "I'm sorry I got home late last night, but no more guilt trips. We don't have time for this today."

Dara bolted from the car before I could gripe any more, and I reached to grab Finn's sleeve before he could do the same. "Five minutes," I hissed as he slipped my grasp and followed his sister.

"Chill, Willa," he shouted over his shoulder. *Gah, I hate it when he calls me by my name.* I resisted the urge to correct him though, knowing it would only prompt him to do it the rest of the day.

Exhaling another impatient sigh, I leaned back in my seat and reached for my purse. I'd allotted an extra ten minutes for the playground stop, but I could *not* miss my morning meeting.

My breath hitched as I watched my beautiful kids stampede through the empty playground like a pair of marauding pirates. They tore up the rope climbing obstacle, their light-up sneakers flashing in the early morning fog. I could almost imagine knives clenched in their teeth and swords at their hips as they stormed the fort. I grinned. Although only seven, they were fierce and determined conquerors. Witness exhibit A—me sitting alone in the playground parking lot while the clock ticked down the seconds to their elementary school start time.

Finn yelled as he leaped from one rope to the next, his blond curls bouncing, while Dara's focused, determined reaching took her higher and higher. Pressing my lips together, I resisted the urge to call her down.

Glancing at my phone, I scrolled through my emails. My boss liked to work late hours, and I'd learned years ago to ignore the annoyance I felt waking up to a full inbox. Still, I flinched when my phone buzzed with another meeting alert.

"Time to go," I called and continued to swipe through notifications, my stress mounting. I couldn't stay late again, but I didn't know how to avoid it. *Finn will kill me. Or demand I install an ice cream machine in his bedroom . . .*

After another long moment, I looked up to call again, only to see an empty playground. I gasped and scrambled for the door handle. Stumbling from the car, I frantically searched my surroundings. The rope obstacle stood empty, swaying in the slight breeze.

"Mama!" Dara called from behind me. I spun in place and spotted her and her brother kneeling at the far corner of the fenced lot. My frozen lungs thawed and, swallowing hard, I trotted toward them. My pounding heart found its rhythm again so that by the time I reached them, I managed an easy smile.

"What'd you find?" I asked as I crouched, smoothing my skirt over my knees. My heels sank slightly into the thick grass.

I expected to see a bug or worm, and my eyes widened as I took in the perfectly round ring of toadstools encircling my kids. In the brightening sunlight, each mushroom cap shone with a pale peach-pink glow, their furling white edges like lacy underskirts.

"It's a fairy ring, Mom," Finn said. "Like Grand-Mère told us about."

"Oh, neat," I said, racking my brain for what I knew about fairies. "Um, remind me again, what's a fairy ring?"

Dara rolled her eyes, a recently learned skill. "It's where the fairies dance, Mama."

"Grand-Mère told us a story about it," Finn added. "If you go inside one on Halloween, you get sucked into the land of the fairies."

I warily eyed the toadstools at my feet before

I stood. "Okay, well, Halloween is in a few nights, so let's not tempt any fairies to snatch you. Time to head to school anyway."

Dara tucked her hand in mine and leaned her head against my arm as we walked back to the car. "Grand-Mère said not to go inside of a fairy ring at all, even if it's not Halloween," she whispered. "I told Finn to stay out, but he didn't listen."

I stroked my fingers through her soft blond curls, my heart aching at her serious tone. "It's only a story, sweet pea. There's no such thing as fairies. Grand-Mère just likes to scare you."

Dara nodded, and I resolved to have a serious talk with Iris the next time I dropped the kids off for a sleepover—no more child-snatching tales. Finn liked her spooky stories, but Dara didn't, though she'd never admit it in front of her brother. And seven was too young for fairy tales that ended the way Iris liked to tell them.

I suppressed a shiver, remembering a story she'd told me when the kids were babies about a woman who trapped a man into marrying her before she turned into a snake and ate him. At the time, I'd thought she was warning me off her son, and I was supposed to see myself as the creepy snake wife. But in the years I'd gotten to know her since, I realized that she merely adored frightening me as a matter of principle, and she didn't want Paul, her son and the father of my children, anywhere near her.

After I checked seatbelts and found a song on

my phone that both Finn and Dara could agree on, I stole one last glance at the ring of mushrooms. I swallowed as I tightened my own seatbelt. The fog had lifted over the rest of the playground, but the corner was still gloomy and dark and, as I blinked, I glimpsed a faint green pulsing light.

Shaking my head, I turned up the music and backed out of my spot. "Okay," I called as we sped off, "what are the rules for today?"

"Tell the truth," Finn started.

"Try your best," Dara added.

"And no fighting!" They finished together in a gleeful chorus.

I crossed my fingers as I dropped them at school and watched their backpacks vanish into the sea of kids. I had a lot on my plate, and I didn't need any more parent-teacher phone calls this week. Finn and Dara were awesome kids, but they were high-spirited and very prone to mischief. Their teacher and I had spent several hours over the course of many conversations talking about how to redirect that energy into schoolwork. The results varied.

I made it to work and, with grim focus, started on the tasks overflowing my inbox. If I didn't clear out a handful before lunch, I'd have to log back in after the kids fell asleep, and tonight was my Ethics class, which I couldn't miss again, or I'd fail the semester.

During the day, I worked as a paralegal at a small law practice next to the courthouse, and in the evening, I took classes online, slowly but patiently earning my law degree.

Paul wasn't in the picture. He'd never been in the picture. I met him one night when I was a freshman in college waiting tables at a small bar near campus. Handsome and suntanned, his blond hair gleaming under the blue and green neon bar lights, Paul had caught my eye immediately and kept it all night. He was my type back then—lean and cocky and a bit of a jerk.

Feeling impulsive and daring, I'd taken him home with me. In the morning, he disappeared, and I hadn't missed him. The sex was good, but I knew I'd only been a warm body to him. I didn't even think he knew my name—he called me *cher* all night.

When the pregnancy test showed positive a few weeks later, I'd cursed my off-brand birth control pills and made a halfhearted attempt to find him, but I only had his first name and I'd never seen him around campus until the night we met. I finished the year, my stomach only starting to show the shape of the twins growing within me and, as the summer turned hot, I made plans to give them up for adoption.

At my office desk, I rubbed my sternum, remembering the ache of that agonizing decision. But there had been no one in my life to help me—no family who could share the load of taking care of twins, or to help with daycare costs so I could finish school or work to support them. I was so young and, despite the frantic love I felt for the quivering, fluttering denizens of my body, I'd known they would have a better life with a real family who could love them *and* take care of them.

At thirty weeks along, I was working my shift at the bar, my stomach poking out like I swallowed a basketball, when Paul walked in the door. He took one look at me and left again. I'd called good riddance to his retreating back, but it was a heavy blow. A part of me hoped that somehow I'd see him again and perhaps he'd be willing and able to help. When the door shut on that hope, I gave into my despair and raced out the rear door of the bar, desperate for air.

In the dark parking lot, I tripped and my placenta ruptured. I nearly hemorrhaged to death before the twins were born later that night.

I shuddered, touching my now-flat stomach, recalling the agonizing pain and the blood—*so much blood*—and the teeny, tiny hands of my babies as they lay in their NICU bassinets.

The day after their birth, however, Iris had knocked on my hospital room door, and that was that. Paul's mother took me and the twins home with her once they were healthy enough to leave the NICU, and nothing more was said about adoption. She watched the kids while I crammed every class I could into my schedule and finished college early, and she found me my job at the law firm. I'd never forget her kindness, despite her being motivated solely by her desire to help her grandchildren—not me.

Iris was complicated, but I owed her, and I

didn't forget my debts.

My phone chimed with a text from the kids' second grade teacher, warning me I owed permission slips for the upcoming zoo trip. Sighing, I made a reminder note and logged back into the case file.

A headache pounded at my temples while I worked. Although I tried to ignore it at first, the pain grew in intensity, spreading from my forehead to the back of my neck. *Don't get sick, don't get sick,* I chanted to myself as I sipped water and gently rubbed my fingertips against the lymph nodes at my neck. Finally, shivering, I swallowed a couple of Advil and dove back into my work. After a bit, the headache eased, then disappeared.

The hours before lunch passed in a blur as I spent them tracking my time in six-minute increments, making my way through my lists, and nodding absentmindedly at coworkers who stopped by my desk to chat. I was not a chatterer, and most moved on after a minute or two.

Most except for Jeremy. My boss had hired Jeremy a couple of months ago, fresh out of law school, and he was a pain in my ass. He couldn't seem to decide whether he wanted to flirt with me or give me all his grunt work and order me around, and the combined approach made him a smarmy mess.

"Did you have a chance to look up those statutes?" he asked, posing against my cubicle wall with studied coolness.

Pausing my typing, I leaned back in my chair and cocked an eyebrow, mimicking his crossed arms. "The statutes you emailed me about twenty minutes ago?"

"Yeah. I need them for my hearing this afternoon."

"Sorry, Jeremy, but no I haven't. And I'll be honest, I don't think I'm going to get to them in time to help you."

"Willa, do I need to talk to Mr. Sharon about your priorities?"

I let my smirk turn a little feral. "Jeremy, I've billed six hours already today. I can't bill for your grunt work. So I think if you want to bring this to Mr. Sharon, you should. But he's going to tell you to ask one of the legal secretaries for help and to stop wasting my time."

His grin wilting, Jeremy straightened his shoulders. "You look tired, Willa. You should think about taking a spa day." He spun and stalked away.

Rolling my eyes at his retreating back, I returned to my documents. "Who has time for a spa day?" I muttered. "I have . . . I have stuff; really important stuff." My brow furrowed. *Stuff? I swear I had something else at the tip of my tongue.*

The light in the office dimmed as the afternoon made way for evening, and my headache returned. Resolutely ignoring the pain, I finished my memo, and when Mr. Sharon stopped by my desk to remind me about my Ethics class, it was with total shock that I looked at the time on my phone.

"It's seven? Oh no!" Jumping to my feet, I updated him on my to-do list, grabbed my jacket, and shut off my computer. Calling out apologies, I jogged for the door.

Ten minutes later, I pulled into the garage of my small rental house and made it to my laptop and the couch—just in time to log into class. Tugging a blanket over my cold feet, I tried to focus on the professor while ignoring my nagging hunger and the vague feeling I'd forgotten something. I crossed my fingers I didn't have a paper due for the course or an upcoming quiz.

The professor's voice droned, and my handwriting sprawled sloppier and sloppier across my notebook.

When I logged off two hours later, I felt like all the energy had leaked from my body, leaving behind only a husk swirling with boring legal terms and gnawing hunger. The headache continued to poke at me, and as I threw off my blanket, I diagnosed that I wasn't getting sick; I was merely thirsty and tired. I ate a quick dinner, pounded some water, and thought about getting ready for bed. But something scraped at my mind as I slipped the dishes onto the drying rack by the sink. Something was missing. I checked my purse by the front door and saw my phone and wallet where they should be. No missed calls or texts. Plugging my phone in, I frowned. Was I expecting a call from someone?

My rental house sat on a quiet street and, as I switched off the lights and double-checked the locks, I tried to ignore the feeling of disquiet continuing to pinch at me. I eyed Shane's dark house; my closest neighbor wasn't home. I had a tiny crush on him and tended to pay attention to his comings-and-goings, so I knew he was home most nights. The soft blue glow of his TV usually reflected into my kitchen when I went to bed. But not tonight. Tonight, my house was black as pitch around me as I walked the silent hall to my bedroom.

I settled under my quilt, and the headache fog, which had retreated after class, returned with a vengeance. The rusty blades of a thousand knives dug into my skull. I was certain I'd forgotten something, but the pain prevented me from getting out of bed again. And I was determined to avoid checking my phone to see if I had new work emails to answer.

I pulled the blankets over my head. I needed a solid night's sleep and more Advil; I'd feel normal in the morning.

SMOKE filled my lungs and my breath stuttered, waking me. I tried to suck in air, but heat clawed at my throat. Coughing and gasping, I sat up in bed. Thick smoke shrouded the bedroom and warmth singed my skin as I stared around me with wide eyes. Flames licked at the bedsheets closest to the window, and I shrieked, scrambling away and falling to the floor.

An alarm screamed, making me flinch. I leaped to my feet. My body felt hot, my skin singeing with heat and dryness as my headache threatened to splinter my skull. I tried to inhale but choked and fell once more to my knees.

Scrambling for my bedroom door, I crawled down the hall and into the living room. There, with the smoke only a wispy current, I jumped up and bolted for the front door.

The night air offered quick cold relief, and the burning sensation eased from my lungs. A deeper alarm blared, and my squinting eyes rounded at the approaching fire truck, its lights and sirens filling the darkness with sound and fury. My bare toes curled in the wet grass, and I panted with confusion and fear, the chilly air painting the skin not covered by my sleepshirt with goosebumps.

Thick figures in fluorescent gear stormed my house as I sank to my knees in the dark front yard, shivering. Something screamed at me; something stronger than my fear and the smoke still clouding my lungs. *Something!*

A loud pop exploded in my ears and a burst of wetness blossomed over my face. Swiping at my nose, my hand came away crimson with blood. I stared, nonplussed, at the red liquid until, with a crash of clarity, my body exploded into action.

"Dara! Finn!" I shrieked, darting for my front door. "My kids! My kids are inside!"

Two firefighters, their shapes hazy in the gloom as they moved methodically through my open garage, burst into motion at my words and sprinted into the flames. The smoke billowed above the house in a growing maelstrom of dark swirling opacity and sparks. I ran to the front door, trying to force my way past the heavy bodies in my way.

"Finn! Dara!" I screamed. I couldn't squeeze between the figures. I ran for the garage again, but it was too full of smoke, and I couldn't see farther than the bumper of my old Toyota. A heavy arm pulled me away from the car, and I struggled, still trying to get inside. "My kids," I groaned, writhing. "Please."

"Willa!" a familiar voice barked. The large hands gripping my shoulders shook me hard. "Willa, stop!"

I froze for a moment, then tilted my head back to see who gripped me so tightly. Blazing blue eyes met mine through the thick sheen of goggles.

"S-Shane?" I stuttered. I'd forgotten he was a firefighter. My hope rallied—Shane would find Finn and Dara! He knew them; he would get them out. "Shane! The kids! The kids are inside!" I struggled in his arms again, but they banded tighter around me.

"What kids, Willa? You're not making sense. Were you babysitting someone?"

I gaped at him. "What kids?" I cried. "My kids! The twins! Shane, my kids are inside the burning house! Let me go!"

Shaking his head, Shane dragged me onto the front lawn. I resisted, digging my heels into the grass to stop him, but he was too strong. He waved at a slim woman in a blue jumpsuit and thrust me at her. "She's raving. Can you get her some oxygen, maybe?"

A tremendous crash echoed behind me, and I spun away, darting toward the house as a massive hole appeared in the roof. Stunned, I stopped, and Shane grabbed me again. With disbelief, I watched the flames leap through the gaping space. I was too late. My heart stopped beating for a long silent moment. Agony ripped through me, digging sharp, grating claws into my soul. My kids. My loves. I'd lost them. With a scream, I fell to the grass, and I screamed until I fell into another coughing fit. I slumped over, watching the smoke swirl with dull, hopeless eyes.

In the abrupt silence following my cry, Shane's radio crackled to life. Two dark figures stepped from the garage, their bulky tanks and masks forming menacing shadows. "We went through the whole house, and it's empty. There are no signs of any kids."

"What?" I said weakly, looking up at Shane's grave face.

He knelt, his heavy equipment creaking and clicking. "Is there someone I can call for you, Willa?"

"No signs of kids? The kids aren't in the house?"

He shook his head, and I slumped over again, my relief incandescent. I sucked in a breath before my throat closed on a knot of tears. Wrapping my arms around my ribs, I sobbed—deep, heaving gasps choked with tears and snot. *They're not in there. They're not in there . . .* The words played in my mind like a song while I rocked back and forth on the cold lawn and flames turned my home to ash.

Shane's bulky gloved hand fell on my shoulder. "Willa, I'm going to ask you to get into the ambulance. You have blood on your face. I think maybe you hit your head really hard. You're not making sense."

This time, I let him pull me up and lead me to the EMT. Over the radio, I vaguely registered a voice confirming city records showed no children living at the address. I blinked. My brain couldn't process the words over the searing relief still coursing through me.

I felt boneless and compliant. The kids weren't in the house. I didn't know where they were, but they weren't dead, which was all that mattered. Maybe I had hit my head—maybe they were sleeping at Iris's house, and I'd somehow forgotten.

I'd figure it out. I would find them. I let the ambulance take me away.

CHAPTER 2

Wiggling my soot-blackened feet, I absently noted the way my pale purple hospital gown clashed with my dark pink toenails. The nurse made a clucking noise with her tongue and finished wiping the blood from my face. She lifted my chin to the light.

"No bruise. No swelling. I don't know where this blood came from."

I shrugged.

"When did the headache start?" she asked, continuing to study my face.

"This morning at work. Look, thanks for helping me clean up, but I really need to use the phone. I didn't hit my head. I don't have amnesia. I just need to find my kids."

Her firm countenance softened, and she waved to the phone at my bedside. "You've got a few minutes before the doctor gets here. I'll give you some privacy." She stepped out of my room, gently shutting the door behind her, and I leaned across the bed to grab the phone.

I didn't have my purse or my cell; presumably they were still in my house, either burned to a crisp or waterlogged, but I knew Iris's number by heart. As the line rang, I wiggled my toes again.

On the ambulance ride to the hospital, while I breathed slowly through the oxygen mask, I'd racked my brain to figure out where Finn and Dara could be, but I'd come up empty except for Iris. And I still had no idea why Shane had sounded so confused when I asked about them.

We'd been neighbors since I moved out of Iris's house when the kids were two, and although we weren't close friends—I had no time for friends—I'd picked up his mail a few times, and he'd shoveled my driveway once or twice. He must have noticed my kids. They left bikes in my yard, chased balls through his, and had gone trick-or-treating at his house.

My brow furrowed as the line continued to ring. Maybe *he* had amnesia.

I kicked my feet harder and the bed squeaked under me. After another minute, I hung up the phone and pushed away my rapidly rising unease. I needed to get to Iris's house, but I had no car—unless mine had survived the fire, which didn't seem likely—and no money for a cab.

Making a quick decision, I hopped from the bed and shuffled to my smoke-covered sleepshirt. Pulling it on over the hospital gown—I'd need the warmth—I crept to the door. With no one in sight down the white corridor, I darted across the hall to the bathroom.

I felt bad sneaking out of the hospital. The

staff was only trying to help me. But nothing was wrong with my brain, and panic fluttered in my chest over my inability to reach Iris. She never left her house. The relief I felt earlier when I realized Finn and Dara hadn't been home was gone, replaced with desperation.

From the bathroom, I could see the front entrance to the hospital and, through the glass, lights gleaming in the parking lot. A bored-looking man reclined at the help desk, and a few people sat in the waiting room chairs. Straightening my shoulders, I pushed out of the restroom and strode down the hall, my bare feet slapping against the cold tiles. The man at the desk turned to watch me approach. I sent him a small smile. He nodded politely before his eyes fell to my dirty toes. I walked faster.

"Ma'am," he called out as I passed him. "Ma'am, did you forget—"

I shoved open the door and took off in a jog, my breath fogging in the chilly air. Glancing back, I saw the man sitting forward, his head cocked as he spoke into the phone. I picked up my pace, wincing as my feet scraped against the sidewalk.

The hospital sat only a couple of miles from my office, and I hurried in that direction as quickly as I could. Goosebumps rose on my skin and my pulse thudded as I alternated between a jog and a brisk walk, keeping out of the lights when possible. In my ragged attire and bare feet, I stood out like a crazy person escaping an asylum—which didn't feel too far from the truth.

When I reached the familiar stone steps of my office building, I exhaled a last shaky breath and darted to the landing, punching the code to open the door. With a sigh of relief, I slipped inside the warmth of the entryway.

My body needed a break, and I wanted to sit for a moment to soak up the heat, but my brain and heart urged me to move faster, faster, faster until I found answers. At my desk, I dialed Iris's number again, my fingers shaking. Listening to the phone ring, I fumbled in the bottom desk drawer for my fleece jacket and spare sneakers.

"Too bad I don't have extra pants tucked anywhere," I grumbled to myself, resisting the urge to check the nearby offices for any other clothes.

Iris's line rang again without answer. I grabbed the twenty-dollar bill from my makeup case and hung up. After calling a cab company, I went back to the front hall to wait.

The minutes I stood in the warm entryway waiting for my cab passed interminably. Rocking back and forth in my sneakers, I inhaled the smoky smell still emanating from my shirt and wondered what was going on at my house—had the firefighters put out the fire? Was Shane sifting the debris, finding children's belongings and feeling stupid for doubting me?

Headlights broke the gloom of the street. I jogged down the stairs and into the brightly colored car, reciting Iris's address as I settled in my seat.

The cab driver's dark hair glinted under the streetlights, and soft, melodic music filled the warm space. Despite my anxiety, my eyes grew heavy and I pinched my thigh to stay awake. My mouth and throat were achingly dry, and I concentrated on that discomfort, willing the cab to go faster. The hospital gown rasped against my skin, scratchy and stiff.

A few minutes later, we stopped at the familiar white house, only a few miles from my own. I paid the driver and slipped out of the cab.

Outside in the cold, I faltered. Iris's windows reflected the black sky; the night around me was still and silent. The porch steps popped and snapped softly under my sneakers as I climbed, and the loud gong of the doorbell made me jump.

I waited, my stomach quivering. No one came. I rang again. It was the middle of the night, but eventually Iris would hear me, or my kids would hear and wake her. I alternated pressing the button with pounding on the door, my palm smacking the wood with an echoing thud.

After a few minutes, I jumped off the porch and ran to the other side of the house. Ignoring the creepy, empty feel of the yard and the rustling of dry leaves along the fence line, I banged on the back door, my blood pulsing with the beat my hand drummed on the wood.

I stopped and forced myself to be still. Holding my breath, I waited. No sound at all came from inside the house.

Desperate, I reached for the doorknob and let

out a squeak when it turned under my hand. The door creaked open and I stepped into the kitchen, swiftly closing the door behind me. Relying on my memory of the layout of the kitchen, I moved through the dark room until I reached the hall light on the far side. I flipped it and waited another long moment, listening once more. Greeted by the echoing silence, I jogged up the stairs.

I went straight for the room the twins shared when they slept over and pushed the door open, a smile already lighting my face. I would wake them up and hug them so hard . . .

But the room was empty. The bunk bed held no small, sleeping bodies and the air smelled stale.

My knees buckled. I sank to the floor, my head thudding against the wall. "No!" I wailed.

The house groaned, echoing my overwhelming despair. I'd been relying on the conviction that Dara and Finn were here, safe in these beds, to get me through the past couple of hours. But they weren't here. Hopelessness sucked me down into its murky depths.

My imagination ran amok with visions of their mangled, bloody bodies. They'd been kidnapped, stolen away from my house while I slept. I couldn't bear . . . *Stop it!*

I pushed back against the door and straightened my spine. Surging to my feet, I marched down the hall to Iris's bedroom. My muffled footsteps echoed hollowly on the worn carpet. "Iris! Wake up! Iris!"

I hesitated at her bedroom door. I'd never set foot inside her room before. On her good days, Iris tolerated me, but mostly she disliked me, and my insides wilted at the idea of storming into her room and waking her. But I had to.

Knocking loudly, I pushed open the door and called again, "Iris! Please wake up. The children are missing."

Nothing stirred in the room. I fumbled for the switch, my fingers bloodless and cold, and gasped when the pale light dimly illuminated the disordered space. The empty, unmade bed mocked me, the center stained with a reddish-brown splotch in the shape of a huddled body. I swayed, my vision blurring, but I had no time for new confusion.

Shaking off my dizziness, I rushed forward and stopped at the edge of the wood frame, the toes of my sneakers thudding painfully against a post. The sharp tang of iron surfaced, overpowering the scent of rosewater—Iris's perfume—and the lingering smell of smoke on my clothes.

"Iris?" I turned to look around the room again. The bureau drawers were open and overflowed with wrinkled clothes. The closet doors gaped; inside, hangers and dresses lay crumpled on the floor, hat boxes and photographs dumped on top. I whirled and ran from the room, thundering down the stairs and into the living room at the front of the house. The couch lay on its side, cushions slashed open to reveal their fluffy white entrails.

"Iris!" I shouted into the deafening silence. No

answer.

I gripped my hair. *What do I do?* My thoughts whirled in circles. I needed to find Finn and Dara. *Where else could they be?* My instincts said the blood in Iris's room and her empty house had something to do with their disappearance, but how?

Pacing, I muttered, "Do I call the police? And say what, 'I forgot about my kids all day, then remembered them when my house caught fire, and when I went to their grandmother's house to find them, I found traces of blood but no kids?'"

I hissed. "Right. And how are those handcuffs fitting you, Ms. Overholt? Not too tight? Good, because obviously you went on a murder spree and tried to cover everything up with amnesia and a house fire."

Pressing my lips together, I put my hands on my hips. I needed to get back to my house, find my phone, if it still existed in unmelted form, and call around the neighborhood. The kids had friends who lived nearby—maybe Finn and Dara had snuck away to their houses. I laughed hollowly. I was a bad mother, prioritizing my work and school over them. And now they were gone. It would be just like them to try to teach me a lesson—although this was a little diabolical, even for my terror twins. Maybe they'd slipped out to the backyard to look at the stars and the fire had scared them into hiding somewhere.

I couldn't spare a thought for the bloodstain in Iris's room or the fact she was missing too. Iris was tough—she could take care of herself.

Stepping out the back door, I shut it behind me and started jogging. I didn't have enough cash for another cab ride, and my house wasn't far. While I ran, I plotted and ignored my tired, aching muscles.

ALTHOUGH I expected it, the sight of my burned, blackened home stopped me so abruptly, I staggered and nearly fell. Smoke saturated the air in my neighborhood with its thick campfire scent, and yellow tape circled the cones lining my driveway—as if the still-smoking husk weren't enough to keep people away. As if the roof weren't a gaping mouth of exposed beams and scorched shingles. As if the lovely pale blue siding weren't stained gray and brown from water and soot.

Stepping carefully over the tape, I walked into the open garage and followed the short hall to my living room. The couch wasn't too badly damaged, though I knew I'd never get the smoky smell out of the cushions. There, behind the small console table, my purse lay on its side, my phone on the floor beside it.

I snatched everything up, slipped the purse across my body, and padded down the hall toward my bedroom, the floor creaking ominously beneath my sneakers. That was where I found a scene of utter destruction. My bed was gone, a jumbled pile of blackened wood and melted mattress coils in its place. The walls sagged, bubbled, and warped, falling away from the studs in some places and burned to a crisp in others.

Swallowing hard, I backed away. I hit the door to Finn's room and spun around, my heart in my throat. I *knew* he wasn't inside, but incandescent hope swirled through me as I shoved the door open. Instead of a small boy's bedroom, the room was a dark, empty space—no bed covered with dinosaur sheets stood against the wall, no bureau littered with clay figurines and soccer trophies beneath the window, and no baseball lamp lit the space when my fingers flicked the light switch.

I darted across the hall into Dara's room, and there I sucked back my scream with a harsh wheeze. My headache returned with raging force, and wetness dripped from my nose again. Swiping away the blood, I leaned my head against my daughter's pale-yellow wall and studied the sterile space. Empty, like the holes in my memory. No sign of her remained. No sign of either of them.

"What's happening?" I whispered into the abyss of my silent, broken house.

The doorbell rang—a deep discordant tone, like a dying, bleating animal—and I muffled a gasp.

CHAPTER 3

Shane stood on my front porch, the splintered fixture above casting weak light over the dried blood that filled the lines on the lower half of his face. I cracked my door, and he shoved an envelope at me. Shocked by his appearance, I ignored it. His thin-lipped mouth was grim and, as I stared, another small trickle of blood dripped from his nose.

"Willa, I have something to tell you."

"Shane! Are you okay?"

Making a sharp cutting motion with his hand, he pushed the envelope at me again. "Focus, Willa." His voice broke. "You need to read this now."

Eyes wide, I grabbed the envelope and backed up.

Shane looked down at his empty hand and curled his fingers into a fist, then followed me inside.

The envelope smelled of roses. I inhaled deeply and ripped it open, my nose warning me about who'd sent the message.

"Willa," I read aloud, "if you are reading this, then I am dead." I swallowed hard, my pulse galloping in my throat. Shane shifted on his feet, but

I didn't look up. "Paul has taken the children, and you must get them back. He can have no purpose other than a desire for power, and no child should pay that price. I have tried to shield them, but I have failed, and now you must steal them away. Trust Shane, he is my *guerrier*, and he knows some of the old ways. I'm sorry."

I stopped reading, my stomach fluttering. The letter fell from my fingers and drifted to the ground. "What"—I sucked in a deep breath "—the hell is this?"

Avoiding my eyes, Shane crossed his arms. "I've been working for Iris for a long time. When the twins were born, she assigned me to be their guardian. I've been watching over them."

A scoff erupted from my throat, and we both jumped at the loud sound. "Their guardian?"

"It's complicated."

"Un-complicate it," I ordered.

Shane sat on the blackened floor of my hall and leaned his head against the wall with a sigh. "I'm a half-blood fae. Iris found me a long time ago and taught me what she knew. I owe her my life—if she hadn't helped me, the blood hunters would have grabbed me long ago."

"Blood hunters?"

Shane shrugged. "The witches. The Slaugh. They search for the half-bloods, and when they find them, they eat their power or drag them to the Green Lands and force them to serve the High Fae."

I blinked slowly, listening but not processing.

His tone sharp and his chin jutting with impatience, Shane continued. “Your children have been taken by the Slaugh. It’s likely their father sold them to a High Fae to gain more magical power.”

His words finally broke through the fog. “What?” I cried. “What are you even saying? I don’t understand half of the words coming out of your mouth. Paul sold the twins? *Sold them*?”

“Your children are part-fae, and the rulers of the fairy lands have stolen them away from you,” Shane said, enunciating each syllable.

“I don’t understand,” I mumbled again. My knees buckled and I dropped to the floor, leaning against the wall opposite him. “You’re talking about fairy tales. There’s no such thing as magic or fae.”

“For most people, that’s true,” Shane acknowledged. “But for those of us with fae blood, no matter how remote in our ancestry, the threat is real. We can be taken to the Green Lands and, once there, we can be enslaved.”

“But I don’t have any fairy blood. I’m from California.”

“Fae blood,” Shane corrected. “And no, you don’t. But your children carry the blood of their father and of Iris, who was once a High Fae until she was stripped of her magic and cast out.”

I shivered. Looking down at my dirty fingers, I rubbed them together. “Iris is truly dead?”

Shane nodded. “I don’t know how. But the guise protecting your home is gone.”

“Guise?”

"The, um, shield? The illusion?"

"Iris was shielding my home? My children? From the Slaugh?" I pronounced the word carefully, imitating Shane so it sounded like a cross between *slow* and *slaw*. My heart thudded in my chest, and I tried to make sense of it all. "I thought you said she was stripped of her magic?"

"She retained a little in the very essence of herself. She feared Paul's quest for power and knew he would sacrifice the children if he could. She used her blood to bind the secret of the kids. But with her death, the binding is broken."

"Paul's quest for power?" I repeated. I hadn't seen Paul since the night at the bar when I fell and nearly died giving birth to the twins. He'd never tried to meet the kids, and Iris never talked about him. I only vaguely remembered what he looked like. I knew the kids got their curly blond hair from him, because mine was stick-straight and dark brown.

"Paul's the reason Iris was exiled. She took the blame for his murder of a female fae. He was trying to gain power with blood magic. As a half-fae himself, he would have been killed for his transgression. When Iris, a High Fae, took the blame, she was only exiled."

"Murder?" Bile filled my mouth. I'd figured out Paul wasn't a nice guy, but a murderer? The father of my children had killed a woman and let his mother take the blame? My stomach lurched sickeningly.

Shane shook his head, scowling. "Away from

the Green Lands, Iris hoped Paul would weaken and assimilate to the humans, but instead he found secret ways to return, while Iris was the one who weakened."

Clenching my fists in my lap, I swallowed harshly. "I can't believe this. My kids are missing. Their grandmother's house has been ransacked. And you're sitting in front of me spouting off about fairies and magic and slavery and death. A couple of hours ago, you denied you even *knew* I had children. You've done something to them, and I'm going to call the police." I stood up.

I closed my eyes against the sudden green light flooding the hallway, and when I opened them again, Shane was gone. In his place, atop a pile of shredded clothes, sat a huge blunt-nosed boar regarding me with weary rust-red eyes. Its coarse brownish-gray coat was topped with a tall mane of darker brown stretching down its back in a stripe, and two sharp tusks curved up from its snout.

The blood left my brain in a rush. I'd never seen a pig that big or fierce looking.

"Don't scream," the boar muttered in Shane's voice.

I bit back a screech.

Another pulse of green light and Shane was back. Only now he was nude.

I stared, too shocked to look away. The muscles of his shoulders and chest rippled with sinewy strength. *Sheesh, who knew my neighbor was a hottie?* Wait, what?

I regrouped, embarrassed at my reaction. *Not the time to think lusty thoughts about the crazy man,* I reminded myself. I opened the closet door at my back, groped blindly, and tossed an old winter coat at him.

Panting slightly, Shane let his head fall against the wall and draped the coat over his lap. "That's about the extent of my power. I can shift to a boar and maintain it for a bit, then I'm spent. I can cast a short-term glamour to change my appearance, and I can ward my house against the fae. Not much use to you, but Iris couldn't risk anyone stronger near the kids."

"You did magic," I whispered.

"I am magic," Shane whispered back. "And so are Finn and Dara. With Iris dead, their blood will have called to the Slaugh and to Paul. We can't be sure who took them, though Iris's letter says Paul. They may be working together for Mab." He rose to his feet and grimaced, his face pinched with exhaustion. "They had power though, whoever it was—enough power to alter our memories, and likely the memories of everyone in town who knew the kids."

His gaze narrowing, he bent his head. "How did *you* remember them? I only broke the spell when Iris's letter showed up on my doorstep. And it wasn't easy. It felt like my brain exploded."

I turned, keeping my gaze averted from the taut muscles of Shane's abdomen. "I had a headache." I remembered the sharp pain and rubbed my forehead. "All day. During the fire, I was so scared and I thought of the children. I got a bloody nose."

Shane nodded, swiping at the dried blood on his face. "Interesting."

My reeling mind stuttered with exhaustion, and I swayed on my feet. Shane gestured toward the front door. "Come to my place. We'll sleep, then in the morning, we'll plan."

"I can't sleep," I protested, even as I followed him through the broken door. "I have to find the children." I staggered when I considered the monumental task before me. "How do I find them? I don't even know where to begin. We can't call the police, right? How do we track them?" My frustrated exhale puffed into the chilly air in a cloud of vapor.

Shane's hand on my back gently steered me through the cold, damp grass. "If I can get to the Green Lands, I can follow them. I have their blood scent, and my tracking abilities should be stronger there. Along with my boar powers."

"You'll help me? Even though Iris is dead?" I asked, my eyes searching his face.

"I've sworn to guard them, and I will. But you can't come with me."

I dug in my heels, stopping our momentum, and crossed my arms. Glaring toward the hazy pale shape of his face in the dark, I said, "I'm coming. I'm their mother."

"You have no fae blood in you. You can't pass into the Green Lands."

Bristling at his dismissive tone, I opened

my mouth to retort, but a memory struck like a lightning bolt. "The fairy ring! There's a fairy ring at the playground, and it's almost Halloween."

His jaw clenched and he cocked his head. "What do you know about fairy rings?"

"Nothing! But Finn and Dara found it this morning. Yesterday morning? And they told me what Iris said the rings can do."

"Did they touch the ring?"

"Finn went inside it, then Dara too."

"Damn," Shane said, pulling me along at a faster clip. "That's what started it. The wildfae must have sensed them and come to investigate."

"The wildfae killed Iris?"

Shane nodded. "Probably. They wouldn't have seen the kids until the blood ward broke, but they would've sensed Iris and gone to her for answers when they crossed the Veil."

"But we can use the ring to go after them, right?"

"I don't need to use a fairy ring," Shane said as we slipped into his dark house. "That's not where my problems lie with accessing the Green Lands."

"What are your problems?"

"Well . . ." Shane pointed to his index finger as he pushed me toward the couch and paced in front of the unlit fireplace. "First, I've never been before, so I have no idea how it will affect me. I'm a half-blood, but the Green Lands will alter my magic, and I don't know in what way." He held up a second finger. "Second, I don't know where anyone or anything is.

I don't have a map, just my tracking abilities. Third, I'm going to stand out like a sore thumb. Iris taught me a little about the fae, but I've never seen the Slaugh before, or a troll, or a wraith, or any other wildfae. I may be ill-equipped for this." He said the last in a low voice and dropped the three fingers he'd been holding up. Straightening his shoulders, he looked at me, his gaze fierce and determined. "But it's my duty, and I'll get them back. I swear it."

Eyeing him, I resisted the urge to groan. I had no faith in his abilities, not even with his power to shift into a scary-looking animal. It didn't sound like he was any more prepared than I was to go to the Green Lands and find Finn and Dara. He was a firefighter—a normal, boring man who sometimes waved at me when he checked his mail. And I was a paralegal. The urge to weep was strong—I was so frustrated with the new information circling my brain and too tired to process it all.

"I'm going to make some tea," Shane said, his tone gentle, "and we can talk more about why you need to stay here."

Recrossing my arms, I watched him step into the kitchen. I wouldn't let him leave me behind. My kids needed *me*, their mother. And if I had to beat up a troll to find them, I would. Leaning my head against the soft cushion behind me, I examined the ceiling as my thoughts churned.

I needed to suspend my disbelief at the nonsensical, ridiculous explanations and trust Shane knew what he was talking about. I couldn't deny I'd seen him do magic. And I couldn't deny the truth of my altered memory, my vanished kids, and their missing and presumed dead grandmother.

Oh, Iris. Tears threatened when I thought of her dying alone, trying to shield her grandchildren from her son. *Why didn't you tell me?*

Shane seemed like a solid guy, and although I wasn't used to relying on anyone other than Iris, maybe I could trust him. The way he'd tried to keep me safe during the fire, despite his altered memory, was reassuring. He wouldn't go alone, though—no way would I let him leave me here.

I blinked slowly. Had the fire at my house been related to the kidnapping? Had the wildfae, the witches, or Paul tried to kill me so I couldn't chase the kids? That made little sense. I sank lower into the cushions, my heavy eyelids drooping. It wasn't an efficient way to murder someone, and they'd already taken the kids by that point. And if not for the fire, I might not have broken the memory spell. I shuddered and a hard knot formed in my throat.

The soft clinking sounds from the kitchen, homey and normal, soothed me, along with the whiff of a sweet herbal scent. Chamomile? *How nice . . .*

My thoughts slowed further, and I closed my eyes. I'd rest for a minute, then drink my tea and plot with Shane. But surrounded by pleasant warmth and darkness, sleep claimed me without warning.

THE buzz of a vibrating phone woke me, and I

blinked slowly at the strange ceiling above my head.

I sat up and looked around. With a frown, I brushed the dark blanket from my legs. The dank odor of smoke filtered into my nose as I moved, and my memory flooded back. I still wore my filthy sleepshirt from the night before.

"Shane?" I called, tripping over my sneakers and stumbling into the kitchen. A note sat on the counter in a spot of sunshine, right next to a house key. I raced forward, my heart stuttering in my chest.

Willa, I've gone after the kids. Stay here. Don't do anything stupid. I'll bring them home.

Crumpling the note, my hands shook. "You jerk," I muttered. I whirled and jogged down the hall, flinging open doors and shouting Shane's name. He wasn't there, of course.

In his bedroom, I found signs of his hasty departure—open drawers and a discarded backpack crumpled on the floor. Shane's scent filled the air. A citrus and pine aroma I'd never noticed before, but now immediately made me think of the tall, quiet man. The tall, quiet *jerk*, I corrected, fuming.

I raced to the living room and dug my phone from my purse. One missed call from my boss, but nothing else. I didn't think Shane had my cell phone number, or I his, but I scanned my contacts quickly, just in case. Nothing.

My fingers trembling, I searched my emails and texts for any communications with the kids' teachers, their doctors, their summer camps . . .

Nothing again. There was no electronic record of Finn or Dara—nothing to prove their existence. I wanted to collapse, but I couldn't. I had to keep moving. If I stopped, I would fall apart, and Finn and Dara *needed* me.

I called my office back and, while I waited on hold, I dug into Shane's drawers, finding sweatpants, a t-shirt, and socks. I didn't want to take his stuff, but I had to get out of my filthy, smoky clothes to go out into the world. So I straightened my spine, marched into the bathroom, and started the shower.

The bathroom was clean but spartan, with soft gray towels stacked on a shelf and a lovely watercolor of a mountain landscape on the wall. It was so vivid; I could almost hear the soft shhhing sound of the gently falling snow. The artist was supremely talented . . . I frowned when I recognized Shane's name scrawled across the corner of the canvas. *Hmm* . . .

As I waited for the water to warm, I updated my boss on my house fire and told him I needed to take a few days off. He was suitably horrified and told me to take the time I needed. I followed the call with a quick email to my law school adviser, asking her to please notify my professors that I would need makeup assignments for the next few classes.

In the shower, I ignored the squicky feeling in my stomach from being naked and vulnerable in a strange man's house. Shane's shampoo smelled like a lush forest, and I focused on that as I scrubbed the smoke from my hair with unsteady hands.

After I dressed, looping the waistband of the sweatpants over several times so the cuffs wouldn't trip me, I grabbed my fleece, sneakers, and purse, plus Shane's house key, and stepped outside into the bright morning light.

I caught sight of my landlord staring at my house, his arms crossed and chin jutting out. I ducked my head so he wouldn't see my face and turned sharply toward town. The playground stood a couple of miles from my neighborhood, and I ran the whole way there, yanking at the baggy pants when they threatened to trip me.

A couple of kids too little for school played near the swings when I made it to the small fenced lot. I ignored the moms sitting on the bench, chatting and drinking from thermoses. At the far side of the grassy area, I found the fairy ring and stared at it for a long moment as the warm sun beat down on my head. The dry brown and red leaves of the park's tall maples skittered across my sneakers in the slight breeze, and I shivered.

Did I believe Shane's story? Did I truly think if I returned here on Halloween, I could step through the ring and enter a fairy land? I wasn't sure, and I bit my lip as I considered my alternatives.

There were no alternatives. To the real world, my kids didn't exist. Everyone's memory of them had been erased. I couldn't involve the police or anyone else without getting locked up as a crazy lady who'd probably set her own house on fire.

And I couldn't bear to sit by and wait for

Shane—if he could even get the job done. Last night was the longest I'd ever spoken to him. He'd never given me reason to doubt him, but I didn't know him well enough to trust him. I couldn't quell the fear that he would cut and run if things got too hard. The number of people I could count on to love my kids enough to risk everything was now down to one—me.

My stomach twisted. *Oh, Iris.* She'd adored Finn and Dara, of that I had no doubt, and she'd supported me during an incredibly difficult time in my life. I hadn't loved her, but I appreciated her, and the kids would miss her desperately. If her son had played a part in her death, my heart hurt for her soul.

Turning away from the pale marbled mushrooms, I sat down in the grass and grabbed my phone from my purse. Starting with Wikipedia, I started reading about fairies.

When my neck developed a crick and my growling stomach grew too loud to ignore, I walked deeper into town and bought a sandwich, then went to search out a sporting goods store.

Inside, I filled my cart with new pants and shirts, underclothes, and thick socks, and I tried on hiking boots until I found a rugged pair that didn't pinch too badly. I grabbed kid clothes and boots too, shoving aside an image of Dara and Finn lost and cold, shivering . . . had they even worn their coats to school yesterday? I steeled myself—I *would* find them.

Consulting the list I'd written while eating my sandwich earlier, I snagged a sleeping bag and tent, along with matches and a water bottle. After dumping an entire carton of granola bars in my cart, I felt ready to check out, only to run back over to a sales bin for a large, scary-looking hunting knife.

I took a cab back to Shane's house and cut the tags off everything with a pair of scissors I found in the kitchen. Grabbing his extra pack from the bedroom, I stuffed it with all the things I'd need. The task filled me with determination, but sitting on the couch afterward, staring at the pack, I hesitated about what to do next.

My internet searches of Celtic lore and fairy tales told me I needed to wait until Halloween night to get through the fairy ring, but I was ready now. My heart would burst if I had to sit around another day. My breath came faster as I tried to control my panic, but it was no use. My kids were out there, scared and alone, and I was sitting on a couch . . . *waiting*. A scream of frustration and rage built in my throat.

Their whole lives, they'd had only me and their grandmother. Now their grandmother was dead, and I was all they had. I loved them so desperately—they were everything good and bright in my life, my reason for opening my eyes every morning, and I *missed* them. If I strained myself, I could almost feel Dara's small fingers curling in mine while Finn's piping voice demanded my attention. *My God, I can't bear it . . .*

A sharp pain exploded to life in my hands and I gasped, swallowing a scream as my fingers turned to fire in my lap.

My hands were on fire! I stood and shook them, but the orange and yellow nimbus climbed to encircle my arms as well. My panic grew to a fever pitch, my heart rate doubling. My hands grew even hotter.

I ran to the kitchen and hit the faucet with my elbow, dousing my hands under the cold spray. The flames extinguished, and I exhaled a shaky sob, closing my eyes as the cool water soothed the burn away.

Shivering, I kept my eyes closed for as long as I could, certain when I opened them, I'd see bloody blisters and shredded, scalded skin. After another long moment, I steeled my nerves and peeked into the sink. I gaped at what I saw.

My hands were fine—a little red maybe, but that could have been from the cold water. No sign of the fire remained. I shut off the water. Had I hallucinated the whole thing? The stress of the last twenty-four hours had broken me open and exposed my weaknesses—I was having a mental breakdown, exactly like my mother.

I squeezed my eyes shut once more, then cracked them to stare at my trembling fingers, white and thin. The heat built again, and my fingertips turned a deep cobalt blue. Before I could blink, pale-yellow flames erupted.

Sucking in a sharp breath, I watched the fire

dance. I felt the heat, but it didn't burn. The sparks danced up my arm, but my jacket didn't scorch. This fire was coming out of me. I could control it. With that conscious thought, the flames vanished. A sharp pain prickled in my chest but quickly eased.

Swallowing, I backed away from the sink and willed myself to settle. Every time my heartbeat accelerated, my hands heated, so I needed to *calm down*. I steadied my breathing and when it evened out, I examined my fingers again. They looked like they always did, slim with unpolished nails and veins flowing with normal human blood.

But what I'd just witnessed had been neither normal nor human.

I retreated until I sat on the edge of the dark couch, my knees too weak to hold me. "I set my house on fire," I whispered. "It was me."

CHAPTER 4

Applying logic to magical powers made no sense, but I couldn't think of an alternative. Once I'd calmed down sufficiently that my hands didn't catch my pack on fire, I slipped it onto my back and locked up Shane's house.

Something was happening; something beyond human comprehension, and I had to assume it was some kind of fairy power. Or fae power. *Whatever*.

Maybe I didn't need to wait until Halloween night to get through the fairy ring.

The setting sun lit the playground with cheerful peachy colors but did nothing to lighten my grim mood. Settling onto a bench, I watched the moms and dads collect their tired, dirty kids, alternating their coaxing promises of ice cream after dinner with threats of no screen time if butts didn't start moving *right now*. It pinched my heart, and I rubbed my sternum, reassuring myself I would have Finn and Dara back soon. Then no more playgrounds for a while. Or forever.

When the last car's headlights vanished from the parking lot, leaving behind a muted landscape of empty equipment and the vague lingering aroma of goldfish snacks, I stood and tightened the backpack straps across my shoulders. Tucking my hair behind my ears, all too aware I needed to stay calm if I didn't want to turn into a living torch again, I moved across the grass toward the rear corner of the lot.

My new boots squeaked as I walked, and I grimaced, hoping the noise would cease once they were broken in.

At the edge of the ring of toadstools, I stood for a long moment, attempting to muster determination that this would work. I couldn't let doubt or fear of the unknown derail me. I needed to succeed, and I required the strength to survive whatever strangeness waited on the other side of the fairy ring.

Straightening my spine, I stepped into the circle and held my breath.

Nothing happened.

The sun continued its downward path, vanishing behind a row of houses in the distance. A dog barked as twilight descended.

I shifted my feet and examined the toadstools surrounding me. They looked like ordinary mushrooms. They even smelled ordinary—musty and damp.

A knot grew in my throat, and I groaned. "This isn't going to work."

My fingertips itched, and I blinked as the flash of an idea coalesced in my head. Staring at my hands in the gloom, I thought of the fire that had raged across my skin a few hours earlier.

Wiggling my fingers, I envisioned them on fire again. Imagined yellow and orange sparks, the heat, and the burning sensation in my chest.

My nails darkened to blue, and I grinned as the fire appeared, bursting to life and burning merrily up my arms toward my torso. Flinching, I blew out, trying to direct the flames away from my face, but they covered me anyway. I was relieved to find they didn't burn my clothes or hair, although the flickering light made it difficult to see the gloom beyond my flaming form.

I waited, feeling a combination of wonder and fear, and watched the toadstools at my feet glimmer in the dancing light of my flames. Still, despite the magic I'd created, nothing happened.

After a few minutes, I noticed a prickling pain under my ribs. It grew until it reached an unbearable level. I willed my fire to extinguish, envisioning diving into a cool pond, and after a beat, the flames vanished and took the pain with them.

I sucked in a dry breath that turned into a hacking cough and tilted my head to stare at the sky, my despair welling again. Blinking away tears, I glared into the blackness above and watched the first stars of the evening appear. It took a long moment of angry sniffs and snotty coughs before what I saw penetrated my dispirited mind.

The stars above me were not in their normal pattern.

My mouth dropped open.

Without the glare of my flames, my eyes pierced the darkness around me, and I stiffened. The playground was gone, and I now stood on the bank of a river. Stumbling back, I narrowly avoided trampling the toadstools at my feet. Slipping and sliding in the damp grass, I fell to my knees.

It worked! I wanted to scream my excitement, but sudden terror quieted the impulse. I was in a foreign, magical place—alone—and I had no idea what to do next. All my energy had been directed at finding a way to the Green Lands. Standing there, I berated myself for not planning what I'd do when I got here. I had no tracking abilities, no idea where the wildfae had taken Finn and Dara, and no clue what magical creatures lurked in the dark or what I would do if I came upon one.

I swallowed.

The river flowed steadily while I sat in the damp grass. The stars reflected off its dark rippling surface, winking at me and flashing every color of the rainbow. Pink and purple constellations appeared above, scattered through the inky darkness and chasing green and blue moons and suns. The night sky looked like a child's drawing of the solar system, with vivid celestial objects spinning in all directions. Watching it made me dizzy, so I dropped my eyes back to the river.

The slick sounds of trickling water and lapping waves soothed me, but I couldn't fall asleep here, exposed and vulnerable. Climbing to my feet, I scanned the still, shadowed landscape and decided to climb the hill above the river to see if I could find a landmark. The neon-glowing sky above lit the ground enough for my eyes to locate the rocks and dips in the grass, and I managed the climb with only a few stumbles.

At the crest, I knelt so my silhouette wouldn't stand out above the tall grass and examined the surrounding valley. Faint green lights pulsed at the edge of a stand of trees on the bank of the river, and on the far side of the valley, a rocky peak interrupted the beautiful skyline with jagged edges.

I didn't see anything that looked like a dwelling. There were no scents of woodsmoke or domesticated animals, no signs of cultivation, like fields, gardens, orchards. I'd entered a pristine landscape untouched by civilizing hands. And I didn't know which way to go.

My stomach churned at the daunting nature of my task. I dropped my pack from my shoulders and dug for my water bottle.

I would sleep here, I decided after I gulped my dry throat away, where I could see in all directions if something strange woke me, and in the morning, I would return to the fairy ring. See if daylight revealed a trail or something I could follow.

Nervous about setting up my tent for the first time in the dark, I pulled out my sleeping bag and draped it around me, settling into the tall grass until I had a comfortable perch. The night breeze blew cool air across my skin, but it felt much warmer than the weather I'd left behind at the playground.

Drowsily, I wondered if the Green Lands had seasons.

I watched the planets spin above me, trailing gleaming comets, until they lulled me to sleep.

BRIGHT sunlight pricked at my eyelids, and I woke with a start, flailing in my sleeping bag and crashing through the tall stalks surrounding me until I lay, panting and sweaty, in a circle of crumpled green growth. The scent of wet grass assaulted my nose.

The overhead sun beamed directly on me like a laser. Curling into a ball, I tried to regroup.

A heavy snort, thick and gruff, broke the silence. I sat abruptly, pulling the sleeping bag away from my face.

A massive boar stood a few steps away, its small rust-colored eyes narrowed, assessing me. It wore a small pack slung around its neck.

I cleared my throat. "Hello, Shane."

The boar shimmered, and in its place stood a familiar nude man. He glared at me, and I averted my eyes, blushing.

"I chased the kids' scent all day. Through the forest, through the swamp, and when the scent screamed to me from the river again, I followed it back. And found you." Shane's voice was angry and hard.

I pulled the sleeping bag tighter across my shoulders.

"I can't distinguish your scent from the

children's. I tried to follow it again, once I realized *you* slept by the river, but all my steps returned me to you."

Shivering, I dropped the sleeping bag and rose to a crouch, gathering my things and stuffing them into my backpack. "I came through the fairy ring. You shouldn't have left me, and you know it."

Satisfied I had everything, I stood and put my hands on my hips. I would not let him bully me, not after I'd come so far. "I'm here for my kids. I told you not to leave me behind." I deepened my tone, trying to sound commanding and assertive. "Now, tell me what you've discovered so far."

"Discovered, damn," Shane muttered and dropped the pack from around his neck. Sitting in the grass at my feet, he squinted up at me, and the fine lines at the corners of his eyes tightened.

I resisted the urge to pat his shoulder. I knew I had to be firm or he'd ditch me again.

"Cool your jets, Willa. I've discovered nothing. I passed through the Veil at Iris's house, and yes, before you ask, she's definitely dead. I found her body in the woods. I think maybe she tried to chase the Slaugh, but she was too badly hurt. I buried her in the Green Lands when I came through, so the police won't take notice, I don't think. Iris stayed pretty well off the human radar."

I shivered.

"I found the children's scent easily enough and tracked it to the river, where I guess, according to you, the fairy ring comes through. I followed it all day, never gaining, and then the scent suddenly blew from the river again, so I backtracked."

I narrowed my eyes, refusing to feel guilty.

Shane stood and leaned forward, breathing deeply and fluttering my hair with his strong inhale. "How did you come through the ring? Halloween?" He sniffed me again. "Willa, what have you done? Why do you smell of blood magic?"

My brows rose. Lifting my hair to my nose, I inhaled, but I noticed no change from my regular scent. "I used your shampoo?" I offered.

Shaking his head, Shane took another deep breath. "Don't lie to me. I can smell the magic in your veins. Blood magic is forbidden. Who did you sacrifice?"

My brows rose higher.

"You reek of witchery, like burned iron and singed hair."

A flush spread across my chest, and I crossed my arms. "I don't stink. I just took a shower at your house a few hours ago."

It was Shane's turn to flush.

"And I didn't sacrifice anyone. I woke up in your house, and—"

I remembered the rest of what happened. "Oh!" I cried, clapping my hands. "I'm magic! Or I did magic! I'm not sure if there's a difference."

"What happened?" Shane's raspy voice still sounded suspicious as he continued sniffing around me.

Swallowing, I ignored the wall of gleaming

golden skin directly in front of me and explained what had happened with my hands, both at his house and at the fairy ring.

"And I think that's why my house caught on fire. My magic was trying to wake me up from the memory spell."

"This is impossible," Shane said when I finished. "You have no fae origins. Iris checked thoroughly. The only way to do magic without any of your own is to steal the magic from someone else first in a blood sacrifice."

"Like what Paul tried to do to the woman he killed?"

Shane nodded.

My mouth gaped. "B-But I didn't! There must be another explanation."

"Well, I don't know what it is. But you reek of magic. Any fae we meet is going to assume you're a blood witch and either run away screaming or try to kill you."

I shivered and wrapped my arms around my ribcage. "What should I do?"

"Go home. Let me do my job."

Scowling, I shook my head. "No."

"Then you're on your own. I can't waste any more time. I'm going to return to my trail, and I suggest you go back home through the fairy ring. If you don't, you're going to die here. Think about that. You're all Dara and Finn have."

Shane crouched and, with a pulse of green light, transformed into his boar form. Ducking his head, he looped his backpack around his neck, snorted at me, and ran off into the tall grass.

Watching Shane lope away, his bristly mane swaying in the wind, a sea of doubts swept over me. Was I being foolish? Or was Shane only trying to scare me so I'd go home?

I shivered in the warm breeze but straightened my spine and slipped my own backpack over my shoulders. Lifting my chin, I followed the bent grass of Shane's trail and began to hike.

As I tramped through the bright green grass, I wondered at Shane's revelation that my magic could only come from fae blood. Unless someone had slipped it into my evening glass of wine, I had no idea how it was possible. But, I reminded myself, Shane had admitted to being only a half-blood, and this was his first time in the Green Lands. He likely knew little more about it than I did, and I knew nothing. He'd already told me his magic would change here. Maybe it was messing with his sense of smell.

Reassured, I marched past the fairy ring at the bank of the river and continued to follow Shane's trail.

An hour later, I paused to drink from my water bottle, and I wiped the sweat from my forehead. I was walking blindly. Shane's trail, a slight path of bent grass and the occasional hoofprint, had vanished a while ago. I now followed the bank of the river, listening to its soft murmurs while the sun grew hotter and hotter overhead.

The river skirted a forest, and I'd never seen such strange trees before. Some were immensely tall with massively wide trunks and thick arching branches covered in richly hued green and aquamarine leaves. Others were slim, with pale golden trunks and drooping branches that swayed toward the ground, their long, purple-veined leaves dangling into the river.

Part of me wanted to cross the water and head into the forest where I might see what other marvelous plants grew there, but the saner part of me said I needed to stick to the open bank where I could see in all directions if any danger approached.

After trudging another few miles, I stopped and adjusted my boots. The heel portion was rubbing a hole into my ankle. Still crouched, I took a deep breath and caught a faint trace of woodsmoke in the air. I straightened and froze, blister forgotten. Where did the scent originate? Not the forest on the other side of the river, I didn't think. The breeze blew into my face, and I moved forward more cautiously.

I crested a small hill and, on the other side, stumbled to a stop and dropped to my stomach. Below me, a campfire crackled, and beside it hunched two small figures. I held my breath.

Liquid heat pooled in my chest, and I fought it, pushing back my burgeoning flames. *They react to my fear*, I reminded myself, swallowing. No need to set the meadow on fire around me—maybe I could sneak past the camp.

A spindly creature stood in front of the campfire, appearing to warm her long wings as she lifted one arm and then the other, slim fingers curling along her purplish-black iridescent feathers. Her human torso, with its small breasts covered in down, morphed into narrow hips above orange-scaled legs that ended in sharp talons. Her bird-like face, round with a curved beak and large dark eyes, glared at the male creature laying bound at her feet. She drew a sword from the sheath at her hip and twirled it at the prisoner in a cocky, aggressive motion.

She chirped, "Did you forget I could swim? Foolish goblin. With your bounty, I'm sure to gain a boon from Queen Mab." She shook her feathers.

I closed my gaping mouth with an audible click as the fairy—or fae? I couldn't remember the term—taunted her captive.

"Shall I ask for you? To serve me?" She trilled a laugh.

The bound creature, dressed in a soft-looking gray tunic, had olive-green skin and dark black hair sprouting into a spiky mohawk. He closed his eyes and turned his head, showing the buds of two small black horns.

An ache grew in my chest as I gazed at him. There were long streaks of red blood on his wrists and ankles where the roughness of the rope had rubbed his flesh raw. The creature—the goblin—was small, but firm muscles defined his bare arms. His bowed head and softly curved ears called to my motherly instincts, and I couldn't turn away.

The bird-fae continued her taunts, and I hunkered lower in the grass. "Did you know I was the one who captured your brother? Oh yes, I recognize you, Kalo Nightspawn. Do you want to know what happened to him? Shall I tell you which fae lord bought him for his blood sacrifice?"

The goblin snarled and lunged, flashing sharp teeth, but the fae danced away, laughing, as the boy sprawled in the grass at her feet.

"Maybe I'll sacrifice you myself. What need have I of a boon if I carry your blood already?"

The goblin stilled his thrashing and sneered. "You'll not risk my curse, foolish pixie-duck."

"Duck!" The winged creature shrieked. "I'm no duck, you jackanapes!" She moved her sword and, with a single sharp motion, slashed a line across his collarbone. "One warning only," she hissed.

Ignoring the wound, the goblin said, "Too weak you are to harness my blood, though you call yourself a hunter. Go ahead, bring me to your queen. I'd rather my blood water the ground at her feet than move through your weak veins."

Another sharp shriek rent the air.

The fae drew back her sword arm, and my breath caught in my throat. There was no question she was a moment away from slashing the young goblin's throat. I couldn't bear it—the fae's cruelty, the goblin's stoic grimness . . .

I jumped to my feet, determined to help. "Stop —"

With a single great flap of her wings, the bird-fae launched into the air and tossed a hand in my direction. A black sticky net fell over me; thick barbs dug into my skin. I screamed, and with a whiff of acid and blood, I fainted.

CHAPTER 5

Pain dug its fingernails under my eyelids and ripped them open.

Exhaling, I tried to sit up, only to be tugged back by the net anchoring my body to the ground. I flailed, my feet drumming against the dirt.

A thin voice laughed. "A human? How rich. The queen will truly delight in me."

I froze and a burning sensation seared my exposed skin. I stared at the cloudless sky above me. My bones ached under the heavy weight of the net. I swallowed my instinct to flail again—every time I moved, the barbs dug deeper into my skin, and blood already trickled from the open wounds on my arms and neck as my heart stuttered and pounded in my chest. The barbs burned like acid, eating into my flesh with an eager hiss in the still air.

Fear pulsed through me as another wave of blackness flickered across my vision. My stomach lurched. Was the net poisoning me? I swallowed but couldn't get any moisture past the knot in my throat.

"Where did you come from, woman?" A dark shape bent over me, blotting out the sun, and a pair of liquid black slitted eyes glittered out of the feathered face.

I couldn't speak—terror stopped my brain from processing anything beyond panic and a desire to escape.

"Hmm, you smell of burned offerings. Did you steal some magic that didn't belong to you, witch?" Sharp claws dug into the skin of my arm, forcing my attention down my body. From the corner of my eye, I saw the fae draw her sword again.

Shane's warning from earlier broke through my panic. I needed to escape immediately—this creature had identified the same blood magic odor, and she wanted to execute me.

I screamed, and as the bird-fae fell back in surprise, my hands burst into incandescent flames. Without thought, I threw out my hands and shot fire down my body, incinerating the net. I scrambled to my feet. The fae lunged forward with her sword, and I shot an arrow of flames at her. Before I could process what was happening, fire engulfed the creature and, in seconds, left behind only a pile of ashy feathers atop an oily black spot on the grass.

Bile filled my mouth as I looked down at my hands. They burned with a bright amber glow. I killed someone. Set her on fire. It had been so easy.

"Are you daft, lady? Or are you trying to immolate yourself?" On the other side of the campfire, the goblin snagged the now-loose sword from the ground and sawed his hands free of the rope.

I blinked at him and the flames at my fingertips winked out. “What?”

“You must always direct the fire away from you. If you turn yourself into a candlestick, you’ll soon burn to ash, like Yaneeka there.” The goblin gestured at the black spot.

My mouth fell open. “You know about my magic? What is it? How do I use it? Why do I have it?”

The goblin snorted and rolled his red eyes. “Stupid, are you? Using magic you don’t understand. Go off with you. I’ve no time for fools.” He gathered loose items from around the fire—the sword, a pouch bulging with its contents . . .

“No, please. I don’t know what’s happening to me, but I have to find my kids. The Slaugh stole them from me.”

“Half-bloods?”

I nodded.

He grimaced. “Best make your peace with it. They’re gone.”

My fingers turned blue and hot once more. “I don’t accept that,” I bit out.

“No, I don’t imagine a dragonkin would.”

I fell silent again, stupefied, until I croaked, “What?”

He rolled his eyes. “Dragonkin. A descendant of the Great Serpents of Eire.”

My lips trembled. “Dragons? There’s no such thing as dragons.” I coughed and stared at the scorch marks on the grass where the bird-fae once stood. “I mean, that's absurd, right?" I mumbled.

"The Cursed Patrick drove the serpents from Eire, yes, but he didn't drive them to the Green Lands. The drakes were of ancient origin, older than the High Fae, no matter what those power-hungry lords and ladies may tell us now. The dragons, when they fled, went west. And where are you from, lady?"

"West," I repeated, thinking of the cold house I'd grown up in along the Northern California coast. A whisper of a story in my father's deep, kind voice stirred in my memory. No way. Impossible.

I shook my head. "I was told I have blood witch magic. Now you're saying dragons? I think you fae are all nuts. None of you know anything."

The goblin cackled. "Well, that's a fact right there." He tied his pack closed and kicked dirt over the coals in the center of the fire ring.

He straightened his small sharp shoulders. "We'll do this the correct way, despite the corruption continuing to stain this land. You saved me, and now I owe you a boon." His red eyes burned into mine, and I resisted the urge to flinch. "I'll not serve you, witch . . . or dragonkin. Whatever you're calling yourself."

His eyes glowed a deeper crimson, and I swallowed my protest.

"But you or your children, if you find them, may call on me for a return service for as long as you live. My name is Kalonymos of the Nightspawn Clan. Kalo for short." He pointed his shortsword at me. "Don't you go spreading that about, now. My name is mine alone. If you misuse it, I'll kill you."

"Noted," I breathed. He was young and small, but he was fierce, and I didn't like the sword pointed at my face.

"Good." Kalo tucked the blade into his pack and turned away. He started toward the deeper grass but hesitated and glanced back at me. "I can smell two children in the forest. There." He pointed at the woods across the river from where we stood. "I assume they're yours. Best get them out of the Green Lands now—if you can. Queen Mab will not relinquish them once they reach Court. Especially so close to the winter solstice and her time of sacrifice."

I nodded my thanks. Before I could wave, the goblin vanished. Did he use magic, or was he faster than the human eye could track? I didn't know. Shivering, I sat back on my heels. I wanted to process the information I'd learned—the possibilities spun in my brain in distorted waves—but if Finn and Dara were across the river, I needed to get to them as soon as I could.

I stood and adjusted my pack, avoiding the scorch mark in the grass as I turned to the water's edge. I shoved my hands in my pockets before they could set anything else aflame.

A sour taste growing in my mouth, I examined the water. The river didn't look too treacherous, but I had no idea if water-dwelling fae lurked within its blue depths.

The welts from the net's barbs ached when I rubbed my arms. I stepped forward and water soaked through my boots like cold fingers gripping my toes. Gritting my teeth, I continued. By the middle of the river, the water reached above my waist, and racking shivers accompanied each step. Forget about deadly mermaids, I was going to freeze to death. I lifted my pack above my head in an effort to keep it dry. Clenching my jaw, I tried to be grateful that at least the frigid water was soothing my wounds.

I finally sloshed onto the grassy bank on the far side and knew I needed to warm up before going any farther. Dropping my pack, I dug through it for a dry set of clothes and quickly stripped and changed, leaving off my wet boots. I wrapped my sleeping bag around my trembling body and stared into the dark woods looming ahead.

The trees, so pretty from the opposite bank, now seemed ominous—their dangling branches looked too much like thin reaching arms, and their brightly colored leaves blocked the sun from reaching the forest floor. From where I stood, I could see vast tracts of glowing mushrooms and toadstools.

A bitter scent wafted from the woods, and my trepidation grew. Everything about this place screamed with spooky vibes, and I was risking my life by entering. But I didn't have a choice. After repacking my sleeping bag and slipping into my wet boots, I cautiously stepped forward.

Leaves rustled above me as I moved from one small patch of sunlight to the next. I didn't want to step on or touch the mushrooms, so I skirted around them. The air under the trees was chilly and occasionally grew frigid, causing my breath to frost for a few paces before the cold eased to merely brisk.

How would I find the children? There were no tracks through the mushroom patches and there were no sounds other than those of a normal forest.

After a while, I paused. My arms and neck ached from where the bird-fae's net had pinned me down and my skin was bloody and raw there too. I shivered, imagining what would have happened if I hadn't burned it away.

The blister on my foot radiated pain and made me stumble. Before I could recover, I brushed against a neon blue toadstool sprouting from the root of a massively wide tree. A puff of blue dust danced in the breeze. Hurriedly backing up, I watched the dust drift a few feet before it settled on a patch of frilly pale flowers. I held my breath and exhaled it in a whoosh as the flowers wilted before my eyes, turning black and stringy and, with a quiver, broke into brittle black stalks.

I swallowed.

Stepping even more carefully than before, I moved to the next patch of sunshine and ventured deeper into the woods.

When the sun began to set and the dark forest became a minefield of toadstool traps, I paused again. Despair ate away at my resolve. I wouldn't be able to move once the sun vanished and, for all I knew, the Slaugh were taking my kids farther and farther away from me with every second that passed.

But I couldn't help them if I touched a toadstool and vanished into a puff of dust, so I forced myself to stop and look for a patch of dirt wide enough to set up camp. I found one and quickly assembled my tent, crawling inside its pale orange walls just as the forest was swallowed by night, turning pitch black around me. Laying on my stomach, I watched through the open flap of my tent as the mushrooms and toadstools turned black too, booby traps prepared for a forest creature to misstep in the night.

While eating a few granola bars and drinking water, I continued to watch the eerie forest. I hated the idea of zipping my door and sleeping, leaving myself vulnerable in the night, but I had no choice. After one last glance at the sky, searching in vain for the bright celestial objects of the previous night, I sighed and closed myself within the thin nylon walls.

Worried it would take me hours to relax enough to fall asleep, I lay on my back in my sleeping bag. But before I could stew over the danger surrounding me, I fell asleep.

I woke in the dark to a tugging sensation in my chest. My frightened gaze failed to penetrate the absolute blackness of my tent, but I knew without a doubt I needed to follow the feeling.

I slipped on my boots, unzipped the narrow

flap, and stepped carefully into the dirt. I hesitated. The sharp pull told me to turn right, but I didn't dare take a step with the mushrooms surrounding me.

The pull turned painful and I gasped, swaying on my feet. My fingertips alight with my flames, I kept the sparks muted and heeded the goblin's warning about burning myself. I followed the tug, picking my way through the black and gray shapes of trees.

After a while, my hands grew hot, and a sharp ache in my chest replaced the tugging sensation. I extinguished the fire and stood in the darkness, my breaths shallow. Fear screamed its shrill tone in my head, but I didn't turn back.

The forest rustled around me, and I waited for the pull in my chest to resume. It didn't.

Crouched in the dirt, I put my hands on the ground and willed my body to keep going, but I was so scared, and now I didn't even know how to return to my tent and my pack. I swallowed hard, the harsh sound breaking the bubble of silence around me.

The hair on my arms lifted and I froze, huddled against the earth like a mouse before an owl.

I risked my fire once more. The scraping of leaves grew louder around me. I shivered and glanced up. My heart stopped beating in my chest. The noise I'd assumed came from leaves rustling together instead came from a colony of massive creatures with leathery wings, all swaying together above my head. They hung upside down, their thick claws anchoring them to the thin boughs of the trees.

Willing myself to remain still, I stared at the bat-like animals. They were enormous, easily the size of an adult human, and they slept only feet above my head. Their claws alone looked to be the size of my forearms.

I knew I needed to quiet my flames, but I couldn't bear sitting in the dark with them dangling above me.

"Mama," Dara's voice whispered. I stifled a shriek and turned my hands toward the sound. The fire illuminated a pair of small, huddled figures clinging to each other at the base of a tree a few feet away.

"Baby," I breathed back, my throat dry. "Shhhh."

Dara nodded, her face ghostly pale. Finn slept, his head lolling against her shoulder.

I risked another glance upward. The dark shapes of the creatures remained mercifully undisturbed.

Beyond Dara, a light green glow pulsed, and I swallowed another startled scream as Shane stepped out from behind the tree.

Placing his finger on his lips, he pointed to the ring of dark toadstools surrounding the kids and mimed an explosion with his hands. I gave him a short nod. I'd seen what the mushrooms could do.

Dara stirred and reached for me, but I held up my hands, telling her to stay still. It killed me not to grab her—grab them both—but we needed to be smart. Her huge eyes filled with tears that spilled down her cheeks before she nodded and resettled against the tree.

Shane tiptoed to my side and gestured at my dimly glowing hands. I didn't know how to convey that I needed to stop the flames soon. The cracking sensation already grew under my sternum. I settled for shaking my head and tucking them behind my back.

My eyes drifted to the creatures sleeping above our heads, and I jumped when Shane touched my elbow and pointed into the darkness beyond where my flickering flames could reach. He mimed sharp teeth in his mouth. My pulse stuttered in my throat.

We're surrounded. The kids are in a minefield. And if I don't turn off my fire soon, I will burn to ash. Great, no problem. We got this.

Shane bent his head until his lips touched my ear. A shiver racked my body.

"Fae hounds sleep beyond those trees. Above us, the Slaugh. If any of them wake, we die."

I exhaled a shaky breath.

"I was waiting for dawn, when their powers lessen. But now I think, since Dara has seen you, we cannot wait."

I ignored the dig. I refused to feel guilty. Every second my child was less afraid was worth the risk.

Turning my head, I whispered back, "I can shoot fire, but I don't know how far or how big. A goblin owes me a favor, should I call him?"

Shane's eyebrows rose in the dim light, and he adamantly shook his head. "No way. Never call in that favor."

I frowned at him.

Pressure grew in my hands, different from the fire sensation. I shook them and flinched as the light around us flickered.

Shane hissed, but I ignored him. Dara's eyes locked on mine, and my hands tingled again as a determined expression moved across her face.

Mama, she mouthed silently. *Make a bigger fire.*

My eyes widened on my hands, which had involuntarily risen in front of my chest. I shoved outward and gasped as an orb of flickering flames grew to encircle the four of us.

The sudden light woke the creatures, and a cacophony of shrieks and growls filled the air. Glowing yellow eyes opened and focused on the children. Giant bats dropped from the tree and landed in the dirt outside my circle. From behind the nightmare fae, a trio of giant dogs ran at us, their fangs dripping saliva, their eyes rolling and wild.

Darting forward, I crouched over Finn and Dara and shielded them with my body. Finn woke up, flailing and screaming, but Dara stood and stepped away. From inside the flaming bubble, she faced the Slaugh on the outside and brought her hands together in front of her chest. With a deep breath, she stilled and closed her eyes, then thrust her arms out with a shriek. Her high-pitched cry raised the hair on my arms.

I froze, stunned by the volcanic blast of air that exploded from my shield to envelope the milling creatures in a fiery, swirling plume. A moment later, the concussive boom of power hit my eardrums before the forest fell silent, and I watched in disbelief as row after row of bodies hit the dirt, writhing and disintegrating to ash.

Shane shouted something, but I couldn't hear anything. Finn and Dara climbed his back like monkeys, and he grabbed my arm, shaking me. I staggered after him, flailing until I found my feet, and we ran.

My fire shield surrounded us still, blasting the toadstools in our path as we ran through a battlefield of smoke and dust. My hearing returned, starting with a shrill whine in my eardrums.

I slammed into Shane's back and looked up to find him staring at me, Finn's and Dara's wide-eyed faces peered down from where they perched on his shoulders.

"—have to find the river," he shouted. "Breach the Veil there!"

I nodded, pushing forward once more, my hands thrusting the flaming shield in front of us. I didn't tell him about the pain in my chest, or the blisters forming on my hands. We needed to get out of the forest. Needed to run.

So we ran.

My breath came in pants, and it was almost

enough to distract me from the fire burning out of my skin and under my sternum like a live coal. Black spots flickered in my vision, but I stumbled on, following Shane's broad back and the frightened, glassy eyes of my kids.

Dara mouthed something at me, and I pushed myself to move faster. But my feet were slowing. The orb of flames surrounding us flickered, the darkness of the night piercing it.

I staggered and Shane grabbed me, lifting me to his chest like a baby. Curling into his strength, I matched my gasping inhales to his and pushed every ounce of energy I possessed into the ring of flames.

When we reached the edge of the forest where the river glistened under the star-brightened sky, Shane dropped me and shouted something, waving his fingers. Dara's small hands enclosed mine and my fire died. I blinked once and felt nothing more.

CHAPTER 6

I floated in a sea of darkness. A story echoed in my memory and a wave of peace engulfed me as I listened to the smooth, low-pitched tone of my father's voice.

"Once upon a time there was a great king, and he was sad because his people were dying. So he gathered his most powerful friends and told them to go west, to where the land remained free of cultivation and they could live without persecution. The king made a pact—"

Another voice intruded—a frosty, hard voice. My mother. I shivered.

"Stop this. Are you telling her another fairy tale about dragons? She needs to go to sleep. She has a math test tomorrow."

Dara called my name and my eyes popped open.

"Mama, Mama, wake up. I'm sorry. I'm sorry."

I shushed her automatically, sitting up and looking around the grassy clearing. The ground under my legs was cold and firm, and I exhaled at the sight of normal-looking trees arching above us. Through the branches, plain golden stars shone down. With trembling hands, I pulled Dara into my lap and buried my face in her neck.

"Oh, my baby girl," I murmured, squeezing her hard before I looked up again. "Where are Shane and Finn?"

"Here!" Finn called, running from the trees and tackling me, knocking me to the ground.

Tears flooded my eyes. I clutched the warm, familiar bodies of my kids and tried to talk, but mostly blubbered and squeezed them tighter. I'd found them. We were out of the Green Lands. I wanted to calm down, to reassure them, but I couldn't stop my sobs.

Finn was the first to squirm away. "Mom, you're squishing me." I let him stand but continued to hold Dara in my lap, inhaling her vanilla scent as I willed myself to settle. Dara let me pet her and rub her slight shoulders, and my strangled breaths returned to normal.

Shane crouched nearby; his stern face relaxed for the first time in days. His blue eyes twinkled at me, and I grinned back, giddy.

"Where are we?"

"In the woods behind Iris's house."

I swallowed. "We need to get them inside, get warm."

"Let's go to my place. It's warded."

With a nod, I rose, slipping Dara's pliant but heavy body onto my hip.

Finn wrapped his fingers through the belt

loop of my pants, and we followed Shane through the woods. As we walked, Dara stroked my hair. Eventually I had to set her down, and she held my hand, her small body brushing against mine with every step.

We followed the familiar sidewalks, exhaustion slowing our pace, until the thrill of reaching our neighborhood perked everyone up.

“Mom,” Finn gasped when we reached our street. “What happened to our house?”

Wincing, I reached down to squeeze his hand. “It’s sort of a crazy story. Let’s get inside. I’ll tell you what happened to me, and you can tell me what happened to you.”

Finn nodded, goggling at the destruction and the yellow tape crisscrossing the scene.

Inside Shane’s house, I positioned the kids on either side of me on the couch and tucked a blanket over our legs before taking their cold fingers in mine. Shane sat across from us and leaned forward, placing his elbows on his thighs.

“Can you tell me what happened to you?” I asked.

Neither kid spoke for a long moment, but finally Finn sucked in a deep breath. “I fell asleep on the bus on the way home from school. In my dream, something icy touched me.”

“I got very, very sleepy too,” Dara said. “I closed my eyes. When I woke up, it was daytime, and I was flying in the air. A bat was carrying me.” She shuddered and a tear dripped down her cheek.

"It smelled bad, and I couldn't see Finn anywhere. Or you."

My stomach twisted. They'd been terrified, and I'd been oblivious. Going about my day at work, my kids already forgotten.

Finn said, "The bats carried us for a while, then we went into the woods and it was dark. There were big dogs following us. Dara cried a lot."

Dara ducked her face into my shoulder.

Shakily, I said, "I'm so sorry, kiddos. That sounds really scary. I'm so proud of you for staying together."

"What happened to the house?" Dara asked in a small voice.

"There was a fire. After the bats took you away. I got out okay, but the house burned down. Then I started chasing after you," I explained.

Dara squeezed my hand. "I'm sorry for hurting you in the woods, Mama. I could feel my blood in you. It whispered to me; told me I could use it."

My brows rose. "Your blood was in me?"

Dara and Finn both nodded. An inkling of an idea coalesced in my head. *The abruption. When the placenta ruptured on the night of the twins' birth. Our blood mixed . . .*

"In the woods," Finn added, interrupting my train of thought, "there were a lot of voices in our heads, telling us to do things."

I cleared my throat and gave Shane a pointed look. He rose to his feet and both kids focused their wary gazes on him.

"Your grandmother had magic in her blood. It passed to you through your father. So you two have magic. With it, you can do special things other kids can't. But it's dangerous, so you should be really careful before you listen to the whispers."

I rolled my eyes at the sparse explanation and took a few minutes to go into greater detail about everything Shane had shared with me about the Green Lands and the High Fae and the blood hunters.

When I finished, Dara asked, "And Grand-Mère is dead?"

I rubbed her knee and nodded. Dara's sniffle broke my heart, and Finn's next words tore it to pieces.

"And we're in danger? The fae are going to chase us again?"

I shrugged helplessly. "We'll figure it out."

"You're safe in my house. The fae can't get in," Shane added. "Why don't you go to sleep—you can have my bed. And in the morning, we'll make our plans."

I helped the twins get drinks of water, brush their teeth with their fingers, and slip into a couple of Shane's oversized t-shirts. They needed baths, but they needed sleep more. Finn's eyelids fluttered as he swayed down the hallway.

I tucked Dara under the blanket, and she grabbed my fingers. Her voice shaky, she said, "I can't feel you. I'm not inside you anymore. I think I burned my magic out of your blood in the forest."

I nodded. "I think when you were born, some of your and Finn's blood mixed with mine. But it was only a very small amount. When you helped me make the explosion to get away from the monsters, I think I used it all up."

Dara's tone turned to a sleepy whine. "It's not fair. Finn can still feel you."

I looked over at Finn, already passed out and snoring. "Oh, sweet pea," I said softly, "you're always inside me. Your magic may be only yours now, but you're in my heart as deep as the deepest part of the ocean."

I stroked her hair for a few more minutes until she fell asleep, then I slipped out of the bedroom.

In the living room, I found Shane smoothing out a pillow and blanket on the couch. He looked wan and muddy, and I glanced down at my own dirty pants with a sigh.

"Sorry to take over your house."

Shane gestured beside him, and we sat, our shoulders nearly touching. My stomach growled, but I was too tired and anxious to do anything about it.

"This is my debt to Iris. I will keep the kids safe. Whatever it takes," he promised.

"Are we really out of danger here?"

He hesitated for a long moment, the lines bracketing his mouth deepening, and my heart sank. "From the fae and the Slaugh, yes. They cannot pass my wards. From Paul? I'm not sure. He's a half-blood, and I don't know the details of his magic. Iris made the ward protecting your house and tailored it to him specifically. But I made this one myself, so I don't know."

"We can't stay here then."

Shane grimaced. "We can stay here until we think of a way to get you past the Rockies. But ideally, no more than a couple of days. Paul will discover the Slaugh lost the kids, and he'll return for them."

"The Rockies?"

"The fae can go no farther west than the Rockies. Long ago, a deal was struck with the original inhabitants of this land, and the fae still honor it, though the enforcement mechanisms have long since calcified. Paul won't be able to track us either. The magic to the west is different than his—older."

"What about his human side? Human ways of tracking?"

Frowning, Shane said, "He's half-human, with more fae blood than the children. If I can pass the divide, then maybe so can he. We'll have to see when we reach the border and, if we need to take more drastic steps, we can consider them then."

"Drastic steps," I repeated, envisioning the treacherous father of my children dead at my feet.

Reading my feral expression, Shane snickered. "I mean like finding a witch and paying them to cast a better ward."

"Oh, okay. Yeah, that sounds good."

Shane's smile deepened.

I felt my body relaxing. Shane's citrus and pine scent enveloped me, and my heart swelled when I thought of all he'd done for the kids. For me. I'd never been able to rely on another person like this before. It made me feel warm. Safe.

I stared at his callused fingers as they scraped at the mud on his jeans, and my throat contracted in a hard swallow. I suddenly wanted those fingers on me and mine on him. I wanted to trace the sculpted abdominal muscles he'd been flashing at me for days. I wanted to follow my fingers with my tongue. I wanted his mouth on me in a way that was tangible and hard and hot, forcing me to feel more than fear and relief. Swaying, I leaned toward him.

"Want to tell me what happened with the goblin?"

I startled, then blushed and straightened. *Sheesh, Willa*, I chastised myself. *Focus*.

"I rescued him from some kind of bird-fae; a blood hunter. The goblin said he owed me a debt now."

"Iris warned me to stay away from the goblins. They have a very violent society. They're very primitive. If you call him for aid, he might decide the best way to pay his debt is to kill everyone nearby. He would be a very blunt instrument."

"Noted." Dropping my head back on the couch, I spoke to the ceiling. "The Rockies, hmmm. I wonder if that's the west the goblin meant when he called me a dragonkin."

Shane's shoulder moved against mine and his

scent flooded my nose again, flavored with a dash of male sweat. I shivered, resolutely ignoring it.

"A what?" he asked.

"He said something about me being a dragonkin; that I smelled like a blood witch and a dragonkin. The blood, I think, is from the twins' traumatic birth. But the dragonkin—I have no idea." I picked absently at the blanket, my thoughts growing hazy with exhaustion.

"My dad used to tell me stories about dragons," I murmured, flashing back to the memory I'd woken to earlier—my father loved to tell me fairy tales, and my mother loved to shut him down. I'd never understood how they ended up together, and I wasn't surprised when he finally left one day. I hadn't thought of him in years.

Shane's rough fingers tilted my chin down, forcing my gaze to his. "Start over," he ordered.

Staring into his warm blue eyes, I explained what I'd learned from Kalo. Shane's fingers on my skin were distracting, but when I finished and he let go, I missed the warmth.

I kicked myself again, working hard to ignore the prickling feeling kindling in my chest. This attraction was not a good idea. Shane needed to guard the kids. And he was too bossy, too big. Too prone to manhandling me. I looked away from him, letting the silence between us grow while I searched for the energy to get up and go to bed.

"Willa, what are these? You're bloody."

I remembered the holes and burns on my

arms from the barbed net at the same moment their sting returned. I stumbled to my feet and ran to the kitchen sink to wash them under the warm water.

Shane followed. "Why didn't you tell me you were hurt?"

I flushed, carefully rinsing the welts with water and soap. The water eased the ache a little, so I swiped at my neck with a wet paper towel. "I didn't want to give you another reason to stop me from helping," I answered softly, turning off the water and shifting to face him.

He shook his head. "Well, lying to me isn't a good way to build faith in your abilities either." He pulled a first aid kit from under the sink and handed me a tube of antibiotic cream.

Ignoring his words, I slathered on the cream and handed the tube back.

"You missed a couple." Shane stepped closer, his toes nearly touching mine, and I tilted my head up so he could gently spread the cream over the remaining spots on my neck. His breath stirred the hair at my temples.

My pulse fluttered in my throat, and I resisted the urge to lean forward and press my lips to his stubbled chin.

"The fae I killed—it caught me first in a net." I cleared my throat, fighting off a shiver as Shane examined the burns.

"Some of these welts are deep." He finally moved away. "Keep an eye on them or they may get infected."

“Yes, sir, Dr. Shane.” I gave him a mock salute. “Hey, what’s your last name?”

Grinning as he packed away the kit, he said, “Shane Casey. Nice to meet you formally, Willa Overholt.”

I smiled back, and when my gaze dropped to his lips, I spun around and hurried down the hall to sleep with the kids.

DARA woke up screaming a few hours later.

I flailed under the heavy comforter, my senses scattered, as she scrambled from the bed and darted from the room.

Sparing a glance at Finn, who slept hard on his stomach beside me, I ran after her.

In the living room, I found Dara sprawled atop Shane on the couch, her thin body quaking with sobs. Shane blinked up at the ceiling for a long moment, getting his bearings. My heart skipped a beat when his arms encircled her, and he held her to his chest. His hand cupped the back of her head and patted it gently before he sat up.

“Sorry,” I whispered, crossing the room to pick her up.

“Leave her, s’ okay,” Shane slurred.

“Mama,” Dara croaked, lifting her tear-soaked face. “The bats smell like throw up.”

Pressing against Shane’s side, I sat beside them and leaned my body over hers so she was cocooned between Shane and me. “The bats are gone,” I whispered. “We’re with Shane. He smells like oranges. And Christmas trees."

Shane stiffened a little, but I avoided looking at him. Stroking my hand through Dara's curls, I added, "Just a nightmare, baby. Mama's here."

Dara's shudders faded, and soon her soft snores filled the quiet living room.

Eventually, I moved to lift her, but stopped when I realized Shane had also fallen back asleep, upright on the couch with his head lolling to the side.

I stared down at them for a long moment, their cheeks pale in the darkness, and I sighed. Dragging a pillow and blanket from the couch, I made a nest beside them on the floor and closed my eyes.

IN the morning, I woke slowly, my body languid and soft. Heat curled in my core like a licking flame, and I reached for my dream, not ready to wake. The line between sleep and wakefulness blurred, and I tucked my face into my pillow. Breathing deeply, my nose traced the soft fabric, and I sighed. My hand slipped between my thighs, chasing the fire.

"Willa," a voice rasped, blowing strands of my hair across my forehead.

I sat up with a start and teetered at the realization that my body lay sprawled across Shane's on the floor.

"Wha—" The memory of Dara's night terror rushed back, and I glanced up to see her sleeping on the couch, her body spread-eagled across the broad cushions.

Shane moved underneath me again, and a small groan escaped his lips.

I tried to scramble off him, but my knee fell between his legs and I froze, not wanting to nudge the hot bulge I found there. My cheeks flashed scarlet.

Shane's arms banded around me. "Don't move," he rasped.

We stared at each other, our faces inches apart, and I traced the gleaming cobalt stripes in his blue eyes as our breaths mingled.

"Mama," Dara murmured sleepily and rolled over on the couch.

Shane shoved me away in an abrupt move that left me sprawled on the floor. His hunched back vanished down the hall, and I huffed and turned to my daughter.

Over the next hour, I managed baths for the kids and a shower for myself in the time Shane took to run to the store for new clothes and shoes for us all. After a massive breakfast, the kids watched Shane pace back and forth in front of the long kitchen counter, deep frowns of suspicion on their faces as he lectured us.

"You cannot leave this house. Don't even open a door or a window. Don't call any of your friends and invite them over to play." He pointed at me. "Don't call or email your job or your friends either. Anyone who comes to the front door is to be treated with the utmost suspicion, even if they wear *my* face and ask to be invited inside."

Finn's expression grew mutinous at Shane's authoritative tone, and I jumped in. "Just for a little while, guys. Until we figure out how to hide you."

"I want to go to school," Dara said. "I want to go to Grand-Mère's house and tell it goodbye." Her eyes filled with tears.

"Well, I wanna go to the playground," Finn said, crossing his arms.

I lifted my hands, palms up. "Okay, I hear you. Now, you hear me. If you don't follow these rules, the bat creatures may steal you again. So please, promise us you'll do what Shane says."

"And why is Shane telling us what to do?" Finn demanded, his lower lip trembling. "He's not the boss of me."

Shane paused his pacing to stand in front of Finn. I prepared to intervene but relaxed at Shane's soft tone. "I'm not your boss. I'm not your mom's boss. Your grandmother trusted me, and I'm trying to honor a promise. Your grandmother saved my life, and it was very, very important to her I keep you safe. Please help me keep you safe." His shoulders bowed as he leveled his intent gaze on Finn's. "I'm trusting you and asking you to trust me."

Finn sat back, slightly mollified, while Dara watched Shane with her mouth agape and stars in her eyes. "I trust you," she breathed.

I rolled my eyes. Shane reached across the counter to tug on one of her curls.

"And it's not forever," Shane added. "When you're bigger and your magic grows, you won't need me. I promise to teach you all I know, so when you're ready, I won't boss you anymore."

"Where's your family?" Finn asked, not willing to let go. "Why aren't you taking care of *them*?"

Shane's eyelids shuttered briefly. "I don't have a family."

Dara's soft gasp coaxed a smile back to his face. "Iris was my new family, so that makes you my family too," Shane assured her.

Her cheeks pinkening, Dara nodded at him. "I'll call you Uncle Shane."

My heart melted. Clapping my hands, I redirected the kids' attention. "We're doing our best to understand what's going on. I know you have a lot of questions. And I know you're worried about what's going to happen next. Whatever we decide to do, it's very likely we're going to move away from here. Maybe we'll go to California, where I grew up."

Finn's eyes lit. "And see the ocean?"

I smiled at him. "Yeah, big guy."

He grinned. "Okay, I'll stay in the house."

Shane threw his hands in the air and stalked away, and I winked at Finn.

We spent the morning sending Shane back and forth to the burned house to bring us anything he could salvage. Finn's and Dara's stuff remained gone, lost in whatever void the Slaugh created to erase the kids' existence. I tried to keep them distracted, making it into a treasure hunt of remembering where in the garage we kept the Christmas decorations and where to find the hot chocolate with mini marshmallows—at the rear of the pantry.

After lunch, Shane brought us downstairs to his unfinished basement. In the center of the space, a large swirly design was painted onto the concrete floor.

Pointing at it, Shane said, "This is the ward on the house. When we get where we're going, I'll teach you how to make your own."

"Teach us?" Dara asked.

Shane nodded. "Both you and Finn have magic in your blood, and although it won't whisper to you here the way it does in the Green Lands, you can still use it a little. You"—he pointed at Dara—"have air magic, I think. The blast in the forest, though you used your mom's fire, you also moved the air."

Dara's eyes gleamed. She lifted her hands and wiggled her fingers in front of her face as she mumbled, "Awesome."

"What about me?" Finn asked.

Shane frowned, looking at him closely. "I'm not sure yet. Your magic has a very familiar scent, so you may shift to an animal, like me. But we'll have to see when you get stronger."

Finn's chest puffed out. "I'm going to be a bear. Or a wolf. Wait, what do you change into?"

Stepping behind a stack of boxes, Shane vanished and reappeared in his boar form. He paced into the open space, and the green glow surrounding him faded. He stood still while the kids patted him.

It took heroic effort, but I held back my snort of laughter. It felt like we were visiting a petting zoo. But I clearly didn't do a good job hiding my mirth, because when Shane shifted back to his human shape, he set me to work.

I practiced drawing the shape from the floor again and again. I drew it on note paper, with chalk on the ground, and with a drawing app on my phone. While I doodled and tried to memorize the loops and whirls, Shane had the kids "focus their magic." Whatever that meant.

Dara kept at it much longer than I thought she could sit still, but it wasn't long before Finn roamed the basement, looking in boxes and distracting his sister. When he found a box of knives and swords, he dumped it out and reached for one, cutting his finger in the process. Shane called an end to the lesson, and we trooped upstairs.

My back ached from crouching and bending, and I wanted a moment to myself to stretch, but I pulled Shane aside as the kids ran to watch TV. "They're smart kids," I said. "But they don't like to be still. I'm sorry Finn didn't listen better to your lesson."

He shook his head and smiled. "Relax, Willa. They both did fine. If Finn is a shifter, his magic will come to him intuitively when he's ready. And Dara already created an explosion with hers. She's miles ahead of what I'd expect a seven-year-old partial fae to do."

I smiled, proud and relieved.

"It's beautiful," I said. "The ward design. And I saw your art in the bathroom."

Shane flushed beet-red to the roots of his hair.

Clearing his throat, he mumbled something I couldn't quite hear, but I grinned anyway. I liked learning these little tidbits about him. I wondered what he was learning about me, and it was my turn to blush. Probably that I was messy and awkward and—

He straightened, and I refocused. "You won't be able to use the ward. But I figured if we ever got separated, you could draw it for Dara, and she could activate it. I'll work on that with her tomorrow."

I nodded. Taking a seat on the couch between the kids, I drew the ward again and again on a notepad while Shane went out to get groceries.

Later, Dara helped Shane make dinner while Finn and I looked at RV rentals online.

By the time dusk rolled around, the kids were hyped about driving west, and I was ready for a glass of wine and a foot massage.

I settled for the beer Shane handed me as I walked into the living room after putting the twins to bed. I dropped down on the couch and tucked a blanket around my feet.

"So that's it?" I asked. "We pick up the RV tomorrow morning and we leave? Never to return?"

Shane shrugged and took a long pull from his beer before rising to put another log on the fire. The bright crackling flames made the room feel homey, and I appreciated the view of Shane's backside. I shifted my gaze to my glass and swallowed hard.

"The fae won't be able to track us in a vehicle," Shane said, turning to face me. The firelight danced behind him, casting him in shadow. "We would have to stop for at least a couple of days before the kids' scents would transfer through the Veil and call to them."

"What if we get to the Rockies and the kids are too powerful to go west? Or you are?" I voiced the fear that had been circling my head all day.

Shane returned to his seat beside me, his thigh brushing against my jeans with a rasp. "Then we try another treaty land. The fae don't cover the world. There are hundreds of different places where their magic can be avoided. We'll find one we can pass. Don't worry."

I nodded my agreement, but I worried anyway. I envisioned our lives, running from one part of the globe to another for years to come, never finding a home. What about the kids' schooling? How would they make friends? How would we find the money to survive if I couldn't work? A tight band of anxiety encircled my chest and squeezed.

"Take a breath, Willa." Shane grabbed my hands and rubbed his thumbs in a circle on my palms. I stared down at our entwined fingers. Air whooshed out of my lungs for a new reason—the memory of my body draped across his this morning. Our limbs soft with sleep, our dreams hot.

The patterns traced by his fingertips simultaneously soothed and aroused me. I kept my eyes on our hands, hyperaware of his body looming over me. A fluttery sensation grew in my stomach.

I peeked at him under my lashes. He licked his lips, his gaze heating on mine. "Willa, this morning I —"

I panicked.

Yanking my hands away and tucking them in my pockets, I jumped to my feet. "Good night!" I said, my voice shrill as I scrambled from the room. I didn't look back, but I felt his smoldering eyes following me, scorching me even from his position on the couch.

In the bedroom, I brushed my teeth and berated myself. It was just biology. A man and a woman in close quarters. Our physical reactions to each other meant nothing. "But oh, what I wouldn't give for a babysitter," I whispered. "And a date night for Mom."

***

The whip cracked. A man groaned.

"Why did you return, exiled one?"

"Please," he croaked. "Brought blood debt. Swear it."

"Where?"

"Lost . . . mercy."

"The queen is displeased with you."

The whip cracked again in the darkness.

Another groan.

"You have forfeited the queen's gift of mercy to your mother. Your mother begged the queen on her knees for your exile instead of your just execution. How dare you return! You will remain here to rot and think on your transgressions."

"Please, try again. Please. I have two demi-fae."

The whip coiled on the floor in a rasp.

"Two?"

"Yes, two. My children."

"You bring your children to the queen?"

"Twins."

A pair of voices whispered near the door. The man dropped his head between his hanging arms. Rage burned in his heart. He'd been so close . . . That bitch. His mother. She'd hidden the twins too well. And assigned a guardian. He hadn't expected to be followed into the Green Lands. He swallowed a harsh cough as the skin on his back ached and bled.

"Very well," an imperious voice echoed in the cell, making him flinch with new fear. "Bring me the twins. You have one week."

"Yes, my queen," he croaked.

CHAPTER 7

Whispers woke me. I sat up as Finn and Dara snuck out of the bedroom, their backs vanishing from sight. I glanced at the clock and winced. Hurrying to brush my teeth, I followed them into the kitchen where they sat, still whispering, with cereal bowls they'd obviously poured themselves.

I mumbled, "Morning, monkeys," and started Shane's coffeemaker. Mild lemony sunlight reflected off the kitchen counters with a soft glow. I swiped up Froot Loops and dropped them in the trash.

"Can I go with Shane to get the RV?" Finn asked, his voice distorted by a mouthful of food. I grimaced at the milk dripping down his chin and tossed him a napkin.

"Uncle Shane," Dara corrected in an undertone. Finn kicked her, and she stuck out her tongue.

I shook my head. "No, we have to stay inside, remember?"

"He already left, anyway," Dara said. "I saw his car."

Frowning, I peeked into the living room. The pillow and blanket he'd used sat in a neat pile at the end of the couch, a note on top: *Back in an hour. Get packed.*

I frowned again. “Pack what?” I mumbled. We had one set of clothes each right now.

I called toward the kitchen that I was going to take a shower and told the kids to go through the stuff Shane dug out of our house to see what they wanted to bring in the RV. “You can bring one box each!” I yelled down the hall.

“Okay, Mama!” Dara yelled back.

After my shower, I threw our meager pile of clothes and toiletries into one of the duffel bags from Shane’s closet and tossed the bag on the ground by the front door.

“Finn? Dara?” I stepped into the kitchen where the mess of their empty cereal bowls and drops of milk remained on the counter. Rolling my eyes, I yelled, “Guys, come on. You’re supposed to put your dishes in the sink when you’re done.”

No one answered. After I cleaned up, I wandered the house, calling their names. When I ducked into the basement and found no sign of them, worry prickled.

Shane wasn’t back yet—no RV sat in the driveway.

My heart pounded as I walked back to the kitchen and leaned over the sink, checking the yard. The kids stood at the edge of the lawn talking to a tall, thin man.

I burst through the door and thumped down the deck stairs, sprinting for the twins. The man looked up at me and smiled, his teeth flashing in a devilish grin.

"Hello, Willa, long time no see."

I stumbled to a stop, my disbelieving eyes taking in Paul's haggard appearance. He looked old —significantly older than the last time I'd seen him —and sick, with sallow skin and sunken eyes. His blond hair, thinning at the top, hung loose to his shoulders, and he wore threadbare jeans and a t-shirt. No trace remained of the handsome, cocky guy from the bar a lifetime ago.

"Paul," I gasped and reached for Finn's hand to pull him back. He stepped away from me, crossing his arms.

"You didn't tell us he was our dad." Finn's voice was sharp and accusatory. He squinted at me. "He says he just wants to meet us. To teach us about magic."

My automatic protest died on my lips. I hadn't told them the kidnapping and their grandmother's murder resulted from their father's greed. I hadn't told them what Iris warned—that Paul wanted to steal their magic. I hadn't wanted to add to their trauma, and now I looked like a liar.

Kicking myself for my shortsightedness, I swallowed. "I should have told you. I'm sorry. But you can't believe him."

"No, I can't believe *you*, Willa."

I winced at Finn's use of my first name.

"I want to stay with Mama," Dara said loudly, directing her wishes to Finn. "He sent the bats after us. He's not nice."

Finn frowned but shook his head. "Maybe the bats weren't so scary."

Dara gasped, and Finn's shoulders drooped. A struggle played out on his face, and it broke my heart.

"Finn, I . . ." I waved my hands helplessly.

"Enough of this. I don't care if you choose me. I only wanted you past the ward line." Paul clapped his hands together, and both kids fell limp at his feet.

I darted forward, only to smack into an invisible wall. I slammed my fists against it. "Stop! What are you doing? Please stop. Please let them go. Please. I'll do whatever you want!"

Paul sneered. "Idiot. I don't want anything from you. But these children will pay my family's blood debt to Queen Mab and end my banishment."

"You're going to sacrifice them?" I gasped. The blood drained from my head in a dizzying whoosh.

"No. I will give them to Mab to replace the fae she lost. She adores demi-fae servants." His lips twisted mockingly as he added in a mutter, "The fool." Returning his hard eyes to my face, he continued. "And at the winter solstice, if they please her, she'll keep them alive for another year."

Pressing myself forward, I reached for Dara's hand, but I couldn't penetrate Paul's magic. I banged my fists against the barrier again as panic built a scream in my throat.

"And if they displease her?" I croaked.

"She'll take their blood and their magic."

"*What*?" I shrieked.

"Relax. They're strong, but not that strong. They're more useful as servants than blood sacrifices."

I shook my head, gritting out, "They're *your* children."

Shrugging, Paul tossed a limp Dara over one shoulder and tucked Finn against his hip. "I don't care. And neither should you. In the Green Lands, if they please Mab, they'll never grow old, never face disease. You should thank me."

"But they'll be prisoners!" I shouted again. Rage kindled to life in my hands, and I worked to calm my burgeoning magic. I couldn't shoot fire at him while he held the children.

Paul traced a quick sketch in the air and a green light flashed. On the other side of the glittering portal stood the Green Lands.

"I will find you!" I screamed as he vanished, taking the children with him.

The invisible bubble holding me back disappeared, and I staggered to my knees, despair clawing at my mind with poisonous claws. I'd lost them again. And it was my fault. I hadn't warned them to be wary of their father. I let them out of my sight, hadn't kept them in the house. And I'd been unable to stop Paul from grabbing them, even though I stood directly in front of him.

An inferno built in my chest and my hands burst into uncontrollable flames. My pulse thundered in my ears. I screamed at the sky. Screamed until my voice turned hoarse. Exhausted, I slumped, and my fire winked out.

The chilly air raised goosebumps on my skin, and I shivered. The kids didn't even have their shoes.

A car horn blared from the front yard, and I staggered to my feet. I needed to regroup. I *would* rescue them again. But my fear and panic trapped me in place. We'd barely gotten them back from the Slaugh. Now that Paul had them, we'd be facing formidable magic. Quicksand composed of hopeless impotency tugged at my feet and threatened to pull me under.

The horn honked again, and I mindlessly staggered around the side of the house. Shane jumped from the cab of the RV, a grin on his face. He saw me, and the grin fell. He jogged forward and grabbed my shoulders.

"Why are you outside? Where are the kids?" he demanded, his fingertips digging into the soft flesh of my upper arms.

I shook my head, helpless tears returning to the surface. "Paul lured them out to the backyard. He told them he was their father. He would teach them magic. When they crossed the ward, he grabbed them. I-I . . . I couldn't stop him."

Shane dropped his hands and stepped away. "Damn."

I missed the warmth of his hands. He probably hated me, but not as much as I hated myself.

Shane waved me into the house. "Tell me

exactly what happened. What he said, word-for-word."

I recited the story while Shane paced the kitchen. When I finished, I added, "I know this is my fault, but you're *not* leaving me behind again to go after them."

Shane halted mid-stride and came to stand in front of me. I glared at his chin, unable to force myself to meet his eyes. I couldn't bear to see the blame there.

Silence echoed in the kitchen. Goosebumps rippled across the skin of my shoulders.

"Willa, this isn't your fault," Shane finally said, and I looked up in surprise. "Paul tricked the kids. Fae are very good at tricks. We can go back and forth with blame—I shouldn't have left you guys here alone—but the bottom line is we need to get moving."

Crossing my arms, I nodded. "Right, yes. Do you know where Mab lives? When is the winter solstice?"

"It's mid-winter, the shortest day of the year. In the Green Lands, it's the one day per year the sun doesn't rise. The High Fae use the cover of darkness to conduct old rituals."

I swallowed hard. "Blood sacrifices?"

He looked away. "For all that it's an outlawed practice, no one gets as strong as Mab without delving into that kind of magic. Iris said she goes mad with it sometimes. The blood hunter lure. No one is safe in her Court."

My mouth dried and my throat convulsed.

"But I can track them again in the Green Lands, like before. We'll get there in time, Willa. I swear it."

I nodded, my eyes staring but not seeing as I envisioned a day of darkness and blood. The screams of my children.

Shane's warm hand on my shoulder brought me back. "I loaded some camping gear in the RV at the rental place. Let's go through it, pack, and head to Iris's gate."

I straightened my spine and followed him.

AN hour later, we stood outside Iris's house. I eyed it sadly. It had only been empty for a few days but already looked neglected. Dry leaves cluttered the wide front porch, and a window screen hung loose, in danger of falling.

We slipped along the side yard, and I thought of the indomitable woman who'd made such a difference in our lives. A sudden wave of grief swamped me, and I stumbled. She'd loved the kids so fiercely. She died to protect them. I knew nothing about her former life in the Green Lands, but she hadn't deserved to be killed for her son's greed.

I wondered if anyone outside of the four of us would mourn her. Had she left any friends behind in the Green Lands who cared?

Shivering, I hurried my pace to catch up to Shane.

He led us down the now-familiar path into

the woods behind the house, and when we reached the clearing where I'd woken only a couple days ago, hurt and bewildered but full of joy to have the kids back, I gritted my teeth.

I'd worked so hard and been so frightened, and it had all been for nothing. Now the kids were lost again, likely even more confused and scared than before, because now they knew their own father wanted to hurt them. The guilt Finn was undoubtedly feeling stabbed at my heart.

Shane sketched out a complicated symbol in the dirt while I fought the impulse to shoot a furious bolt of fire at the sky. It would accomplish nothing except making me look like a lunatic, and I didn't want to give Shane any excuses to leave me behind again.

Sucking down a sharp breath, I focused on remaining calm. Adjusting the straps of my backpack, I knelt beside him. "Can I help?"

His fingers moved across the ground with delicate strength, and I was momentarily mesmerized enough to forget my anger.

"Nope, all set."

Shane's design was intricate and beautiful, the artist living inside his soul readily apparent.

Standing, he pulled a long knife from the sheath at his belt. He dug the tip into his thumb and spattered a few flecks of blood on top of the key.

My mouth dropped open as the symbol flashed a deep emerald-green. A crack in the air appeared above it, like the one Paul had created in the backyard. Through the rent was a languid river.

A firm hand pushed me forward, and I stepped into the Green Lands.

At the riverbank, we pulled off our sweatshirts and packed them away. The warm sun on my skin felt more like late summer rather than early November, and the robin's egg blue sky stretched endlessly without a cloud in sight.

I looked at Shane. "Okay. What's the new plan?"

Inhaling deeply, Shane tilted his head and stood still for a long moment.

Resisting the urge to fidget, I breathed in the gently flowing river. Its burbling murmurs soothed my anxiety a little, and by the time Shane straightened, I felt more in control than I had since I lost the children.

I'm coming, babies, I promised.

"I have a scent trail. They're far off—very far. I have a feeling Paul used magic to take them directly to Mab's Court."

I swallowed. "Then we better get going."

We shouldered our packs, and Shane set the pace. I followed and tried not to imagine my children in a High Fae's castle, terrified and hopeless. Shane's news about how far we needed to travel had burst my bubble of peace.

As we hiked, I quizzed Shane on what Iris had told him about the Green Lands, but quickly I realized he didn't know much. His quiet frustration made me stop pushing him for answers. Why hadn't

Iris been honest with me? If I'd known the risks, I would have moved us west long ago.

I staggered to a stop. "She didn't tell me because she didn't want me to take the children where she couldn't follow. If I'd taken the kids west, she wouldn't have been able to pass the Rockies. That's why she hired you and kept me in the dark."

Shane stopped as well and stared at the sky. His shoulders drooped. "I suspect you're right," he murmured.

I kicked the grass at my feet and let out a growl. "How selfish! You know, that's so typical of her. She couldn't stand me, however much she doted on the kids. Of course she'd prioritize her time with them over their safety."

Shane spun to face me. "Don't talk about her like that. She's dead because she tried to protect them."

"But she wouldn't have *had* to protect them—she wouldn't have died if we'd gone west," I argued. "Look, I get you think you owe her your life, and I'm grateful you feel that way because it means you're helping me, but I think Iris was a selfish woman, and I'm pissed at her right now." Closing my eyes, I sighed. "But I know it doesn't matter anymore."

Shane frowned for another long moment before nodding. We resumed hiking.

My eyes stayed on the back of his neck, which turned a darker shade of red with every step. Did he understand where I was coming from? How did it feel to realize the woman he revered wasn't so saintlike after all? My stomach churned with guilt, and I resolved to go easier on Shane about the Iris thing. He had enough on his plate. And I was sure his grief was real.

I skipped forward and patted his arm. His fingers briefly grasped my hand.

I cleared my throat. "You said she saved you. How?"

A muscle ticked in Shane's jaw. He bent his head to look at me, and his eyes reflected the blue of the sky, making them glow cerulean. "I always knew I was different. My mom told me stories when I was little about the handsome man who found her in the woods and took her to a place of magic and beauty. When he dropped her home after he was finished with her, she found out she was pregnant. But he never came back. I never met him."

His gaze turned distant, and he grinned. "I transformed into my boar form for the first time as a toddler. My mom found me in the crib, curled up, and she knew I'd gotten some of my dad's powers. She was so excited for me. We played with the magic all the time, just the two of us. But . . ."

After a beat, I prompted him. "But?"

"But then she got sick and died, and I stopped using the magic. I didn't like it anymore. It hadn't saved her. It was useless."

I reached to grip his arm again, my throat burning at his grief.

"After I hit puberty though, I couldn't control it anymore. If I didn't use it, it leaked out of me at school, at my foster home. So I would sneak into the woods at night and transform and run around, just enough to exhaust myself."

Frowning, I interrupted. "Finn doesn't do that. Are you sure that's his magic? Shifting?"

"Finn's blood is more diluted than mine. Remember, Paul's a half-fae."

"Oh yeah."

"So I was in the woods one night, and a blood witch caught me. He told me he was going to eat me to steal my magic." Shane shivered and the warm skin of his forearm tensed under my fingers. "Then Iris popped up, killed the witch, and took me home with her."

"And that's it?" I asked. "She adopted you?"

"No, but she started teaching me about myself. I would go to her house after school, and she would talk to me. She was really sad and lonely, I could tell. She told me about being an exile. And I think I reminded her of Paul a little. Before he turned into a total asshole."

"And now you don't have anyone," I murmured, absently stroking his arm and staring down at my boots swishing through the grass. *Poor Shane. Poor Iris.* The horrible things I'd thought about her earlier weren't totally fair. She'd played a critical role in Shane's life, and he obviously loved her.

Firm fingers enclosed mine and I flushed. I started to pull away my hand that still gripped his forearm, but he tugged me closer until our hips bumped. We stopped walking, and I craned my neck and looked into his eyes, holding my breath.

"I have you," he said, the corners of his eyelids crinkling with his lopsided smile.

I exhaled a puff of air and wrapped my arms around him in a tight hug. "You have me," I agreed. "And Finn and Dara."

His hands warmed my skin as he squeezed me back. The moment offered a peaceful respite from everything going on around us. He'd lost Iris, but he wasn't alone. I'd lost the kids, but I wasn't alone either. We had each other now, and we'd get through this. Together.

WE hiked for hours, though the sun remained in the same spot in the sky. Then, in a blink, the yellow orb dropped and a brilliant sunset rippled across the western sky.

Shane drew me to a stop, and I admired the peachy glow the sun cast across his face.

"I could only find one tent in the RV, so you can have it. I'll shift to my boar form and sleep by the fire."

Part of me wanted to protest, tell him we could share the tent, but the smarter part of me knew separate was a better idea.

Shane dug the tent from his pack, along with a rigged fishing line.

Striding to the water's edge, he called over his shoulder, "You set up camp, and I'll catch dinner."

Following him, I gathered a pile of driftwood

and branches from the bank and built a fire with my magic. The flames shot so quickly from my hands to the wood I almost singed my shoes. My power was stronger in the Green Lands.

By the time I had the tent set up, Shane was cleaning a string of fish. I dug through his pack to find a pan and set it up for him.

"This is going to be a simple meal," he warned while he fried the fish. The delicious aroma made my mouth water.

"I don't care," I told him. "Last time, I just ate granola bars. This is way better."

He grinned at me, his cheeks creasing. My fingers itched with the desire to trace his features. I looked away.

After our feast and the cleanup, we sat together in the grass by the tent. My worries returned with full force, swamping me. Here I was with a full belly and a companion who would protect me, while my kids were probably in a dungeon somewhere or sobbing in the grip of giant bats flying through the sky.

I imagined them being chased by the hounds, their wide mouths salivating. Or by some other ravenous wildfae—like a troll.

"We'll find them," I whispered. My fingertips went white from the force I used to grip my elbows.

"We will," Shane affirmed, his voice gruff and solid.

His determination should have soothed me.

It didn't.

CHAPTER 8

"Are they poisonous?" I stared at the nest of swirling tentacles.

"I'm not sure."

A squirming mass of thorny vegetation lay across our path. The leaves and vines rasped against each other with an echoing hum. It was like someone had carelessly and callously dumped a massive potted plant, and the roots came alive with a vengeance. They writhed at our feet, some as thick as my leg, with serrated barbs and venous red and purple leaves. There was no easy way past them.

The mushroom forest waited to the east, full of deadly toadstools and dark shadows.

To the west, the land dropped away into a sweltering swamp. The stench emanating from that direction burned my nose.

We'd risen with the sun and hiked all morning, only to run up against this obstacle in our path.

"I vote we cross the river and risk the toadstools," I said. "We've done it before."

Shane shook his head. "We were lucky. More than mushrooms live in those woods."

"Like what?"

"Trolls, ogres, pixies . . ."

I shivered. Pixies didn't sound too bad, but no thanks on the trolls and ogres. "There have to be creatures in the swamp too," I pointed out, kicking away a stem that reached for my boot.

"Yeah." Shane closed his eyes and sighed.

"I can maybe burn it up?" I offered, gesturing toward the writhing plant monster. "It's a big area, and I don't have Dara's air magic anymore to make that exploding shield, but I can try."

"Those vines cover at least an acre." Shane scratched his chin and looked down at me with his eyebrows raised.

"Let me try. If it doesn't work, we can debate the forest and the swamp."

Shane backed up a step and made a go-ahead gesture.

I assessed the vines but couldn't tell where the roots dug into the ground within the writhing bulk. Concentrating, I imagined flames engulfing my hands. They sprang to life, and I threw my fire outward, trying to remember how I'd directed it when I shot at the bird-fae. It had been easier when Dara ripped it out of me with her magic. Now, I needed to figure out the logistics myself. I imagined a hose and grinned as a jet of bright orange blasted the snaking leaves.

The vines screamed, and I flinched but kept going, directing the flare in a sweeping arc, back and forth. The green mass curled away from the fire, turning to ash where it didn't move quickly enough. The screams grew louder.

Marching forward, I cleared a path in front of us. Shane followed close behind.

"Keep moving," he shouted, his voice barely audible over the shrieking plants.

My hands grew hot as I spread the fire, but the tell-tale ache in my chest was absent. Hopefully that meant I was doing a good job sending it away from my body like Kalo had warned. I was tiring though. Sweat beaded on my upper lip and at my temples.

A few tense steps later, we stood in the middle of the mass. Behind us a swath of charred leaves and ashes lay unmoving, but we were only halfway through. My eyes widened as the vines ahead appeared to rise into the air in front of us, the shoots whirling in a frenzy as they formed a barrier.

"Hurry," Shane urged.

I pressed on. The unending howl rose another octave as I moved the fire steadily forward. My pulse pounded through my veins and echoed in my ears. My foot slipped, and Shane grabbed my arm to steady me.

My hands grew impossibly hot, and I lost my footing when black spots popped in and out of my vision. Shane scooped me up, and I made sure to keep my hands away from his body.

"More, Willa," he shouted. His voice reached me as if traveling through a thick wall, the vibrations from his chest reverberating against my ear. The plant's wails had reached a deafening crescendo. The green matrix in front of us stood chest-high, limbs whipping about with agitation. The vines recoiled from my flames, and the barrier continued to grow taller.

My fire died down again, and I reached deep inside my core to find the coal of magic. The hard pulse felt like a second heartbeat, and the heartbeat was slowing. I closed my eyes, stepping inside myself to examine it. It emanated a dim light. My magic was almost spent. I wanted to remain, to examine the coal and feel its power, but from a great distance I heard Shane screaming my name.

He shook me until my teeth rattled.

I opened my eyes. Green vines wound through the air inches from my face, and I recoiled, pushing myself harder into Shane's chest and blasting my fire outward with every bit of my remaining magic. It flared incandescently bright, forcing me to close my eyes again. Shane staggered forward at the same moment the screams cut off.

Blinking, I looked around. We were out of the nest. The field ahead stood clear. Shane dropped me to my feet and fell to his knees. I spun to see the remnants of the vine creature coiled into a tight ball, edging toward the swamp and avoiding the burned patches of ground. Its voice was a muted wail, and my skin crawled at the sound of its cries.

Swaying with exhaustion, I dropped beside Shane, but I gasped when I saw the state of his legs. His jeans were ripped to shreds and revealed bloody, oozing gashes along his flesh.

"Shane!" I shrieked and reached behind him, but my hands found only empty air. "Where's your pack!"

Closing his eyes, his face pale and sweaty, Shane muttered, "Fell off when I grabbed you. The vines swept it away."

I looked over the field of ashes but didn't see his bag.

"Oh no, the first aid kit," I moaned. What if we needed to disinfect his cuts? Maybe it wasn't too bad. "Strip. Let me see."

Shane pulled off his jeans, and I held back a cry at the state of his legs. The welts along his shins and thighs were deep, and blood ran in rivulets from several jagged gashes, likely from the barbed thorns.

Grabbing my pack, I dug until I found a towel. I dabbed at the cuts. "Some of these are bad, baby," I said. I blew on one, trying to soothe his pain. "I think you need stitches. What are we going to do?"

I looked up and found him watching me with a peculiar expression on his face.

A flush swept over me. "Ah," I scrambled. "Sorry. Force of habit with kid injuries."

Shane gave a short, jerking nod and inched away from my hands. "Give me a little space. I'll shift. That usually gets rid of any mild injuries."

I sat back on my heels and looked everywhere but at Shane as he stripped off the rest of his torn, soot-stained clothes and made a neat pile by my pack. A pulse of green light and a snorting noise made me turn my head. Shane's boar form watched me with red-rimmed eyes.

"You're bigger here," I blurted, and flushed again. "I mean, your boar. You're bigger. Do you feel any different?"

The pony-sized boar snorted at me again, filling the air with a musky scent. Did the Green Lands not only make Shane's boar form larger but also remove his ability to speak?

He trotted in a slow circle, sniffing the ground, and raised his head to scent the air. Spinning quickly, his hooves spattering clods of dirt, he looked into the dark forest. It was closer than I'd realized. The river had slowed to a trickle and the woods loomed only a few yards away from where we rested.

I stood; my legs wobbled.

A deep baying sound penetrated my still-ringing eardrums and a chill raced down my spine. The sound grew louder, singing of danger and sharp teeth, wilder than a wolf's call.

Shane snorted and moved in front of me, scraping the ground with a pointed hoof.

I dove for Shane's clothes, pulled out his knife, and unsheathed it. The boar and I kept wary gazes locked on the forest.

When the source of the chilling sound came into sight, my brain refused to believe what I saw.

Three monsters sprinted out of the woods—three monsters with sharp claws, bright white fur, and jagged teeth in gaping red mouths. They paused at the river, and I held my breath, only to lose it in a strangled gasp when they forded the shallow water and headed straight for us.

They looked like a cross between gorillas and wolves, with long lupine snouts and shaggy-haired, muscular chests. They ran on two feet and used a third limb every few steps to push off the ground in a burst of speed. Their long bays changed to high-pitched, excited barks as they neared.

My knees knocked uncontrollably. My knife was barely as long as one of the claws tearing up the ground. They would rip us apart.

Shane's boar squealed a warning, but the monsters paid him no heed. Straightening my spine, I swiped a shaking hand across my forehead and brushed my hair behind my ears. The boar squealed again, the sound deepening into a roar, and I spared a glance at him, only to fall back a step.

The air around Shane blurred with a faint shimmer of green, and I gaped at his change. The boar was gone. Covered in hulking, grotesquely veined muscles, his shoulders almost stooping with the weight of the load, Shane looked like a cartoon-version of his human self. If the cartoon were designed by a psychopath. He turned, and I flinched back from his swollen face. One eye bulged in its socket, and the other gleamed like onyx, a pupil-less black. Sharp canines dropped into place, protruding over his bottom lip and curving out, like smaller versions of his boar's tusks.

A long white spear appeared out of nowhere, and he gripped it in one hand. Straight, smooth, and topped with a jagged point, the spear stood as tall as Shane, and Shane now stood close to seven feet. My mind whirled.

Stomping massive feet into the earth, he roared at me, and I dropped to the grass, covering my head with my hands. “Shane!” I screamed.

He snorted and the hair on the top of my head blew back. Just when I thought he would attack, he turned and roared again, this time at the monsters. Peeking through my fingers, I watched the attacking creatures hesitate.

Hope kindled in my chest, but it burned out a moment later as the beasts resumed their charge. Shane dropped into the same three-limbed stance and ran at them, and they met in a clash of fur and snarls.

I jumped to my feet, ready to help, but wavered. New-Shane didn’t need any help. His initial spear thrust caught one animal in the center of its chest. It fell with a howl, blood pulsing from the wound. The other two scraped at Shane with razor-edged claws, but he didn’t even flinch as he knocked them back and thrust wildly with the spear. His movements were brutal and ugly but effective. In moments, the monsters lay still on the ground, their white fur now matted red and black with blood and gore.

Shane didn’t stop, however. He continued to hack at their bodies, his growls interspersed with wet snorts. The muscles of his back rippled as he stabbed, and the deep claw marks on his thighs and forearms closed.

I started to call his name, but I hesitated. He didn't appear capable of reason at the moment, considering the way he kept stabbing at the dead wildfae. Was he mincing them up to eat them? My gorge rose.

Eventually, the wet squelching noises of his attack slowed, and Shane stood, swaying on his feet, above the mutilated bodies of our would-be attackers. Mustering my courage, I approached and quietly spoke his name. The blood on his body gleamed starkly crimson against his tan skin, and there was no way to tell which bloody streaks belonged to him and which belonged to the monsters he'd killed. My heart stuttered as I got closer.

The misshapen eyes met mine, Shane's gaze dull and unfocused.

"Are you hurt?"

He growled at me, but it was halfhearted. I stayed out of reach of his spear and dropped the hunting knife to show him my empty hands. "Okay, big guy. Come on. You know me."

A deep shudder racked his huge body, and he dropped to his knees. The spear vanished from his hand, and his bulging muscles shrunk in a slow-moving ripple as the tusks over his lips receded into his mouth. With a final massive groan, Shane toppled the rest of the way over and lay flat on his face in the blood-soaked grass.

Darting forward, I dropped by his head and

pushed my fingers against his neck. His pulse thudded slow and steady under my touch. Shifting my weight to my heels, I sighed and crossed my arms.

I didn't like where we were, so close to the forest's edge. The smell of blood and death would attract predators and scavengers in no time. But I couldn't carry Shane, not even in his normal size.

I settled for dragging him a few steps at a time away from the woods. When we passed the burned acre, I grabbed my pack and his ruined jeans. Drag and rest. Drag and rest . . . I repeated the steps so many times that when I finally stumbled to a halt, I was surprised to find the sun low in the sky. Looking backward, I estimated we'd probably made it a mile from the fight scene.

Dropping the pack, I dug out the tent and set it up. Then, with one last wriggling heave, I got Shane inside before I collapsed flat on my back in the grass and stared up at the sunset sky. Purple clouds drifted across my field of vision. Stretching my aching muscles, I took deep breaths and tried to slow my galloping heart.

We'd barely made any progress toward the kids today, and we'd nearly died twice. And I didn't know what was up with Shane's new shapeshifting magic or how to wake him from the coma-like sleep that showed no signs of easing.

Finn and Dara had spent another day lost in the Green Lands without me, and I was no closer to finding them. I rubbed my cold hands together.

Hopefully they were together, wherever they were.

IN the morning, Shane was still unconscious. I'd spent the night by his side, checking his breathing every few hours until the sun rose. He looked peaceful, but nothing I did roused him—not pinching, not splashing water, and not kissing his lips.

I grimaced and scrubbed my face with my palms. I felt bad about kissing him without his consent, but I'd decided it was worth a try, considering the fairytale nature of my life recently. His dry lips hadn't moved under mine.

Frowning, I clenched my hands into fists then loosened them. My mind raced with possibilities, each scarier than the last—Shane's new power had drained too much of his strength, and now he didn't know how to wake up. Or some unknown fae had cursed him, and he was frozen in time. What if Shane had been poisoned, either by the white-furred monsters or the barbed vines, and now he lay dying while I sat and watched?

I closed my fists again. *I don't have time for this! Can I leave him behind?* I stopped cold. That would be murder. Shane was unconscious and vulnerable. He'd used his new power to protect us, and he deserved my help in return. I felt despicable for even considering it. But oh, the delay chafed at me, and I had to swallow a frustrated scream.

How many days had we lost already? How many days until the winter solstice? My thoughts circled as I counted and stared at Shane's still form.

By mid-day, I'd resorted to pacing in front of the tent, kicking the grass and trying to ignore my empty, quivering stomach. The sun burned hot overhead and, despite the chill in my heart, my body was coated in a fine sheen of sweat. Shane still hadn't moved—he hadn't so much as drawn a deep breath. It seemed more and more likely that something was seriously wrong with him. *Should I try to drag him back through the fairy ring and get him to a hospital?*

My shoulders slumped. It would be impossible. We were miles from the fairy ring, and Shane outweighed me by at least sixty pounds, all of it solid muscle. I crawled into the tent and checked on him again. His chest rose and fell in a normal rhythm and his skin felt warm against the back of my wrist; not hot. But his hand fell limply to the side when I picked it up and dropped it.

I needed help, but I had no one.

The ache in my chest intensified and I absently rubbed my sternum. Maybe . . . no. But what other choice did I have? Shane had told me not to do it, but Shane was in no position to make decisions.

Exiting the tent, I flung my arms wide and called out into the sunshine, "Kalonymos of the Nightspawn Clan, I need you!"

STARING at the campfire, I shivered and nibbled absently at a granola bar. The cold night air whistled past me, stirring my hair and sending plumes of smoke toward the river. I needed to sleep, but I couldn't bear to lay in the tent next to Shane's immobile body.

Kalo hadn't answered my call. Shane was dying. I didn't know how I knew, but I was certain. I would wait with him until he passed, and then I would go on. *Somehow.*

The knot in my throat had grown into a boulder, and it was all I could do to force the dry food down. Tears burned in my eyes, but I blinked them away and watched a vivid purple comet hurtle across the sky. I hurt for Shane, who would die in the Green Lands; I ached for the life cut short because of my actions, my choices, my family . . .

My guilt ate at me with scraping, grating teeth.

I would never get to take that final step toward him and see if his mouth tasted sweet or carnal. In my heated imaginings, it had been both.

Sucking in a sharp breath, I willed myself to remain steady and calm. *How long can a person live without food and water?* Shane had been unconscious for over twenty-four hours. Earlier, I tried to force water down his throat, but I hadn't even been able to open his mouth. It was like he was made of stone.

The wind shifted, blowing the smoke into my face, and I stood to change positions. Blinking away the gray haze, I stepped into a hard body. I fell back with a shriek, and my heartrate exploded into a stampede.

Firm hands gripped my forearms and stopped

my fall into the fire pit. "Shush, lady."

I stopped screaming. "Kalo?" I rasped, looking up at the man hovering over me. Familiar olive-green skin gleamed at me from an unfamiliar body. Tall and broad-shouldered, this goblin was no child. His bare chest, planed with muscles, narrowed into slim hips shrouded by a leather kilt. He wore a sword at each hip, and the hilt of a third blade protruded over his shoulder. I swallowed.

High, angular cheekbones stood out under a furrowed brow, and two sharp, gleaming horns curved out of the dark mane of hair atop his head. His red eyes met my wide and staring ones, and I struggled to repress a shiver—a shiver of what? Fear? Or something else? I swallowed again.

"You called me."

Taking a calming breath, I nodded. "I did. I need help."

Kalo let go of my arms and stepped back. Moving over to the tent, he poked a finger into the nylon and stooped to peek inside.

"Where are the children?"

Tears filled my eyes, but I furiously blinked them away and scrubbed my cheeks. "We got them out. Three days ago. Four? We got them home and planned to go west. Then their father stole them again."

Kalo frowned. "We?"

I gestured to the tent. "Shane is the children's guardian. He's a half-blood." I stumbled over the words and cleared my throat, then quickly explained

Shane's relationship to Iris and to the kids. Kalo's eyes continued to gleam at me in the darkness.

When I got to the part where Shane had shifted into a monstrous man to fight the wildfae, Kalo growled.

"Drows, most likely. Very vicious. Good thing to have a berserker at your side."

"A berserker?" I bit the inside of my cheek, racking my brain to remember the Wikipedia article I'd read before I entered the fairy ring. Had that been a term I'd seen? I didn't think so.

"Did you not know?"

I shook my head. "I thought . . . I thought he was a boar. And I think he thought he was only a boar? But after he shifted back to his human form after the fight, he lost consciousness. I can't wake him. I think he's dying." My voice quivered.

Kalo stroked a hand through his dark hair, pushing it back from his horns. "A boar is a common form for a berserker. Likely the Green Lands pushed the third form on him when he reached for more power. He'll be fine in a day or two, once he sleeps it off."

A deep exhalation exploded from my lungs. My relief was quickly swallowed by frustration. "A day or two! I don't have a day or two! I have to find my kids!"

Kalo watched me as I paced in front of him. Warring feelings battled in my chest. Shane would be okay—thank goodness—but I could *not* wait another couple of days for him to wake.

"Do you wish my help?" Kalo's voice was deep and smooth, so different from the piping tones I remembered from a few days earlier.

I stopped pacing to stare at him. I frowned. "Why are you so much older?"

He shrugged. "Time moves differently in the goblin caves. Where my clan resides, in the Crystal Caves, we live years while a day passes aboveground."

Biting my lip, I considered his answer. "Are you saying in the handful of days since I saw you last, you've lived years?"

Kalo nodded.

I studied his size, his features, and his attitude. He had to be telling the truth, no matter how shocking the truth may be. "Shane didn't know that, and supposedly Iris taught him everything about the Green Lands."

Shrugging, Kalo glanced at Shane's still form. "Told him less than nothing, I presume, wanting to keep him under her thumb. Typical High Fae."

He straightened and put his hands on the hilts of the swords at his waist. "I will help you. We will go to the Crystal Caves. You will stay there for one year, and you will train to fight the High Fae. In one year, we will return here, and the guardian will still be sleeping. He will wake, and you will continue your quest, but with more power and more knowledge."

Speechless, I shook my head.

"If you go to Mab now, as you are, you will die. A berserker is no match for a High Fae Court. You will need more."

"You can help me."

Kalo shook his head. "I'm no match for a High Fae Court either. Facing one or a handful, yes." He shrugged. "But a Court? My magic is darkness and deceit. Coldness and fury. A High Fae's magic aboveground in the Green Lands is wicked power. Mab will devour your mind before I draw my sword."

I fought the despair churning in my stomach at his words.

"But if I train you—a dragonkin, a blood witch, a mother . . ." Kalo stared hard at me. "Yes, I think this is a good plan."

My mouth fell open. "Wait. I'm not a blood witch."

"You have the blood of demi-fae in you; your children, I assume. It's not a lot but it may be of some use." He smirked. "It's your choice, of course. I stand by my vow. If you demand my life now in a pointless sacrifice, I can take you to Mab and you can die in front of your children."

My knees weakened, but I forced my spine straight. "Who will guard Shane if I go with you?"

Kalo's eyes gleamed with satisfaction, and he whistled sharply.

I flinched as two new shapes materialized beside the fire. Kalo barked a few commands at them, and the figures melted into the shadows before I caught a clear look at them.

"Bren and Mael will guard the boar."

I stared into the darkness outside of the fire's

glow. Conflict raged. Shane had told me not to trust the goblins, but Shane's information about the Green Lands came from Iris, and I had a feeling Kalo's assessment of Iris had been correct—she absolutely would have held things back from Shane to ensure his dependence on her.

I glanced at Kalo again and met his crimson eyes. My instincts told me to trust him, but that made no sense. I needed to discount those instincts. However, if I studied my situation logically, it wasn't like I had many options. My children were gone, and I didn't know how to find them without help. Shane was out of the picture—hopefully only for a little bit longer, but maybe forever if Kalo was wrong or deceiving me.

And I couldn't deny the evidence standing right before my eyes that time passed differently in Kalo's caves. I needed that extra time before the winter solstice—time to get stronger.

My stomach roiled. Despite Shane's warning, I would trust the goblin.

I straightened my spine. "Let's go. You train me. I fight. One year." Furious intent filled my eyes. "If you're lying . . . if you betray me—I will burn you to ashes."

White teeth flashed at me in the darkness. Callused fingers grabbed mine. "Hold your breath, lady."

I sucked in a gasp and the world went black.

PART II

CHAPTER 9

Water splashed onto my face, and I flinched. Rolling over on the sleeping platform, I yanked a fur over my head. The Crystal Caves dripped—something I'd discovered in the six months of my residency. You never knew when a stalactite would let loose with an eyeball-burning drop, and I'd learned to sleep under the furs. Unless I forgot.

The fur tickled my nose. I sneezed and sat up with a groan. My forearms and wrists ached from Kalo's sword drills, and my fingertips burned from expending too much fire yesterday.

The dim cave surrounding me stank of iron and damp. The goblins, fiercely protective of their homeland, laced every door and pathway with iron ingots to keep the High Fae away. It made for an unpleasant sleeping environment, but anything was better than an invasion from aboveground. Or so I'd been told.

I spent my first few waking moments as I always did—imagining my kids safe and warm, somewhere above me, unafraid and waiting for rescue. Although months had passed for me, I held on to the hope Kalo had been truthful and only moments had passed for them in the Green Lands.

The hope hurt my heart, but nothing I'd seen in the Crystal Caves yet made me doubt my trust in my goblin rescuer. So every morning, I sent a powerful thought toward Finn and Dara—*I will see you soon.*

My second thought was for Shane. I hoped he was asleep and healing, safe in the tent where I'd left him. *Maybe he's dreaming of me.* I smiled.

My chest grew heavy, and the smile vanished. I needed to compartmentalize those sentiments and worries. The weight grew to a sharp pinch under my sternum. It was getting harder and harder to ignore the deep pull I felt to return to the surface. But to do so now would be foolhardy—I wasn't nearly ready to face Mab.

Every morning I practiced with an iron sword. Every afternoon I worked to strengthen my fire magic, and every evening I listened to Kalo lecture about the perfidy and menace of the High Fae.

Apparently, the goblins hadn't always lived belowground in the caves, and there used to be great civilizations full of other magic-wielding fae creatures. But now there were only High Fae, the goblins, and the wildfae in the Green Lands, and the goblins and High Fae were at war—not an all-out conflict with battles and armies, but an unending guerrilla campaign of assassinations and kidnappings, poisonings and thefts—perpetrated by both sides.

Another drop of water plopped onto my

shoulder. I shivered and got out of bed to dress quickly in the cool, moist air. My human pants were long gone—lost to the damp, dirt, and sword slices. After pulling on a pair of fur-lined leathers, I scrubbed my teeth with the paste Kalo had given me when I first moved in—it tasted like charcoal and tea—then ran a brush through my hair and braided it out of the way.

In the dark corridor, I followed the familiar path to the storeroom and snagged the goblin-version of a granola bar, a hard bread mixed with seeds and nuts.

I didn't live with the goblins—I'd hardly seen more than a handful of them during my stay. Kalo told me they didn't like humans, and while he had enough clout in their society to decree me off-limits and safe in his portion of the Crystal Caves, he didn't want to push my presence on them and tempt anyone to harm me.

It was a lonely existence, but I had a job to do, so I focused on learning everything I could and not on the fact my voice had grown rusty with disuse.

Munching my breakfast, I hurried farther along the tunnel—the wide and smooth rocks glittering with water and delicate flashes of silica—until I reached the open cavern marking the boundary of how far I was permitted to roam unaccompanied.

Kalo waited for me with an unhappy frown on his austere face, and I released a sigh. My sword lessons were frustrating and demoralizing for both of us. I wasn't progressing quickly, and when I sparred with other goblins who were hand-picked by Kalo, even the young ones beat me handily. With the iron blade in my hand, I wasn't graceful or deadly or intimidating—I looked like a jester at a Renaissance festival. I flailed. I tripped. I staggered.

The cavern around us glowed with pale-yellow torchlight, the floor sloped but smooth, and a rack of weapons rested along the wall. I spent hours in this room every day, and I'd come to learn every bump and groove of the floor—both as my body slid across it and as I collapsed into an exhausted heap atop it.

"Today, we try something new," Kalo said, striding forward and circling me. Turning my head to keep him in sight, I ignored the way his muscled chest gleamed in the torchlight. Goblins had no problems with nudity, and Kalo walked around in his kilt most of the time. The magnetic distraction of all that velvety-smooth green skin continued to make me blush, so I resolutely kept my eyes on his face. The sharp tips of his black horns glinted as he rocked back on his heels.

"You're halfway through your time in the caves, lady. And you're nowhere. You're tentative, scared, and weak. I train you every day, and when I push, you fold."

I swallowed, straightening my spine as I raised the tip of my sword.

"You don't attack. You barely defend. You hear my words, but you don't *react*." Kalo crossed his arms, his swords still strapped to his hips. "We will begin to push harder now. You must awaken more than your fire to face the High Fae. The time for coaxing is over."

Coaxing? He's been coaxing *me?* My burning muscles and callused palms begged to differ. I raised my eyebrows, and Kalo drew his swords across his body and lunged for me.

Air exploding from my lungs, I dove to the ground to avoid the blades whistling toward my head. Before I could think, Kalo reversed his thrust and dropped his aim. Two swords froze millimeters from my bare throat.

Kalo shook his head, and I resisted the urge to wilt under his crimson glare.

"It is not enough to dodge. You must fight back."

I nodded and returned to my feet, adjusting my grip on the hilt of my sword. I knew that. I'd been drilling every day for months, working on sword combinations and blocks, on thrusts and parries, and on footwork. But as soon as an opponent stood across from me, my training leaked from my ears. I reacted on instinct—and apparently my instincts demanded I duck and cower.

"Again," Kalo demanded. "This time, you attack me first."

I stared at the large muscled body in front of me and noted Kalo's relaxed shoulders, his hands resting on the hilts of his sheathed swords. I never attacked first. The idea of it frightened me to death, and that was precisely the problem. Exhaling, I chose one combo I'd been working on, and before I could talk myself out of it, I lunged and tried to stab Kalo in the gut.

My ears barely registered the shushing sound of his sword being unsheathed before his lightning-fast parry rang up my arm. I staggered, barely keeping my balance.

I spun and brought my sword up to block the thrust I expected, but Kalo stood still, sword back in its sheath, and watched me catch my breath.

"That was better," he said slowly. "Weak and lagging, but you didn't cower. We will do this again."

And we did. Again, and again. For what seemed like hours, I struck at Kalo while he stood before me with his swords sheathed. The ease and speed with which he pulled his blades, blocked me, and sheathed them again irritated me.

He wasn't even breathing hard; his movements were so fluid. Meanwhile, sweat pooled under my breasts and trickled down my hairline. My face had to be bright red with effort and frustration. The moist air of the cavern fogged my lungs as my attacks morphed from practiced lunges to wild swings. I stopped thinking about my feet, forgot about the heaviness of exhaustion in my limbs. A new blister formed under my thumb—I ignored it, determined to reach Kalo.

It wasn't fair he expected me to learn how to sword fight in six months when I'd never even taken a kickboxing class. It wasn't fair he expected me to compete with him—a male who'd wielded a blade his entire life and whose thigh muscles were the size of my waist. It wasn't fair I was in the Green Lands at all, desperately trying to learn an impossible skill in time to rescue my kidnapped children. *Again.*

My motions grew choppier. I lunged for the goblin, swinging and thrusting, arcing my sword in overhand blows. It wasn't *fair.* It wasn't *right.* And I would make it stop.

Words slipped from my lips—words I didn't understand—guttural and harsh. The torches flared around us, and a sheen of sweat formed on Kalo's chest. He'd stopped sheathing his swords between my strikes and was meeting my blows with grunts of his own.

I snarled and attacked harder. My skin burned, but it didn't feel like my fire magic, so I ignored it, concentrating all my attention on my sword arm and the taut patch of green skin at Kalo's navel I was determined to strike.

He was too fast for me though. I couldn't reach him. In six months, I still hadn't struck an opponent. They played with me and toyed with me. Mocked me. I would never succeed. *I must succeed. I must* fight. *And I must win!*

Frustration and determination boiled over, and without thought, I screamed, "Korra!"

My skin flashed with blistering heat and hardened. I hesitated, the lightning sensation alien and strange. I glanced down at my arm, and my mouth dropped open as my skin turned gold. Large scales formed, rippling up my sword arm and—I gasped—my other arm too.

I dropped the hilt and stared, open-mouthed. Scales covered my fingers, and my nails were becoming razor sharp, with ridges growing along my knuckles. I felt the scales forming, hardening, expanding over my body. Without touching myself, I knew my neck and face were now armored.

Raising horrified eyes to Kalo, I shrieked, "What's happening to me?"

Kalo's eyes, I noticed through my terror, were not horrified. In fact, if there were a word for the gleam in his crimson gaze, I would have to call it satisfied.

A bolt of agony ripped through my chest, and I fell to my knees. Blackness swirled in my vision, and Kalo called my name from a great distance. The pain in my chest grew into a burning, aching blast of heat. There was movement in my core—the source of my fire. The coal had kindled to a flame, and the flame was black. Darkness swept over me, and I collapsed.

"LADY," Kalo's voice whispered. "Wake. We have much to discuss."

I shivered, and warm arms wrapped tightly around my body for a long moment then released me. I blinked. A drop of water from the cavern's ceiling fell into my eye. I blinked again.

I sat up and a moan trembled from my lips as a wave of remembered pain raked along my flesh.

I swallowed it back and examined the hands in my lap. The gold scales were gone. My fingers spasmed.

A shadow moved, and I looked up at where Kalo stood over me. "Did I faint?"

"Yes, you collapsed at my feet, dropping your sword first, of course."

My eyes narrowed on the goblin. "What happened to me?"

Kalo crouched and poked my arm with his firm fingers. "Your dragon roused. Finally. I was beginning to think I was wrong about you."

My eyebrows drew together. "My dragon?"

"Told you, didn't I? That you were dragonkin. I smelled it in your fire. But I have to say, after six months of watching you flail, I was beginning to doubt it." Kalo frowned. Rising to his feet, he dusted off his hands. "Now we may begin to train in earnest."

"What?" I repeated, my voice weak. "In earnest?"

"Aye. You've the basics of swordplay already. And now we know how to rouse your dragon spirit. We will begin to train with your armor and your fire. You will need both to fight the High Fae."

"My armor?"

"The golden scales on your skin—impenetrable to fae magic and highly useful against blades. I've seen it in books. I hoped it would manifest in you."

I stood and planted my fists on my hips. "We need to talk. What books? You were expecting this?

Why didn't you warn me? Why did I faint? Why—"

"Cease, lady. You don't ask the right questions. Get your sword. We will not call Korra again today, but we will still practice." He adjusted my stance and shoved my sword into my hand. "Fix your feet."

I corrected my balance, automatically centering my weight and raising my sword in front of my body. My mind whirled with questions and my bones ached, but my muscles knew the drill.

"Focus and defend yourself," Kalo barked. He lunged at me, drawing one of his swords in a swift motion that normally would have made me flinch and duck.

Now, however, my brain caught his motion and calculated, too fast to explain in words. Leaping to the side, I raised my sword, blocked his strike, and shoved forward with my body weight so that, as his blade swung wide, I struck at his ribs.

My blade nicked his green flesh, and I froze.

Kalo froze too, then met my eyes with a gleeful smirk. "Yes!" he crowed. "Again, lady!"

He shoved me back, and I shifted my feet. We began again. Repeatedly, Kalo attacked, and I defended. I didn't always land a responsive blow, but when I did, my blood pulsed and the torches surrounding us flared. Kalo's chest gleamed red with blood as my small nicks and gouges accumulated.

I pulled a blow just before it sliced along his ribs, and he slapped the back of my head as he spun past me. "No mercy, lady. You will not injure me. The time for practice is done."

He swept his blade toward my head again, and I dropped low, parrying the strike. I twisted my wrist to slide my sword along his, the rasp like the whine of a rusty whistle. The sword's tip penetrated the skin of Kalo's upper thigh, and I released my grip.

My sword clanged on the rocky cavern floor, and my fingers cramped with the newfound instinct to reach for the hilt and resume my attack.

My body felt out of my control, like something else pulled my strings—only the something else was *inside* of me. My molten core of magic waved tendrils of black fire, and the tendrils burned both hot and icy cold. I sucked in a harsh breath.

"Enough," I said, staring at the blood oozing from the wound on his thigh. "I don't understand what's happening, and I will *not* strike at you again until you explain."

Grinning at me, Kalo straightened. His white teeth gleamed, his gaze sparking with exhilaration. And something else; something I couldn't name. Grabbing my wrist, he drew me forward until we stood chest to chest, and he stroked a finger along my jaw. "I will explain, yes. And you, lady, you will learn. You are the one; the catalyst. And I knew it."

I frowned.

His fingers flexed on my chin. "You will begin the battle."

CHAPTER 10

"Thousands of years ago, the Green Lands teemed with magic and creatures. There were no High Fae, just fae of varying degrees of power and varying appearances. There were dragons, and the goblins walked aboveground, though of course we had our caves too."

We sat on the rocky floor of the training cavern, sweat cooling on our skin, while Kalo explained. I watched his face as he spoke. Excitement leaked from his usual taciturn expression, and his long-fingered hands sketched images in the air, weaving together the shadows cast by the torchlight so I could picture the creatures in his words.

"The fae easily traveled the paths between the human world and the Green Lands, sharing their magic, their love, and their depravities with the humans—with little care for the future. Over time, however, the fae began to realize the more time they spent with the humans, the more powerful their magic grew in the Green Lands. The power of human belief in the divinity of fae, whether that divinity was good or evil, created fractures and dividing lines in our society for the first time. Suddenly there were rulers, and there were slaves.

"As other human religions took hold, belief in the fae began to fade, and our rulers grew power hungry, desperate to hold onto their waning magic. Blood hunters and witches appeared for the first time, and the fae learned certain sacrifices led to new temporary powers. It was a dark and violent time."

Kalo fell silent, and I watched his chest move as he visibly reached for a calm breath.

"The dragons vanished first, fleeing to the west. But soon, some of the wildfae, like the unicorns and the merrows, disappeared as well. And no one knew where they went—they were just gone. When the goblins began to vanish as well, our queen, Gevah, began to investigate. She discovered the fae rulers, the so-called High Fae, were murdering the wildfae and the goblins in secret and stealing their magic."

I gasped, and Kalo raised his eyes to mine. I flinched at his fierce glare before I remembered he wasn't mad at me. He wasn't even seeing me as he told his story, his mind too full of remembered grief and loss.

"Gevah declared war on the High Fae. But our magic wasn't strong enough. The High Fae, drunk on stolen blood, butchered Gevah and her army. The goblins who survived fled to the belowground, where we've lived ever since."

"I'm sorry," I whispered. His hands clenched

on the sword hilts at his waist. My words were hollow, but I didn't know what else to say. Kalo hadn't been alive for the lost war, but I could see how greatly the story affected him.

Kalo gave a short nod in my direction. "A reckoning is owed, and the High Fae know it. While they've lived slow years in the Green Lands, we've built a new army below. While their magic may still be more powerful than ours, we will overwhelm them with our numbers and our brutality."

Seeing Kalo in the torchlight, his expression fierce and his arched horns casting long shadows, I readily believed it.

"How am I the catalyst for your war?" I asked.

The tension in Kalo's shoulders fell away, and he grinned, showing off sharp white teeth. "You will be an excellent distraction. While you battle Mab for your children, my goblins will come from below and swallow them all down."

My insides quaked at his words and a stinging sensation grew in my chest. I knew Kalo hadn't been training me out of the goodness of his heart—he was fulfilling an oath—but it hurt to hear his intentions. He would subsume my new skills and my children's rescue to further his own ends once our year was up. It felt like a betrayal. Flushing, I called myself stupid. I should have expected it. Kalo wasn't my friend. I was using him, and he was using me. My hand clenched on the hilt of my sword.

I stood abruptly and avoided looking at Kalo. "Thanks for the story. I'm going to turn in. See you tomorrow."

Keeping my gaze averted, I dropped my sword on the rack and hurried away from the cavern as fast as my legs could take me. A bowl of hot stew waited for me in my sleeping cave, and I snatched it up, starving. I hadn't caught sight of the goblin who brought me dinner each day, but I appreciated the gesture, and I tried not to think of what animals constituted the protein in my meals. Aboveground, I hadn't seen anything resembling a cow or chicken.

Kalo's words churned in my head while I ate. I remembered dining at Iris's house with the kids one night about a year ago. She'd told a fairy tale of a great battle, full of magic, danger, and brave warriors fighting green-skinned monsters. The stew soured in my stomach. Had Iris fought in that war? Had she killed some of Kalo's ancestors? She was old and frail when I knew her, but she'd possessed a steely heart. It didn't require a stretch of imagination to picture her young and fierce, wielding a sword. I shivered.

Finn had loved the story. Eyes wide with wonder, he'd brandished his fork in the air and imitated Iris's war cries. But I remembered Dara hadn't shared his excitement. Dara didn't like violence, not even in stories.

Stirring my stew and blowing on it, I pushed away the memory and tried to banish an image of her witnessing violence in Mab's castle.

My shaky exhale stirred the steam wafting from the bowl. I set it down, my appetite gone.

Grabbing a change of clothes and the absorbent fur I used as a towel, I left my room and made my way to the bathing springs. Once there, I stripped and scrubbed the inside furs of my sweaty leathers, then set them to dry and dropped into a hot pool. I hoped to soak away my sore muscles along with my confused thoughts.

I could no longer trust Kalo to act in my or my kids' best interests—not now that I understood his plans. I never should have trusted him. But I'd lacked options. I trusted Kalo from the moment he'd shown up at my campfire and took me to his home—when he told me he'd keep me safe from the other goblins, when he told me he'd help me unlock my powers, and when he told me I had a chance against the High Fae.

But I was merely a pawn in the game Kalo needed to win—a distraction. A good one, if Kalo trained me well. At least I no longer doubted his commitment to train me to the best of my abilities. He had a strong enough incentive. But if I failed, Kalo still got his distraction, and Dara and Finn would be lost to the Green Lands—never aging, never dying. Slaves forever. If they survived the winter solstice.

My heart ached and hot tears pricked at the corners of my eyes. I leaned back in the water and stared at the weeping stalactites above me that swirled with muted tones of gray and butterscotch. The silica in the rocks glowed, flashing silvery glints at me as the torchlight around me rippled with a slight breeze.

Shane had been right about trusting the goblin. But it was too late to reconsider. I needed to train harder and remember that a spectacular failure would please Kalo as much as my success.

THE next evening, after a long day of training, I resolved to talk with Kalo again. I wanted a new promise from him that he would act in my kids' best interests, regardless of what happened with his war.

I placed my stew bowl down beside my sleeping pallet and straightened my spine. Kalo's rooms were a few tunnels away. I'd never sought them out, and I only vaguely remembered the direction from when he first gave me a tour so many months ago.

Every step toward his chambers strengthened my resolve. I'd been a fool to consider Kalo my friend, but he'd manipulated me by waiting so many months before pressing me hard enough to reveal my true nature. I could have learned about my armor months ago if he'd wanted me to know.

I could only assume he delayed to ensure my reliance on him. My cheeks burned with anger and humiliation. Starved for attention, I'd lapped up his lessons and his friendship. *When will I learn?*

I found the corridor I thought led to Kalo's quarters and slowed, my brow furrowing. I counted the torches on the wall and studied the shallow alcoves. Head cocked, I paused.

In the cool, damp air, a throaty moan echoed. I

shivered at the sound.

Stepping carefully, I reached the opening I sought and hesitated again. Rustling sounds, like callused fingertips scraping across leather, rose in the air. Another soft murmur reached my ears.

With eyes as wide as saucers, I peeked around the doorway and froze, dumbstruck.

Kalo reclined on his sleeping platform, his legs spread wide and knees cocked. A female goblin knelt before him, her hair as black as a raven's wings as it moved in time with her bobbing head. Her hands dug into the hard muscles of his thighs, her blood-red fingernails garish against his olive-green skin.

Swallowing hard past my dry throat, I watched her look up into his intense, imperious face. Kalo's eyes smoldered, his jaw clenched. His lips parted, and he groaned for her.

I flinched, and his gaze shot to my face. We stared at each other, my heart stampeding in my chest and my face as red as the woman's fingernails. Then Kalo came, his head bowing back, and the woman at his feet strained to catch it all in her dark lips.

I fled.

A week later, my training once again stalled. My armored scales wouldn't come when I called. Not until I'd expended hours of brutal effort and reached the limits of exhaustion. Only after all that, when frustration burned like fire in my veins, would the power break through my sword strikes, and my molten core would explode with black magic.

But once it was out, I became a fierce and powerful opponent, dodging Kalo's sword strikes and evading his magic blasts—for a few minutes at least. Then I would collapse, magically spent and physically exhausted.

Rousing from another such episode, blood like ice in my veins as my magic turned frigid and restless in my core, I blinked at the cavern ceiling and took a moment to wallow in my fatigue. Finally, I sat up and watched the scales slowly vanish from my hands as Kalo paced a few feet away.

"This isn't enough. This won't rescue my kids. Or start your war." Bitterness dripped from my words.

Kalo crouched across from me, and I looked up to meet his restless gaze.

"You have made enormous progress," he said. "We still have time to learn more. It's not good to accept defeat before we've begun."

"Easy for you to say," I muttered, climbing gingerly to my feet and stretching my sore muscles.

I squeaked when Kalo moved into my personal space. He lifted my chin with his callused fingers and scrutinized me.

"This should be a time of great excitement. You're discovering your magic. But instead, you mope, and you glare." He flicked my forehead with his index finger. "What's wrong? What are you thinking?"

Narrowing my eyes, I resisted the urge to back away. I wasn't used to him standing so close without swords in our hands. His scent—sweaty and rich—swirled around me. I took short, shallow breaths through my mouth and ignored the memory pressing against my mind—the way his face had twisted with pleasure and the sound of his passionate groan as that goblin woman had sucked him dry in front of me.

"Nothing's wrong," I ground out.

"Liar." Kalo pushed closer, and my gaze dropped to the muscular green chest inches from my face.

"It's none of your business what I'm thinking."

Still gripping my chin, he scoffed. "Also a lie. I am your teacher and your friend. I can't help you if you keep secrets from me."

Wrenching my face from his touch, I glared. "You're not my friend."

Kalo flinched. With a sinking, sick feeling in my stomach, I watched his face shut down. He stepped away.

Frowning, I watched him stride down the far corridor and out of sight.

Turning in the opposite direction, I dropped my sword on the rack and muttered to myself as I wandered to my room. "What was that about? He knows we're not friends. Making me feel guilty when he's all up in my face. Jerk." Snatching up my towel and a change of clothes, I hissed the last word.

In the cavern with the hot springs, I soaked for a long time. In one way, Kalo was right—I couldn't keep training with a defeatist attitude. Something would happen; another breakthrough in my magic maybe, and I would figure out a plan to rescue Finn and Dara.

I needed to find a way to call the dragon magic to my fingertips, and I needed to increase my magical stamina. Spending hours a day in the training cavern with my sword helped with both of those things, but maybe I could do more in the evenings as well. Resolving to call the scales again as soon as I finished my bath, I relaxed into the hot water with a sigh.

"I *am* your friend, lady." Kalo's sharp voice pulled my eyes open with a start, and I gasped, covering myself under the water.

"Kalo! What are you doing here?"

Kalo, standing at the edge of the warm room with a fur over his shoulder, looked at the numerous pools with a grimace and scratched his chin. "What do you mean? I'm going to bathe."

Searching hastily for my towel, I muttered, "Okay, let me get out of your way."

I spotted my towel and reached for it, but before I could grab it, Kalo stripped off his kilt and slid into the water of my pool. I caught a flash of velvety-smooth green skin and tilted my head to stare at the ceiling.

"Please close your eyes for a moment. I need to get out."

"No. We will talk first."

I swallowed and looked at him. He sat on an underwater ledge across from me. The steam from the hot spring shrouded his face, but I could easily make out the stubborn tilt of his chin.

"I don't want to talk now."

"Too bad. You rescued me when I was a child. Now I'm helping you train to rescue your children. I've spent every day with you for half a year. I care about you. You are my friend. Am I not your friend?"

Sucking in a breath, I inhaled steam and smothered a cough. He would not make me forget why I was angry. "You're using me. You don't care what happens to me after our year is over, as long as you get your distraction to start your war."

Kalo raised his brows. "By that definition, you're using me as well, lady."

"I know. But it's different," I mumbled.

"How is it different? I owe you my life, and I'm repaying my oath. That doesn't mean I don't care about you or the fate of your children."

"You care about me?"

Kalo's eyes gleamed, and I shrank against the warm stone at my back.

"You are brave and loyal. You work hard. You tell me funny stories sometimes. It's not a hardship to spend time with you. I could have brought in another teacher and still fulfilled my oath, but I choose every day to train you."

The rigid band around my chest that had grown tighter each day over the past week loosened at his words.

"Why do you never say my name? Why do you only call me 'lady?'"

A wry smile pulled at Kalo's lips, and he dropped his chin closer to the water. He didn't answer right away, and I'd decided he didn't intend to answer me at all when he looked to the side and rasped, "I must keep a line in place. I cannot see you as a female." He met my eyes again and my breath stopped. The expression in those red irises scalded. I *knew* he was remembering the scene I witnessed in his room.

"You are not for me. And so, I will not call you by your name."

He rose abruptly, the water sluicing down his green skin, and made an easy leap out of the pool to grab his fur. Averting my gaze as he dried off and dressed, I ignored his low chuckle.

"It is a pity, I agree," he murmured.

With that, he strode away. Blushing furiously, I sank into the hot water until it reached my ears. My heart beat a wild staccato in my chest, and I bit my lip.

With a sharp inhale, I ducked my head under the hot water and scrubbed my face. I was an idiot and a fool. I rose to the surface and stepped from the hot spring with new determination to put more distance between us.

"Okay, so we're friends," I said to myself as I dressed. "And we're *helping* each other, not using each other." *But that's all.*

Later, as I lay in my furs, I muttered darkly to myself. "Men! They impregnate you and vanish, or they try to leave you behind on a rescue mission, or they act all sexy but only call you a friend, or . . ." I sighed. "Or they raise you until you're seven and then disappear. And you never see them again." My heart shrank to a hard nugget, and I rolled onto my side and forced myself to sleep.

I was surprised the next morning when I reached the training cave and found Kalo waiting for me, a heavily laden pack in his hands.

"No sparring today?"

Kalo shook his head and handed me a sheath. "Bring your sword. We're going on a journey."

Fingering the smooth leather, I strapped it to my waist and slid my iron sword into place. "Where?"

"To find some answers."

Peering at Kalo's determined face, I shrugged. "Okay. Let's go."

White teeth gleaming, Kalo reached out a hand. "You know what to do."

I grasped his warm fingers and closed my eyes. With a sickening lurch, we vanished into the cold, empty darkness. I'd traveled this way with Kalo a few times since our first night at the campfire, and I didn't like it any more now than I had then.

I shivered at the sensation of icy fingers skating across exposed skin. Kalo called it never-space, and I knew only a few goblins possessed this *walking* magic. It was a secret I'd promised to keep. I once asked Kalo why he hadn't used it to assassinate Mab himself. He explained that it only worked in the caves or the space directly above them. And where the caves ended aboveground was still weeks of travel from Mab's Court.

Kalo's warm hand on my back anchored me, but still, the air froze in my lungs. With another lurch, my feet hit the ground, and I smashed my cheek into Kalo's hard shoulder and opened my eyes.

We stood in another cavern and, based on the pressure in my head, we were deep underground. I yawned, trying to pop my ears. Kalo dropped my hand and spun in place. The walls sparkled, illuminating the cavern with shimmering light.

His shoulders relaxed as he glanced at the empty space around us. He grinned at me, and I smiled weakly back, my stomach still churning from the trip.

"Where are we?" I asked.

"Deep. I've never been this deep before. But our stories say the dragons lived far below the surface, so we will start here and search for signs."

"Of dragons?" I spoke in a hushed tone, my eyes darting around the dark cave.

"They're long gone, if they were here at all," Kalo reassured me. "I want only to find where they once lived in hopes of provoking a species memory in you."

I swallowed and sucked down a few calming breaths. When I spoke, I managed to keep my tone casual. "Lead the way."

Kalo moved forward.

"No torches?" I hurried my steps, wanting to stay close—I could barely see the cavern floor in the vague glow of the walls' pale-yellow phosphorescence.

"No," Kalo confirmed. "They would ruin our vision if something stalked us outside of the light."

"Stalked us?" I squeaked and pressed close to Kalo's back, frantically looking around.

"We're outside of the goblin caves. The dragons are gone, but that doesn't mean some other creatures haven't taken over their ancient homeland."

Gulping, I nodded. "Okay, right. No torches."

"Don't worry, lady. I'll protect you."

"Right." *Sure, no worries.* I peered into the darkness as Kalo strode toward a tunnel opening on the far wall. The air smelled stale and reminded me of minerals, maybe limestone. A drop of water plunked onto my head, and I stifled a shriek. I couldn't see it, but I *felt* Kalo's smirk.

I straightened my shoulders. I was a badass. Not only did I have fire magic and magical armor, thanks to Kalo, I possessed powerful sword skills. I could handle this. Wrapping my hand around the hilt of my sword, I followed Kalo, attempting to mimic his confident stride.

We walked for hours, wandering through tunnels—some narrow, some wide—past glowing green and milky blue pools. The air continued to smell old and dank. Had any creature passed this way in the last hundred years, they had left no signs of their presence.

Occasionally, we stumbled into wide caves where the ceilings loomed miles above, invisible to the human eye. Those caves were my favorite, and as we stepped across the rocky floor, I stared up, searching the gloom for light—or something else; something I felt I should see. But I glimpsed nothing other than darkness. The whispers of our footsteps echoed high above and reverberated back down, building into a chorus of sighs.

Kalo kept quiet as we walked, and I copied him. I knew our murmurs would carry far, and I didn't want to alert anyone—or anything—to our presence. In the past half-year, I'd gotten used to goblin scents and goblin bodies. Now, I remembered the fearsome teeth of the drows as they ran at Shane and me near the river. I didn't want to think of similar creatures hunting us in the darkness.

That encounter felt like a lifetime ago.

My stomach gurgled loudly in a narrow tunnel, and Kalo passed me a seed bar. I munched it as silently as I could.

After another few hours, we entered an enormous chamber, and I hesitated, staring up into the black. The air smelled fresher here. Instinctively, I knew the ceiling opened to the sky miles above us. The phosphorescence on the cave walls glowed a golden-green color with streaks of cobalt and lavender. The beauty of the swirling pattern made me reach out a hand and touch one of the pale striations. The wall glowed brighter, expanding outward in an undulation of luminosity.

Kalo hissed at me, and I backed away from the wall. My mouth dropped open. The wave of light grew until the entire cavern glowed with it, leaving us standing in a space lit as bright as a summer day.

Large and small boulders in varying shades of earth tones littered the wide, sloping floor. I looked up. The light faded long before it revealed the shadowy sky above. My contradicting feelings of safety and exposure raised the hair at the back of my neck.

Skirting the chamber, I stayed close to the wall and ignored Kalo's footsteps behind me. I reached an alcove hidden by a handful of stalagmites sprouting from the floor like brown bulbous fingers. I inhaled.

Something enticing swirled in the air—cinnamon and campfire smoke.

"Lady, keep moving," Kalo said.

I shook my head.

Moving to the glowing wall, I found a tiny indentation in the rocks—a slightly different shade of lavender than the streaks of light surrounding it. Before I could stop myself, I stretched out my hand again and pressed the indentation.

The alcove wall vanished, gone in a haze of purple and blue, and I gaped at the marvels inside the hidden room.

CHAPTER 11

The space, about the size of a two-car garage, lit with faint phosphorescence that brightened as I stepped inside, revealing heaps of glimmering gold and jewels interspersed with stacks of books. The smell of cinnamon intensified. I swallowed a sneeze and gazed with wonder.

"A hoard," Kalo murmured, stepping around me and crouching to lift a gold coin. He inspected it and said, "Roman." He dropped it to grab another. "Gupta." Digging his fingers through another pile, he added, "A very old hoard."

"A dragon hoard?"

Kalo nodded. "Likely the dragon died on the surface. If they'd gone west, they would have taken the riches. This is good. This is what we wanted to find." He stood and swept calculating eyes around the room.

"How much do you think it's worth?" With a pointed toe, I poked at a green gem—an emerald?—the size of my fist.

Shrugging, Kalo said, "To the goblins or High Fae? Not much. Jewels and gold mean little in the Green Lands where many have illusion magic. And

I have no idea how to calculate human wealth. But those"—he pointed to a stack of books—"are priceless."

He plucked the topmost book from the pile and opened it with careful fingers. The smell of cinnamon exploded into the room. "Preserved," Kalo gloated.

Kneeling, I found a tube and opened the top. Inside, a scroll lay curled up like a snail.

"Dragon history?"

"Dragon, fae, goblin, and other creatures we've since lost. The dragons collected priceless objects, and nothing is as priceless as knowledge."

"This is what you wanted us to find?"

"I'd hoped. It's been some years since an intact hoard was uncovered. We will spend the night here and dig out all the books and scrolls. In the morning, we'll return to the Crystal Caves, and I'll send my people back for them."

Kalo paced reverently around the hoard, kicking priceless gems out of the way to examine one book, then another.

A wry smile crossed my lips, and I cleared my own space and sat, opening the scroll in my hands. Carefully unrolling it, I found words in a language I didn't recognize alongside beautifully colored images of monsters and creatures. *No*, I corrected myself. *Not monsters—fae*.

A blue dragon hovered in the air over a field of battle. On one side, humanoid creatures cowered under shields, their lances bristling toward the flying beast. On the other, a phalanx of white-robed women stood, their arms linked.

I rolled the scroll back up and set it aside, grabbing a book next. The pages, thick and heavy, separated slowly as I flipped through. Another language I didn't recognize scrawled across the paper, which I thought might be papyrus, and showed more depictions of dragons. In one picture, a red dragon stood on a green field, a man crouched before the magnificent creature. The man looked pale as death; his hands ended in sharp claws, and his mouth glowed with red paint.

"Are there vampire fae?" I asked, the air suddenly too thin in my lungs.

Kalo's voice echoed from the far side of the room. "Um, vampire? Ah, you mean a bloodletter? Dearg-Dur. Yes, though they are rumored to be extinct. I've never met one."

I swallowed. Closing the book, I set it aside and sat back on my heels. I used my wrists—the only clean part of my body I could find—to scrub at my eyes. This room wasn't damp like the others we'd passed through, and a thin layer of dust covered the surfaces. I examined my black fingernails and tried to avoid thinking about vampires lurking in the dark tunnels we'd traversed.

"Aha," Kalo muttered. He was crouched against the far wall; his hands cradled an open scroll. Our eyes met, his brimming with excitement. "Come here, lady."

I crossed the room, stepping carefully around

slippery coins, and knelt by his side.

"This is a dragon legend. I've heard it before, but not this version. Listen."

Images unfurled in my mind as Kalo read aloud.

"Once there was a great serpent, Diaevan, who kept her home in Eire and patrolled its skies with fire and blood."

The image on the scroll captured my attention —a beautiful gold dragon flying over an emerald-green countryside, her long, sinuous neck curved with lovely grace. The colors in the picture were so intense, I could almost see her wings glide over the rough paper.

"Diaevan did not like the other dragons of Eire. They were stupid and vicious, and she was wondrous, and the knowledge of the ages shone in her eyes. She swore she would never mate. Instead, her hoard would fall to dust when she passed to the Beyond.

"The male dragons took affront to her decree and vowed to woo her or kill her and steal her hoard."

The next image showed the golden dragon hiding deep underground as numerous other dragons—green, blue, and purple—searched the lands above her.

"Lorcan, a great human warrior, heard of Diaevan's hoard and announced he would be the one to find it. He searched the lands of Eire, and one day by the sea, he saw a huge golden shadow in the sky.

“Diaevan looked down at Lorcan, and her soul yearned for him. Tall and strong, with a high brow and a beautiful voice, Lorcan stood as a prince among men. With her extraordinary powers, Diaevan changed her shape to that of a human female and walked onto the beach to be with him.”

The scroll showed a beautiful nude woman smiling shyly up at a tall warrior.

“Diaevan kept her new shape and followed Lorcan as he traveled the land. But she did not reveal her true nature. One day, when danger threatened, she took her dragon form to defend her love.”

I caught sight of the next image, and the sensation of cold fingers tickled the back of my neck. I struggled to breathe around the sudden lump in my throat. Tears formed in my eyes, but I didn’t know why. I bit the inside of my cheek to distract myself.

“Lorcan saw her and, in his fear, slayed her.”

Sadness gleamed in the jeweled eyes of the golden dragon.

“With her dying breath, Diaevan cursed Lorcan and all his descendants to madness. From her belly, their child, the Red Korra, burst free and flew into the sky with a despairing shriek.”

The final image of the scroll showed the man, Lorcan, watching the sky, a heartbroken expression on his face. At his feet lay the body of the gold dragon.

“She cursed her own child.” I gaped at the scroll. “Wait—Korra is what I say to call my armor.” I stared at Kalo with wide eyes. "Am I one of her line? Am I cursed? What does that even mean—*cursed?* Like . . . doomed?"

He didn't answer immediately, and my blood turned to ice.

"Kalo?"

Giving a minute shrug, Kalo said, "I recognized the name when you called it the first time while we sparred. Red Korra was a fierce and dangerous serpent, but whether you're her descendant—I have no idea. We speak of creatures from centuries before this time. All we have are these books and any stories we may remember."

I nodded slowly. "Point to where it says her name, and I'll search for more books."

Kalo showed me the words, and I memorized the swirling, looping letters. The artistry reminded me of Shane's ward, and sudden tears threatened again. I swallowed them back.

While he sorted through the manuscripts and placed them in piles, I sat next to a stack and flipped through the pages, looking for images of red dragons or references to the name.

After what seemed like hours, I raised my head and flinched at the muscles seizing in my back and neck. I groaned, trying to straighten my hunched body.

Kalo called me and gestured to the larger cavern outside the treasure room. "Come, lady. We will eat and sleep and begin again in the morning."

Blinking bleary eyes, I agreed and staggered to

my feet. I carried a couple of books with me to the doorway where he waited. "Can you read me some of these passages later?"

Kalo nodded, and I gave him a tired smile.

Back in the main cave, I turned and watched with amazement as the wall appeared to close over the hidden space, camouflaging it once more. The strong scent of cinnamon I'd grown used to inhaling diminished to a mere trace.

"We will eat cold rations," Kalo announced, digging through his pack.

"Would you like me to build a fire?" I flexed my fingers and my flames tingled under the surface of my nails. For the first time in months, I'd gone a whole day without using my magic, and my molten coal burned with excess energy.

"No." Kalo grabbed my hands and smothered them with his larger ones. "The smoke would travel too far through the tunnels, alerting any to our presence here."

"Okay." I extracted myself from his warm grasp and sat on one of the large rocks littering the ground.

Kalo unpacked a few wrapped items and shook out a handful of furs. After handing me more of the seed bread and a waterskin, Kalo ate his own meal in silence. The bright glow from earlier had long since faded, leaving the large cavern dimly lit once more.

I finished eating and a wave of weariness swept over me. We'd walked for hours to reach this cave, then spent several more crouched in a dusty room examining books. My eyeballs felt gritty with fatigue.

Kalo shook out the furs and motioned for me to come lie down. I eyed the sleeping area and bit my lip. Kalo smirked at me.

"Relax, lady. We will share body heat only."

I suppressed a shiver. The cave was cold, and Kalo's large body radiated a lot of heat. Still, I wasn't sure I would get any sleep snuggled up to the muscular goblin.

Much to my surprise, I was out like a light seconds after Kalo's warm chest pressed against my back.

"DON'T move," Kalo whispered in my ear.

My eyes whipped open, and I froze. The dim light confused me, but then I remembered we were in the cave.

I lay curled underneath Kalo's crouched form, the heat of his body surrounding me. I tracked the direction of his gaze. It was locked on the open space behind me—his eyes slitted, hiding the glow of his scarlet irises.

A hissing scrape in the darkness almost made me flinch, but I remained still. My heart pounded. What types of creatures lurked in these caves? I had my back to whatever it was. The tiny hairs covering my body stood on end.

Uncurling my fingers from where they pressed into Kalo's chest, I slowly inched my right hand down my body and reached for my sword. I'd tucked it under the furs before I'd fallen asleep, and the hilt dug into my hip.

Kalo didn't move.

The space beyond Kalo's head began to glow, and I spun around in his arms. A slim eel-like creature crouched against the cave walls and the seven unblinking eyes along its spine watched us. Each eye emanated a sickly green light. The creature hummed a bell-like noise and moved a couple inches closer.

"It's a cave wyrm. Stay away from its teeth—it's venomous," Kalo warned.

"How do we kill it?" I pushed Kalo away to sit up. I dragged my sword out from under the furs so it rested in my lap, still sheathed.

"You cannot kill it with a sword. It will only reassemble itself. But we can chop it up into small pieces and scatter them. It will take a long time for it to put itself back together, and we'll be long gone."

"Okay, let's do that."

"But," Kalo continued, "it will never stop hunting us. It has our scents now. If we hurt it, it will track us until it catches us again, no matter how long it takes."

I swallowed hard.

"Normally, I would leave it in this cave to live in peace. But we can't if we're going to take the books. It's too dangerous."

My rising fear sent lightning to my fingertips, and they glowed a dark blue.

"You cannot incinerate it," Kalo cautioned. "It's fireproof."

"Jeez," I grumbled, stifling my power. "So what are we supposed to do?"

"We could drown it, but there's no water in this cavern deep enough. We could try to trap it, and then release it when we leave and hope it doesn't hold a grudge."

"Can it be crushed?"

Kalo cocked his head. "I'm not sure."

"Explosion? Acid?"

Kalo dropped his chin to grin at me. "Both good ideas. But I don't have any acid or explosive materials."

"Does it have any natural enemies?"

"Dragons. To a dragon, a cave wyrm is a tasty treat."

I grimaced at the creature on the wall, noticing it had moved a little closer to us while we talked. Its small legs and tiny toes wriggled against the stone. The trill of a bell sounded again.

"Well, I'm not a dragon," I said shortly.

"No," Kalo agreed. "But sometimes you smell like one."

I raised my eyebrows. "I don't think we have a couple of hours for you to pound on me until my armor comes out."

Kalo shrugged, and I narrowed my eyes at him.

With a sudden, explosive movement, the cave wyrm skittered down the wall and ran for us.

Without time to think, I leaped to my feet and built a wall of fire between us. An unfamiliar word exploded from my lips, and the wyrm rolled over, exposing its pale green underbelly with another chirping ring.

I stood, shoulders straight, my flames blazing white-hot. The air in front of my face stirred with a breeze that blew my hair backward, and I barked another unfamiliar word at the creature. All seven eyes closed at once and the light surrounding its sinuous body flickered until it changed to a lovely pale blue. The wyrm mewed, curled into a ball, and lay still. The small stalks sprouting from its face like whiskers settled flat against its scales.

I rubbed my eyes. Kalo crossed his arms.

"So, that's also a choice," he said in a measured tone. "To make it a pet. Though I have to say, I don't know if it's a good idea, lady."

Clearing my throat, I mumbled, "I didn't mean to do it."

The wyrm unfurled and winked its numerous eyes at me, emitting a tinkling sound my mind classified as a purr.

I dropped the wall of fire and warily watched the still purring wyrm inch toward me.

"This is a terrible idea," I said, but something inside me responded to the little creature. The eyes on its spine shone, and I swore I read devotion in the pale gray irises.

"Do you have any meat in your pack?" I asked.

"Dried rations."

Kalo handed me a small piece, and I tossed it in the wyrm's direction. Faster than I could track, the wyrm snatched the meat out of the air and inhaled it. A small bulge passed along its slim body as it swallowed. Its eyelids drooped and it wound back into a ball. With one last chiming purr, it fell asleep.

I sat down on the furs and studied the creature. It *was* kinda cute. In a salamandroid way.

"We will take turns resting now," Kalo said. "You first, while I watch the creature."

I nodded and curled up on my side. I felt Kalo moving, and another fur settled on top of me. Gazing at the wyrm glowing softly in the darkness, I counted its breaths until I joined it in slumber.

When Kalo woke me to take his turn in the furs, the wyrm still slept.

Keeping a wary eye on the creature, I stretched my sore muscles. My back ached from so many hours hunched over the books. Sleeping on the hard rocky floor hadn't helped.

I reached for one of the books I'd carried out of the alcove and fingered the leathery cover, wishing for a flashlight. The wyrm stirred in its sleep and its glow intensified. Staring at it, I frowned, and thought of the darkness. The wyrm's shine diminished until only a faint outline of its curled shape broke the gloom. Scooching closer to it, I wished again for a flashlight and gasped when the wyrm lit up once more.

Ignoring the implications of what just

happened, I bent my head over the book and flipped carefully through its pages until I found the illustrations of the red dragon.

I studied the images, searching for evidence of a curse, or anything to hint at how the Red Korra changed her shape, but nothing jumped out at me. Did I truly believe the story Kalo had read? Could I change my shape? Was I cursed? My thoughts ran in circles. After a while, I gave up and put the book aside to wait for Kalo to read the strange language.

Leaning my back against a large rock, I divided my attention between the wyrm and listening for any sounds in the vast cavern. Other than an occasional drip, I heard nothing.

My eyelids grew heavy, and I told myself I could listen just as well with them closed.

I dreamed of sad red dragons and falling scales. I didn't feel the cold sensation of the wyrm curling up on my thigh or the small pads of its feet kneading my leathers as it purred itself back to sleep.

CHAPTER 12

To say Kalo was unhappy when he woke up to find me sleeping with the wyrm in my lap was a vast understatement.

"When we trade off resting so one of us is on guard," he barked as he glared and paced, "that means one of us is *on guard*. Not sleeping. And definitely not sleeping with the creepy monster we're guarding *against*."

"It's not creepy!" I protested. "Look, watch this." I held out my hand where the wyrm lay curled up on my palm, his tail wrapped around my wrist. I thought of light and grinned as the creature glowed. The contrast between its cold scales and the warmth of its soft blue light soothed my soul. A sweet chime tinkled from its mouth.

"Lights out," I whispered, and the wyrm dimmed.

Looking up at Kalo, I expected to see excitement on his face, but the scowl remained. "What? That's not cool? I communicated with it! It's trainable!" I frowned, struck by a sudden thought. "Is it intelligent?"

Kalo huffed. "It's not trainable, and it's not

intelligent. It's a cave wyrm. It's a venomous pest at best; a killer at worst. And no, you are not taking it home with us."

Tucking the wyrm close to my chest, I shook my head. "It's mine. I want it. It likes me."

The wyrm uncurled and climbed up my shirt to perch on my shoulder. Kalo shuddered.

I stood slowly, careful not to jostle the creature, and crossed my arms. "Let's get to work." The wyrm's mouth tentacles flicked against my throat, tickling me. While a part of me knew I should be revolted by the sensation, a larger part of me enjoyed it. The tentacles were endearing, like a puppy's wet nose nudging my cheek.

"Your heart's too big, lady. It's a fierce thing of teeth and pain, but despite your hurts, you love easily. I admire that about you."

I froze, staring at Kalo's baffled face. His brow furrowed, as if he regretted his admission, and his lips twisted into a grimace when he caught me watching him. A faint red flush crept across his bladed cheekbones.

"It's the same impulse that told you to save a goblin child, though you were afraid and didn't know him," Kalo continued slowly, almost unwillingly. He paused, then added in a lower tone, "Such an open heart is both a blessing and a hardship, I think." He rubbed his hand against his sternum.

Part of me wanted to attest that anyone would have saved a child, but I wasn't so naive. "Don't you love anyone?" I asked.

Kalo's face shut down. "My love for my people is cold, made of duty and sacrifice."

Reaching a trembling hand forward, I rested my fingers on Kalo's chest, right above his heart. Its steady thrumming reassured me, and I stroked a finger across his velvety-smooth skin. My hand tingled when I pulled away.

Kalo's hand twitched, like he wanted to grab my retreating fingers, but he clenched his jaw instead.

With a warning to myself not to scare him off, I spoke quietly. "I think you have a warm heart, Kalo, though you hide it away. You didn't have to take care of me or help me. You could have left me by my tent with a sword and a list of instructions to fight Mab. You could have left me in some other goblin's care."

"I'm no more capable of that than you are of leaving the wyrm behind. Don't think I can't read your mind and see what you're planning."

I grinned, letting his joke defuse his obvious discomfort at our talk of *feelings*. I believed what I'd said though. Kalo had love in his heart, even if he called it duty and honor. And like me, he would sacrifice for that love.

My thoughts suddenly went to Shane and what he'd sacrificed for duty and honor. Was there love in his heart as well? My face flushed at my foolishness.

We returned to the secret hoard room, and Kalo put me to work. We stacked all the books and scrolls by the door before scouring the space to make sure we hadn't missed anything. That involved shoving heavy chests of gold and jewels around until we were both sweaty and covered with dirt and glittery jewel dust. The wyrm left my shoulder early on, but I could feel its presence nearby. When I thought of it, my nose tickled, and I knew it had retreated to the main cavern to avoid the mess.

I tried not to dwell on the implication of being able to read its feelings, or to wonder if it could read mine as well.

"Cursed her descendants to madness," I muttered aloud as I worked. To Kalo, I said, "Do you think that means I can transform, but I'll go insane if I do?"

A memory poked at me—my childish voice echoing a man's warning. I was so distracted by the errant thought, I missed the first part of Kalo's reply.

"—how diluted, we don't know," he was saying. "You carry your fae son's transformative blood, however. And it may kickstart something."

I blinked at him, rubbing my chest. "Finn's blood?" I recalled Shane's guess that Finn's magic involved changing into an animal form and shivered. "Maybe Finn's a dragon?"

Kalo shrugged. "Does he smell like one?"

I wrinkled my nose. "I don't think so?" Finn smelled like sweaty boy and fruit snacks.

"Then his fae magic is likely the stronger force within him."

My thoughts a thousand miles away, I

returned to work. A while later, I sat back on my heels, panting. "I think we got them all."

Kalo dropped next to me and extended his long legs with a groan. "Aye. I'll not lie, lady, this is a treasure for sure. The old books, untainted by High Fae revisions, do much to teach my people the way the world used to be before we fled below. In one of them, perhaps, there is a story or a spell that will instruct us how to remake the Green Lands."

Nodding, I rested my head against the bumpy wall. "And hopefully, some more information about Korra."

"Of course," Kalo agreed. He stretched one more time and rose to his feet, extending a hand. "Come, we'll return to the caves and send my people for the books."

Grasping his callused fingers, I used his strength to pull myself up and suppressed a whimper as my back muscles spasmed. Kalo stepped into the main cavern, and I straddled the boundary to the hidden room and passed him stacks of materials through the invisible wall.

While he was bent over arranging the bindings of one of the stacks, I sent out a call. Keeping my expression serene, I watched the wyrm creep into my pack.

The creature's contentment rumbled through me as it inhaled my scent inside, along with excitement when it discovered a broken piece of seed cake.

We checked the cavern one last time, and I

stuffed a few books I wanted Kalo to look at into the pockets of my pack, careful not to jostle the now-sleeping creature. I stood and looked at Kalo. His wary gaze searched the room, and I suppressed a grin.

Taking another look at the infinite darkness above, I wondered about the cave's long-dead inhabitant. It had been large—that was obvious—and learned. An ancestor? There was no way to tell. That rankled. My home life was harsh when I was growing up, with my mother's mercurial moods and my father's long absences. That he might have had a good reason to leave—that maybe he'd been dealing with problems bigger than our human world had space for—made me feel no less abandoned. But perhaps I'd discovered empathy for him. *A little,* I admitted with a sad twist to my lips.

When everything was in place, Kalo held his hands out, and I stepped easily into his embrace, hefting my pack over my shoulder. I closed my eyes, and my stomach clenched as the world dropped away. In the infinite darkness, the wyrm released a contented purr. Unbothered by the never-space for the first time, I smiled.

CHAPTER 13

We landed in the training room. Kalo immediately stiffened and pulled out of my arms. A woman stepped into the light, and Kalo's shoulders relaxed.

Tall, with dark teal skin, the woman wore her long black hair in a mohawk and carried an ax. Her horns were short but sharp, and she filled out the standard goblin female attire—a kilt like Kalo's and a leather corset top—with generous assets.

"Kalo," she said.

"Renfri."

"Your father has requested your presence at the Ma'adar."

Kalo gave a short nod and turned to me. "I will send for the books. Remain here and train. I will be gone no more than two days of your time."

"My time?"

"Different caves have different times. Closer to the Ma'adar, time will speed up for me."

I swallowed.

"I'll stay with her," Renfri offered, giving me a small smile. "I will keep her safe."

"Willa, Renfri is my cousin's mate's sister. She

is family."

The corners of Renfri's lips fell at his words, but she smiled again before Kalo saw her reaction. I frowned.

The cave wyrm squirmed in my pack, and I clutched the bag in front of me. Maybe a couple of days away would be good—he wouldn't know I'd brought the creature with us. I would need to find a way to conceal it in my sleeping room . . .

I looked up to say goodbye, but Kalo vanished, the sword on his back catching the torchlight before he winked out of sight. My lungs constricted, and I blinked rapidly at the empty space.

Renfri sidled closer as I clenched empty hands at my side. I turned to her, and her steps faltered. "I've heard all about you, of course. The human woman who saved Kalo when he was a child."

I met her red eyes and read only friendliness there, so I gritted my teeth and straightened my spine. It was ridiculous for me to feel hurt that Kalo had left without saying goodbye. Just because he'd been at my side for over half a year didn't mean he owed me anything. He was fulfilling his duty, and he would return soon enough.

"Yeah, that's me." I told her the story of how we'd met and the promise he'd made.

"And now you have dragon texts? How exciting. I can help you translate them if you want. What information are you searching for?"

"I only have a couple with me." Crouching to dig through my pack, I sifted through the contents carefully, working around the wyrm. It let loose a dim glow so I could find the books, and I sent it a silent warning to stay out of sight. The wyrm chimed at me, not a tinkle, but a low, rumbling tone.

I sat back on my heels, my scalp prickling. The torchlight flared and my mind conjured sinister shapes in the shadowy corners of the room. I shook my head. *Sheesh*. I was losing it over Kalo's disappearance. I needed to put on my big girl pants and remember he wasn't my bodyguard in this frightening, unfamiliar world.

"Just general history," I said slowly as I ran a soft finger along the wyrm's spine. I straightened and stood. "Maybe stories of the High Fae before they became so powerful."

Renfri closely examined the books I handed her, sharp fingernails tracing the image of a green dragon. She leaned forward and inhaled the lingering scent of cinnamon on the pages.

I changed the subject. "What's going on with Kalo and his dad?"

Renfri shrugged and handed the books back. I caught an odor of sweat and iron. "King Jotvar moves us to war. Kalo has been trying to stall him."

"Stall him?"

Renfri sighed and traced a knuckle along her ax's hilt. "We're at war against the High Fae, yes? You know this?"

I nodded.

"We have been growing our numbers for centuries now, and training for battle. We outnumber the High Fae ten-to-one."

I shivered, imagining those numbers in the caves around me. Savage and armed to the teeth.

"The king, Kalo's father, is ready to begin an earnest war. He believes we will crush the High Fae with our numbers alone." Renfri shook her head. "Kalo and his supporters believe numbers will not win a fixed battle. Goblins have magic, yes, but the High Fae command powers that change your thoughts, your memories. In a war of soldiers and magic, the High Fae will destroy us."

"You believe what Kalo believes?"

Renfri's face clouded with a mix of anger and regret. "I have seen a High Fae. Long ago." Her shoulders twitched, like she fought off the urge to slump.

"My parents and I journeyed above, in the Green Lands, to seek a match for me with one of the goblin clans to the east." Renfri's lips twisted. "My father stepped into a trap, and my mother refused to leave him. They ordered me to run away, but I couldn't." Her chin jutted. "I was young."

I resisted the urge to pat her shoulder. Something told me Renfri wouldn't appreciate the gesture.

In the agitated motion of her hands, I read the anguish of a child learning for the first time that her parents were not all powerful.

"I hid. My mother worked to free my father, and a beautiful High Fae lady appeared, trailing magic from the train of her dress. She was"—Renfri sucked in a breath—"the most exquisite creature I'd ever seen. I found myself lulled, watching her talk to them. But I was a fool. She enjoyed their struggle, and then she killed them. She absorbed their magic like a siphon, pulling it from their bloody bodies while I cowered in the bushes."

A dark cloud hazed the air behind Renfri's head, and in the opacity, electricity sparked. I didn't know if she controlled the magic or if it were a byproduct of her emotional turmoil, but it raised the hair on my arms.

Renfri's voice wobbled. "I hid and they died. A single High Fae killed my parents, goblin high commanders, with the ease of a cobra devouring a pair of mice. So yes, I follow Kalo."

I crossed my arms and squeezed my elbows. "I didn't know there was dissension in the goblin ranks. Kalo told me . . ." I trailed off, suddenly confused. Was Kalo's belief that I was the catalyst a secret? He hadn't introduced me to his family or any of his friends—only sparring partners who left as soon as they finished pummeling me. Would I get him in trouble if I shared his plan?

Renfri's scarlet eyes focused on me. "What?" she prompted. "Told you what?"

Squeezing my lips together, I leaned away. "Nothing important."

She studied me for a long moment. Finally, with a small smile, she gestured toward the weapon rack against the wall. "Do you want to spar?"

My instincts screamed no. I didn't want to

spar with this goblin. But I hesitated, unsure. I didn't know if residual fear of her frightening appearance gave me pause—the goblin form was still alien to me —or if my instincts warned of something sinister below her friendly exterior.

But, I reminded myself, I was training to fight High Fae soldiers. I was learning all I could about swordplay and my dragon magic so when I made it to the High Fae Court, I left with my children. If Renfri was as she professed to be, sparring with her would be good practice.

And if she were other—a traitor, a spy, an assassin—what greater test of my skills?

I wet my lips.

"Sure," I said, moving my pack out of the way and drawing my iron sword from the sheath at my hip. "I've never fought someone carrying an ax before," I admitted, eyeing her weapon.

Renfri flashed a sharp grin. "Well, this will be good practice. While the High Fae at Court love their rapiers and sabers, the guards and common soldiers will have axes, crossbows, and broadswords. And the blood hunters will have stolen magic, though they will keep it hidden. If you truly mean to rescue your children, you will need to learn to think on your feet."

I bristled at her words. Of course I meant to rescue my kids! My mouth opened on a retort but snapped shut again at her attack.

The ax whistled toward me, the sharp curve of its blade glistening with deadly intent. With a yelp, I dropped below its arc and rolled to the side, scraping my forearms on the rocky floor.

I scrambled to my feet and swung my sword through the air to parry her next blow. The reverberation of the strike rattled my bones. Gritting my teeth, I backed up a few steps and pointed my blade at her, panting as if I'd sprinted a mile.

"What are the rules of the match?" I asked.

Renfri's eyes glittered. "First blood."

Then she was attacking me again, with formidable whistling blows that knocked me back with every parry I managed. Her ax bore down on me like an unstoppable train. I blocked, ducked, and evaded. I tried to strike where I could, but I knew from the start I was overmatched. Renfri was a goddess of war with her blade, and she toyed with me.

Retreating from one end of the room to the other, I did my best to land a blow, but all my strikes slammed fruitlessly against the backside of Renfri's ax. Sweat poured from my brow and into my eyes as I tried to call my dragon scales, but my body was still operating at the fight or flight stage of my reflexes and I couldn't seem to coax the black flames from my coal.

A few times I thought I heard the wyrm's worried chimes, and I silently urged it to stay hidden. I didn't truly believe Renfri was trying to kill me—despite all evidence to the contrary.

My shirt turned to ribbons, and I took a moment to wish I wore the female goblin uniform of a leather vest. At least it would have protected my torso from the sharp edge of Renfri's ax.

I ducked beneath a violent overhand blow and raised my sword to lunge at Renfri's muscled thigh but froze when a pricking sensation penetrated my panic. Glancing down, I saw Renfri's small dagger pressed into my stomach. A thin line of blood snaked along my skin.

I blinked rapidly, confused, my ab muscles quivering under the cold metal, then I looked up to search Renfri's face for answers.

She smiled at me—a lazy grin—and pulled the knife away from my abdomen and sheathed it at her hip. "Don't forget to watch both of your opponent's hands."

I nodded, my breath coming out in bellows, and sheathed my own sword. Adrenaline racing through my veins, I paced and shook out my hands, taking deep breaths through my nose, breathing out of my mouth. My lungs burned and my muscles felt coiled and tight. I wanted to attack her again, but that was stupid, not to mention outside the bounds of our sparring match.

She drank from her waterskin, and I wanted to drive my sword through her skull.

Tilting my head, I blinked up at the rocky ceiling and worked to steady my breathing. My hands shook as I ran them through my hair, and a new wave of despair crashed over me. I wasn't ready. My battle skills were those of a novice in a training yard. When faced with a real opponent, someone who actually wanted to beat me—instead of Kalo who wanted to draw out my dragon powers —I couldn't even last five minutes.

Tears pricked at my eyes. I didn't stand a chance against Queen Mab's Court. Maybe it was a good thing Kalo planned to attack simultaneously. Maybe, instead of him using me to distract Mab, I could use him to distract the soldiers. Otherwise, I would die and take Shane with me, and Finn and Dara would be lost forever.

SINKING to my chin in the torrid water of the springs, I fought the reflexive urge to close my eyes. I couldn't relax. While the sparring session had ended in a ceasefire at Renfri's win, my instincts screamed that she wasn't my friend.

I knew without question that if she'd struck a mortal blow, she wouldn't have lost any sleep over it.

"These books are full of stories of the Red Korra," Renfri said, stepping into the steamy chamber.

I blinked at her, taking in her fresh clothes—a soft-looking robe—and the absence of her ax. She sat on a ledge at the wall and flipped through the pages of the first book I'd shown her.

"Yeah, Kalo said she was cursed, the daughter of a dragon who shifted to human and was killed by her mate."

Renfri nodded absently.

"Does the book talk about the curse?"

"Not really. Korra was mad, and everyone

knew it. She kept no hoard and refused all potential mates."

I sighed and swirled my hands through the water, ignoring the sting of my numerous scrapes.

"There's a page ripped out here." Renfri showed me the book. "The page before says, 'For her mother vowed until . . .' And that's it. The next page after the torn one talks about a different dragon."

"Until what?" I whispered to myself.

"You smell like a dragon now, your body relaxed and pliant," Renfri said, leaning forward and pinning me in place with the gleam of her red eyes. "Like cinnamon and campfire smoke. Is this why you wanted these books?"

My mouth parted.

"Has Kalo found a dragonkin?"

I shook my head, mute.

She stepped to my pool and stroked a finger through the water, flicking a few drops at me. I'd never felt so vulnerable in my life, and I cursed my stupidity for giving into my urge to take a bath after our fight. I surreptitiously slid a few inches closer to my pile of clothes on the ledge and the small dagger I kept in my pocket at all times—its presence a small comfort.

The steam of the pool distorted the lines of Renfri's body, and she seemed to grow in size in tandem with my fear.

Renfri's eyes held mine captive, and my body quaked under the water. I looked for my molten core but found the coal of my dragon magic merely smoldering. I didn't know how to call the black flame and build my scales at will now any more than I had during our sparring match. And something told me the goblin would not wait around for me to get angry enough for my instincts to do it for me.

"What about the other book?" I asked desperately. "What's in that one?"

Renfri stared at me for several beats then glanced away and returned to her ledge. With a nod, she picked up the other book. "Yes, this one I've read before. In the library at the Ma'adar."

"Ma'adar?"

"Where the goblin king and queen hold our Court. And the armies train. It's a vast underground space; a city beneath the earth."

"And that's where Kalo went?"

Renfri seemed to peer past me, lost in her thoughts. "The king told me to call him home—that battle plans were being finalized—but I think it's more." Her black fingernails tapped a steady rhythm against the book's spine.

"I think," she continued, "his marriage has finally been scheduled. And the king wishes to ensure an heir before we march to war."

A sharp pang blossomed in my chest. "His marriage?" I croaked.

Renfri sent me a tight smile. "It was arranged when he was a child."

I stared at her, reading the same hurt in the slope of her shoulders I was sure echoed in my own. I remembered Kalo's words in this same room, and I blinked away stupid tears.

As much as I tried to tell myself I didn't care, it was a lie. He was not for me. I agreed with him about that. But it had felt like he was mine for the year he'd promised me. And I wanted him by my side—to train me, to teach me, to—

"A goblin prince needs a goblin princess," Renfri interrupted my musings, "if he wishes to command the clans as the next king."

"Princess," I murmured, finally closing my eyes and sinking to my ears in the hot pool.

Through the muffled gurgle of the water, I thought I heard Renfri say, "A princess. Or a wife with powerful magic."

CHAPTER 14

The scent of blood woke me. I coughed and tried to sit up, only to fall back on my sleeping platform as the rattle of chains filled my chamber. I blinked at the stalactites above and searched my memory for an explanation of what was happening.

After eating stew with Renfri and showing her an empty cave nearby to set up her sleeping area, I'd gone to bed, exhausted and more than a little heartsick.

Now I was manacled in my own bed—my arms and legs stretched so I lay spread-eagled. The room was dark, my torches long since burned out, but in the blackness, I sensed movement and malevolent intent.

Sucking in a breath, I prepared to scream for Renfri, to warn her to run or hide, when a small light flared, and the goblin's grinning face appeared by the doorway. The shadows etched deep grooves into the planes of her face and her scarlet eyes flashed at me.

I exhaled. "Hurry," I whispered. "I don't know what's happening. Unchain me."

"Oh, I think not." She strode forward to relight the torches, and the chamber glowed with their flickering golden light.

My mouth went dry, and I tugged at the links encircling my hands.

"This isn't personal," she confided, drawing a long knife from a leather sheath. "But Kalo is mine, and I'm tired of waiting for him and his parents to realize it. If I take your blood"—she licked her lips—"then I'll possess the power he needs to win this war."

I shook my head. "He'll know it isn't your power. He'll know you killed me to gain it. He'll smell that you're a blood witch." I hated how my voice shook, but the sight of her long blade glinting in the torchlight sent my adrenaline into overdrive. My fingers flared hot as I called my fire, but something about the vulnerability of my position made my willpower falter, and I couldn't produce a flame. My pulse hammered in my throat, and I tried to swallow. My hips moved restlessly, the rattling chains an echo of the desperate thoughts clanging through my mind.

"He's never smelled it before."

With another shake of my head, I said, "Kalo likes me. He'll be angry if he returns to find me dead."

"But what if you're just gone? I woke up, and you'd vanished? Feeling petulant and abandoned, you must have returned to the surface to find your berserker."

Her conviction made me doubt my position, but I tried again, attempting to draw strength from my words. "He's relying on me to do something. He'd know I wouldn't leave him."

"What?" Renfri pounced, dragging the blade along my calf. "What is he relying on you to do?"

The ice-cold blade made me shiver, but I pressed my lips together, biting back my cry of terror.

Renfri struck, and I screamed. The blunt force of agony rendered me speechless. It felt like she'd severed my leg, though a quick glance showed she had merely embedded the knife into the fleshy part of my upper thigh.

My eyes locked onto the dripping stalactites, and I groaned and writhed. The chains securing me in place rubbed my skin raw, and the sensation of hot blood pooling on my skin and dripping down my leg nauseated me. Flexing my fingers, I tried again to access my magic, but I only tore the flesh at my wrists. Desperately, I reached for my flames, and my fingertips finally heated.

A slurping sound raised goosebumps all over my body. Panting, I looked down and found the goblin crouched over me, licking the edge of her knife. My stomach lurched.

"Ah," she exhaled, her eyes rolling back. "Definitely dragonkin. I think"—she licked again—"I could get two transformations out of you."

Was she talking about using my blood to transform into a dragon? My mind whirled with confusion and pain.

"Cursed." I bucked my hips and dislodged her

perch. She hopped to the floor. "My blood is cursed, remember? Korra."

Renfri frowned. "You can't transform?"

I shook my head.

Tapping the tip of the knife against her chin, Renfri shrugged. "Okay, I'll only use your blood for the power boost."

My fingers ached, my fire at the ready to blast her, but she stood at my feet and my chained hands pointed at the walls. I didn't have a direct shot. I needed her to unchain me.

"Please," I said, breathless but trying to maintain an air of confidence, "don't do this. I swear to you, Kalo will find out and kill you." I wasn't sure that was true, but it was worth a shot. Kalo liked me; he needed me. Still, would he kill a family member to avenge me? It didn't matter if he would or wouldn't—I only needed her to believe he would.

Renfri's lips curved into a knowing grin. "I think not, human." My hope died as she leaned over me and ripped open my old t-shirt. The tip of her knife pressed between my ribs, and she angled her hand until she had a direct shot at my heart. I braced myself, sending a desperate plea into the night as I closed my eyes. *Shane,* I shouted into the abyss, *rescue Finn and Dara. Tell them I'm sorry.* My words would never reach him, but I needed the comfort of them. He was a good guy. He'd wake and do the right thing.

I waited for the pain.

Renfri's shriek wrenched my eyes open, and

I watched the cave wyrm crawl across the goblin's arm, its small tentacles waving delicately in front of its bow-like mouth. Renfri's face went white and rigid with fear. The wyrm blinked at me, chimed, and bent its head, sniffing Renfri's skin.

"Stop it," Renfri strangled out. "Please."

I sent a thought to the wyrm, and it struck fast, its sharp teeth sinking into the green flesh of the goblin's arm before Renfri could bat it away.

Silky stalks floated through the air, waving at me, and the wyrm flashed me its bloody fangs. Renfri screamed. Her dagger fell from limp fingers, and she staggered away from my bed. The wyrm dropped to land on my stomach and curled up there as the goblin woman convulsed on the ground.

The skin on Renfri's arm blackened and flaked away, and foam dripped from her mouth while her legs drummed on the ground.

I glanced down at the wyrm. "You're pretty venomous, huh?"

I tried to summon pity for her, but I couldn't locate any. She'd been about to kill me. I shivered. If not for my pet, she would have succeeded.

"Thanks," I whispered. The wyrm purred its sweet tinkling sound.

Straining, I worked to loosen the chains binding me to my bed, but my movement did nothing more than rattle them and cause more damage to my irritated flesh. The clinking sound echoed ominously, and the torch closest to the doorway flickered, then blinked out completely. My stomach settled in my throat. It wouldn't be long before the rest of the torches burned out, leaving me trapped in the dark with Renfri's body on the floor next to my bed.

I didn't know how much time had passed since Renfri died. The room was dark, the torches long since burned out. My mouth was as dry as cotton and the pain in my body had settled into a dull ache. My arms and legs remained anchored, stretching and pulling me down into my fur bedding.

My stomach had stopped growling a while ago.

The wyrm still slept on my chest, its occasional purrs and chimes waking me from fitful dreams. I didn't bother asking it to light up anymore—nothing in the room could help free me from the chains.

Renfri's body was beginning to stink.

IN my dreams, I heard my father's voice. *Willa . . .*

I swam in an ocean of navy-blue and black waves, unlit by the moon or stars, with the taste of salt on my lips. My heart thumped sluggishly in my chest and my tongue swelled in my mouth. I tried to call out but barely a whispering gasp escaped my mouth.

My father stepped into the room; his body lit by a soft golden haze. I squinted at him, and the glow jabbed a spear of pain through my eyeballs.

He wore jeans and a t-shirt, and his hair was long. He looked young, probably only a decade older than me now, and his eyelids crinkled as he smiled at me. My chest ached, remembering the last time I'd seen him. The day he left.

"Willa, have you been practicing?"

I nodded at the apparition, my eyes burning with tears my body couldn't produce.

"What's the rule?"

I opened my mouth, but this time not even a gasp cleared my parched throat.

"Don't use it," my father said, and I mouthed the words with him, remembering the long-ago lectures.

"Don't touch it."

I nodded again, his deep, calm voice echoing in the room and in my memories.

"And never, ever—"

The light winked out and my father vanished.

My frantic eyes searched the room. He was gone. My neck was too weak to hold my head upright for long, so I resettled myself on the furs and dredged my memories for the rest of the lesson. What had he been teaching me? What wasn't I supposed to touch or use?

My thoughts scattered from the hammering beat of a headache pounding against my skull. I closed my eyes once more and let the soothing purrs of my pet wash the pain away.

MY eyes popped open on a wheezing breath. In the blackness, I mouthed the words again. *Don't use it. Don't touch it.*

I reached for the core of my magic, the black coal still smoldering in my chest, though the shifting light that emanated from it barely broke the darkness. It was so weak—*I* was so weak.

I stretched my fingers toward it, imagining the shape of my hands in the dark cavity of my soul. I touched the coal and heat seared into me. A silent scream shredded my throat as my armor formed over my skin, the scales rasping against the chains.

The wyrm sang, chiming a beautiful, aching melody, and I strained with every feeble ounce of energy I could summon.

The chains binding me broke at my wrists and ankles with an abrupt shatter and catapulted me from my bed.

Landing in a heap in the darkness, my head smacked the stone floor. Blackness swamped me once more.

THE sensation of something cold crawling across my throat activated my instinct to swallow. Pressure at my head and chest roused me, and a rumbling voice echoed from far away. I couldn't make out the words.

SOMETHING plinked onto my face, and I startled awake. Yellow light flickered across my eyelids, and I blinked and stared at the damp stalactites dangling above my head.

"Lady," a light, feminine voice said. "You wake." The voice was muffled, like it came from deep underwater. Or maybe it was muted by the blood rushing in my ears.

I turned my head and swallowed a moan as the movement shot agonizing pain all the way down to my bones. I blinked again and met a pair of pale pink eyes that belonged to the goblin woman standing beside my bed. A gentle hand patted my arm through the furs.

I startled at the rumbling, chiming purr under my chin but settled when I remembered the wyrm curled against my neck. Its delicate vibrations soothed me, and tears pricked at my eyes. How long had it been? How many days was I left with only the wyrm for company, the only thing to keep me sane in the darkness?

I opened my mouth, and the pink-eyed woman shook her head, her long, unbound black hair rippling in the candlelight.

"Don't speak yet," she murmured. She helped me sit and brace against the furs then handed me a goblet of water. "Sip slowly," she warned.

The cold, slick miracle trickled down my throat. After a few swallows, I tried again.

"Who?"

Movement at the corner of my eye made me flinch, and water splashed on the furs and the wyrm. It grumbled and shivered against my throat.

I sent the creature an apology with my mind.

"Lady."

My shoulders straightened at the sound of Kalo's voice, and I bit back a cry.

The woman made a clucking noise with her tongue and pushed me back down. "Shhhh," she admonished and turned her head. Speaking to the shadowed shape by the door, she said, "Don't frighten her."

Kalo stepped into the light, and I was struck by a sense of vertigo. He looked haggard, his olive-green skin faded and his eyes heavy.

Clarity flashed into my brain, and I frantically searched the room. Renfri's body was gone.

"I didn't kill her!" I blurted. "She tried to kill me. She chained me and was going to use blood magic. The wyrm bit her."

Kalo flashed me a hollow smile. "Yes, lady. We noticed."

"I'm sorry," I whispered, suddenly remembering she was family to him.

"No," Kalo stepped closer, placing a hand on the woman's shoulder as he leaned toward me. I was distracted, staring at his lean fingers pressing into her skin, so I almost missed what he said next.

"My fault. I was gone too long. And I left you with someone who betrayed us all."

The female goblin patted his hand. "My fault, too. I selfishly kept Kalo with me. I didn't know you were waiting for him."

I stared into her striking eyes and found

only kindness and empathy. Confusion swirled. I swallowed.

Kalo cleared his throat. "Lady, this is my wife, Syfa."

My blood pounded in my ears. Reaching for the goblet, I took another long swallow of water while I gathered my thoughts. My arms felt weak as twigs and my hand shook, but I managed not to spill this time.

"Time enough for stories later," the woman—Syfa—said and held up a steamy bowl of liquid. "For now, drink some broth and sleep."

Kalo gave a short nod and spun on his heel. He strode out of the room, and I noticed a new scar across his back, the six-inch wound red and raw.

Syfa fed me spoonfuls of hot salty soup. My eyelids fluttered, struggling to remain open, before I gave in to the warmth reaching for me. Her soft murmur broke through the haze. "Sleep, lady. I'll watch over you." Her gentle tone soothed me, and my mind stuttered and went blank.

When I woke again, Syfa sat beside my bed still, though she now slept, her head lolling to the side. I took a moment to study her. She was beautiful, I admitted easily, with golden brown skin and a slim, elegant neck. She wore a long green dress and simple jewelry at her throat and wrists. An ornate iron knife rested in a sheath on her hip.

I tried to sit up and she woke with a start, blinking away sleep. Her pink eyes widened, and she leaned forward to help me.

"I have more broth," she said. "And water."

I let her help me eat and drink a little more. My head felt clearer than it had earlier, and my hands didn't shake when I clutched the goblet to my chest between sips.

The wyrm emerged from the furs and nestled into the curve of my arm. Syfa recoiled.

"It won't hurt you," I whispered. "It's my friend."

She nodded, her lips thin.

I called the wyrm to my hand and resettled it on my chest.

"I didn't know Kalo was married." My face flushed bright red.

Syfa's cheeks pinkened also, and she smiled at me, flashing sharp, dainty teeth. "It was arranged a long time ago by our families. Kalo and I grew up together. My father is a general in the army, commanding the First Legion."

I recalled Renfri's bitter words and realized she'd been correct about Kalo's father's plans.

"So you march to war?" I asked.

Kalo stepped into the room again and, this time, I resisted my instinct to jump at the unexpected movement.

"Yes," he said, answering my question. He crouched beside my bed and placed a warm hand on my forehead.

I flashed a look at Syfa, but the serene expression on her face remained unruffled.

"I will return you to your boar," Kalo said,

rising and patting my shoulder. "I have failed my oath, and I cannot promise your safety if you remain with me. We march on the Court, and I must go with the armies."

"What about your plan?"

Kalo's gaze shifted. "I don't know," he muttered. "Perhaps the timing will align. I will do what I can to stall our troops' deployment, perhaps give you another week aboveground, but I cannot say for sure. And I cannot gainsay my father on this. It is my duty to my people."

I shook my head, my hair rasping against the fur beneath me. "B-But . . . I need you. I need you to distract Mab. And you . . . you need me. You said it."

Frustration etched deep grooves in the lines of Kalo's face, making him look both fierce and old. "Unless I dethrone my father, which I will not do, this must unfold now. I have tried to delay, and this is the end." His crimson eyes locked on mine. "I must believe this is happening as it should."

Helpless despair grew in my chest. Without Kalo's goblin armies, how could I possibly get through Mab's Court? I'd learned to use my sword and my dragon scales to a small extent, but Kalo had said the High Fae could affect my mind. I remained vastly outmatched, and I'd run out of time to discover the secrets of my heritage.

"The books—"

"I have no one to spare to retrieve them." Kalo crossed his arms. "And from the information we read about the curse, I'm not sure you should ever try to reach your dragon form."

My mouth fell open.

"You found a way to call your armor at will"—Kalo gestured to the broken chains at his feet—"and that is a powerful weapon."

Betrayal curdled in my gut, and I looked away from Kalo's implacable form.

Syfa placed a hand on Kalo's elbow and met my eyes. "I will wish you luck on your journey to your children. Though I will remain in the caves with our people and it will be many years before we hear the news of the battle, I will think of you."

My thoughts trailed off, my stomach quaking. "But you just got married. You will age, and Kalo will —" I broke off, flushing.

Syfa flashed another sad smile at Kalo. "Yes."

My brows furrowed and my eyes darted between them.

Kalo abruptly stepped away, his shoulders tight, and I settled against the furs with a heavy heart.

"Gain your strength, lady," he said, moving toward the door. "Let Syfa help you. And in a few days, when you can lift your sword again, I will return you to the Green Lands."

STANDING in the training room, my sword a heavy weight at my hip, I stared at the scales I'd called to my skin.

"Your father taught you to avoid the fire," Kalo said, stroking a finger across the burnished ripples.

"Perhaps the answer to your bloodline's curse lies with his knowledge."

He dropped his hand, and I shivered. "I haven't seen my father in almost twenty years. He left when I was still a child. My mother was"—I swallowed—"difficult to live with."

I vanished my scales by removing my fingers from the coal of magic in my chest.

"More fool him," Kalo said, lifting my chin. His red eyes traced the features of my face, and I fought off another shudder. I longed to return to the Green Lands, to my journey and my plans to rescue my children, but a part of me wished I never had to leave these caves. Desperation, and a sensation of immense loss, clawed at my throat.

I shook my head. "I'm not ready."

His lips twitched in a shadow of a smile. "You broke the chains. We must war with the resources we have, not those we wish we had."

I flinched, and he winced.

"I don't mean you, lady. You are not a resource." Kalo's stark face warred between warmth and firmness.

"What am I?" I held my breath.

"An ally. A friend, I hope."

I released the breath and nodded. "Friend."

Kalo lifted my chin again, and this time I couldn't read the expression in his scarlet gaze.

The wyrm squirmed in my pack, chiming at me, and I stepped back.

"Do you love her?" I asked softly.

"Love," Kalo mused. "You said it has many forms, yes? Syfa is a good woman, and she will be a good ruler in my stead while I war aboveground. I trust her. If we have children, she will be a strong mother."

I mulled over his words as I stared past him, down the dark corridor to where Syfa waited for Kalo's return, and my pulse pounded with agitation and—something else. Something I couldn't label. Or maybe I didn't want to.

"But you'll leave her," I confirmed. "And be gone for years. You'll age differently."

Kalo's eyes grew watchful as I paced.

"I don't . . ." I hesitated, rubbing my sternum with my fist. "I thought—"

"Our time was always finite," Kalo said, his tone measured, and I stopped pacing to glare at him. "You knew this, lady."

I rubbed my chest again, my ribs creaking under the heavy pressure of my hand. I was a fool, I admitted, watching Kalo scrub his fingers through the messy hair between his horns. I was easy to walk away from—I *knew* this. At least he'd warned me . . .

Straightening my spine, I pushed the sting away. I was good at it by now, after more than half a year spent ignoring the pain of being separated from my children. This was just one more hurt to brush aside.

"I'm ready," I said.

Kalo opened his mouth then shut it.

I moved into his arms, and his smooth skin

flexed under my fingertips as he circled his arms around me. With a deep inhale, I relished his familiar scent of musk and stone before we winked into the unending darkness of the never-space. In the frigid emptiness, a ghost of warmth traced across my lips.

PART III

CHAPTER 15

The campsite I'd built in a flurry of fear and despair appeared untouched. The tent where Shane still slept sat in the shade of a hill, and two goblins waited by the dead firepit, watching us with unreadable expressions.

I stepped from Kalo's arms and shook off the cold of the never-space, reminding myself barely a few hours had passed here. My hand moved of its own volition to rest on my sword grip. My skin crawled from being out in the open again, and I resisted the urge to draw the blade and wave it around.

The sun on my skin felt unnatural.

Kalo spoke a few words to the guards, who shook their heads in response. One, the female, said something in a questioning tone. At Kalo's head jerk, matching savage grins stretched across their faces.

"There is no change in the berserker," Kalo said to me. "He should sleep one more day, I estimate."

"Goodbye, Kalo," I said. "Thank you—"

He made a cutting motion through the air. "Do not thank me. I didn't fulfill my side of our bargain. If I'm still alive at the end of this war, I will owe you another boon."

I swallowed. My fingers itched to reach for him, but I restrained myself.

"I go to gather my father's armies. Make haste to Mab's Court. I will give you as much time as I can, but you shouldn't delay. Once my people reach the surface, the High Fae will know we are at war, and they will tighten their defenses."

I nodded. "Good luck. Remember—there is love in duty."

He frowned, then flicked a glance under his lashes at the guards. I hid my smile behind a cough.

I absorbed the final sight of him—his strong features, stern in the bright light, and the slightly mocking twist of his lips—and my breath hitched.

"I will see you again, lady."

Without another word, Kalo placed a hand on the shoulder of each guard and they vanished, winking out of the sunlight before I could blink. A whispering breeze raised goosebumps on my arms, and I stared at the empty space.

Shaking off my reverie, I moved to the tent to check on Shane. His chest rose and fell with even breaths, and I fought off the disorienting déjà vu as I crouched next to him. I'd been gone for seven months, give or take a few weeks, while he'd remained here, asleep and oblivious. He looked the same, with his heavy brow, straight nose, and thin lips. His clothes lay in tatters, and he still had drow blood smeared on his skin. I placed a gentle finger against the pulse in his neck and sighed at the reassuring flutter. My heart swelled with a wave of pain and worry and grief, and I closed my eyes before it swept me under.

I'd missed him—his solid presence, his steady blue eyes . . . his open heart. Unlike Kalo, Shane didn't hesitate to show me his emotions. And I'd never doubted his devotion to my family, despite his sometimes-aggravating methods. Breathing the same air as him again felt like a second chance.

I remembered waking on top of him that morning after Dara's nightmare, and I let myself wonder what would have happened if Shane had held me close when he'd opened his eyes instead of tossing me aside and running.

I sighed.

Would he notice a change in me when he woke? Would he like it? Or would he prefer me as I was—weak? The question soured my stomach, and I sat back on my heels, frowning at his still form.

I felt changed—transformed. Yet the same. Sure, I could hack at people with a sword and call on my dragon magic to make armor, but a hole—filled with regret and loss like I'd never known before—burned in my heart.

Smiling ruefully, I called myself a fool and stood. I would get more firewood and scrounge up a meal while I waited for Shane to wake—maybe I could try fishing? He would probably be starving.

HE slept for almost another twenty-four

hours, and I spent the time avoiding thoughts of Finn and Dara by gathering firewood, catching fish, and practicing with my sword.

The open landscape bothered me for longer than I thought it would. Trilling birdsong and the passing shadows of clouds made me twitchy, and the scent of grass crushed underfoot during my swordplay distracted me. The cave wyrm, curled up in the shade cast by my pack, gave a discordant chime whenever a ray of sunlight fell on its skin.

Walking on the surface again ignited the embers of my anxiety, which had lay dormant for months. In the caves, I knew I had time on my side. Now, every second I gulped the fresh air around me, I had to deliberately shove aside worry for my children. The clock had resumed its countdown to the winter solstice, and every second that ticked by reverberated in my chest.

Was Paul being nice to them? Was he even still with them? Or had he dropped them at the High Fae Court, collected his prize, and vanished again? Were they hungry? Hurt?

When I didn't keep my thoughts in check, they spiraled into a deep, all-encompassing fear, freezing me in place for indeterminate periods of time.

As sick as it was, the easiest way to distract myself was to wonder what Kalo and Syfa were doing—I imagined the underground city of Ma'adar, full of goblin soldiers training for war. A day had passed, which meant months or years belowground.

Was Kalo already on his way to the battlefield, leaving Syfa behind? Did she miss him the way I did?

The direction of my thoughts stopped me in my tracks, and I returned to my sword practice.

When Shane's groan broke the late afternoon silence of the campsite, I ran to his side, desperate for both distraction and reassurance.

The cool air inside the tent caressed my overheated skin. I sighed his name. "Shane."

His brow furrowed, and he groaned again.

Patting his shoulder, I said, "It's me, Willa. You're safe. You're okay."

Pale blue eyes opened to gaze at the nylon ceiling of the tent. His mouth pursed. After a moment, the fog cleared from his eyes, and Shane glanced around. He saw me and gave a crooked smile. "Willa. I was having the weirdest dream."

I smiled back. "I bet. Come get something to eat and drink and I'll tell you what I think you dreamed."

He blinked owlishly at me before staggering to his feet. Looking down, he studied the dried black blood flaking off his skin. He inhaled the ripe aroma and made a face.

I waved him toward the unlit fire and handed over a water bottle and a granola bar. Kneeling, I lit the fire with my fingertips, sending the flames to the kindling with an easy toss. While he ate and drank, I prepared the fish to fry and told him about his fight with the drows.

Frowning, Shane scratched at the black

smears on his forearm. "I don't remember anything past when I changed to my boar."

"Kalo said you're a berserker. That the Green Lands built on your boar magic."

"Kalo?"

I faltered under the odd note in his voice. Looking up from the silvery filets sizzling in the pan, I swallowed and gave a little shrug.

"Who's Kalo?"

"The goblin I helped against the bird-fae hunter."

"You called him?" Shane asked, his voice was raspy from disuse.

I straightened my shoulders—I wasn't afraid of his disagreement with my choices.

I told a succinct version of my last months. Concentrating on the fish, I avoided his eyes and the way his hands flexed and released in his lap. When I finished, he remained quiet, and I looked up to find him staring at my sword with a pinched expression on his face. Feeling self-conscious, I covered the hilt with my arm and gripped my elbows.

"I can't believe you called the goblin. I can't believe you *trusted* him. I can't believe you went to their caves."

Shane sucked in a deep breath, visibly reaching for his calm, and I interjected. "You were unconscious; maybe dying. I made the best decision I could. And it worked out fine! I'm stronger now. I don't need you to turn into your berserker form to protect me."

Shaking his head, Shane skewered me with a piercing glare. "You were strong before, but you didn't realize it. And I didn't transform to protect you because I thought you were weak. I did it because you're important."

I gaped at him, my throat suddenly dry.

Shane turned away to look across the wide meadow and ground his teeth together, his jaw flexing ominously. His deep sigh echoed in my ears. "It's done, I suppose," he muttered.

I was both stung by his rebuke and stirred by his words. *I'm important to him?* I wanted to dig further, but his stomach rumbled audibly, and I hurried to dish out the food.

Shane ate most of it. My own appetite was curiously absent. Too many worries swirled in my mind, building a knot in my throat too large to force food past. He finished eating and went to clean up in the creek while I washed the pan. I kept my eyes away from his muscular nude form, cursing myself an idiot. *Again.*

When we're back home, I promised myself, *I will ask him out on a proper date. With no pressure to save me or my kids. We can eat Italian and talk about art. I can wear something sexy. Until then, stop staring!*

I glanced up and flushed at the sight of Shane drying off. Looking down, I doused the fire—literally and figuratively. His next words redirected my thoughts with eerie precision.

"We've lost what, two days? We need to hurry up. Let's pack up the tent and get moving."

I took care not to jostle the wyrm as I hefted my pack—that revelation could wait until later. I didn't know how much more Shane could tolerate, and I didn't want him to leave me again. Not that I had a leg to stand on, considering I'd left him this last time.

I shook my head. Finn and Dara still waited for me. I needed to concentrate on them at the expense of all else. They needed me, and I would sacrifice everything to reach them and get them to safety.

WE hiked for a few hours, Shane's nose guiding us steadily south, and I hoped that meant the kids were in one place and not moving anymore.

Shane asked lots of questions about the goblin caves, and it seemed like he became more relaxed about it the more I shared. I showed him my scales too.

"But you can't transform?" he asked.

Shaking my head, I kicked at a tuft of grass in front of me. "I don't know if it's only a matter of figuring it out, like I figured out the armor? Or if I can't do it at all because of the curse."

"Your father warned you not to do it, so I bet you can, but you shouldn't."

I frowned at him. "We don't know the reason he warned me. Maybe it was just because we were in the human world."

"Or maybe it's because if you transform, the curse will kill you. Or drive you mad like the red dragon."

My mouth dropped open, and blood whooshed in my ears. Clearing my throat, I nodded slowly. "That's a good point."

"Look at me." Shane waved a hand down his body. "I transformed into this berserker guy and lost my mind. Then I slept for two days. We shouldn't be trying to use strange, unfamiliar magic. Especially in the Green Lands."

Shane's serious expression and his careful words made me doubt myself, but a part of me rebelled against his assertion that my dragon form was too dangerous for me to use, although Kalo had warned against the same thing. We had to be missing something.

In my pack, the wyrm sent out a tiny tinkling sound of agreement, making me frown harder.

As the sun dropped in the sky, a dark shadow smudged the horizon. A forest lay in our path, still a few miles away, but the sight of it sent a cold splash of fear through me.

"Let's camp here," Shane suggested, eyeing the purple tree line with the same skepticism I felt.

We quickly set up camp, mindful of the rapidly vanishing sun.

Dropping my head back after dinner, I watched the brightly colored stars and moons circle in the navy-blue sky. The movement lulled me, like a slowly spinning kaleidoscope. I relished the warmth of Shane's presence by my side, and I inhaled his unique scent.

"You look different," Shane said.

I turned to him with a raised brow.

He flushed and cleared his throat. "You're acting differently too. Not so scared."

Bristling, I sat up straighter. "There's nothing wrong with being scared in the face of a completely unknown reality."

Shane smiled at me, and I relaxed my attitude a little, glancing down at the fine white scars crisscrossing my arms, remnants of months spent sword training. I traced one with a callused finger, feeling my blood vessels pump on top of strong, lean muscles.

"Yeah, I guess I do look a little different. No more mom bod."

"Your mom bod was hot, Willa."

I grinned at my lap, my cheeks turning pink.

"But," Shane continued, "I must admit, these muscles are pretty badass." His finger followed the path of mine, and I shivered.

We sat in silence for a long time, and I returned my gaze to the sky. I'd forgotten the intensity of the constellations in the Green Lands, and witnessing it all over again stole my breath—as it had the first time I saw it. With a pang, I wondered if Finn and Dara had seen it. If they'd looked up at the moons and stars and felt the immense wonder.

I turned to Shane and tugged on his arm. He looked away from the incredible view to focus on me, his expression open and sleepy.

"Don't be gentle with me."

His eyes narrowed, flashing a darker shade of

cobalt.

"I mean," I said quickly, "don't sugarcoat—"

Shane leaned forward and grabbed me, pressing firm fingers into my back and my hip so my body arched into his. His lips found mine in a hungry, devouring kiss.

Intensity and desire pulsed in the air, and for a moment, I lost my head and kissed him back. Wrapping my arms around his neck, I opened my mouth to his, and the growl he released and the way his grip tightened around me sent waves of molten heat through my body. I kissed him with every fragment of pent-up frustration I'd been fighting against for months, and he kissed me like he felt the same. His mouth tasted of passion and a trace of citrus, and I shivered and quaked under the onslaught.

After an achingly long embrace, I leaned away, pressing my fingers into his chest when he moved to follow me.

"Stop," I gasped. "We can't do this."

Shane sat up straighter and looked down at me with a wolfish grin. "Too late."

"No, I'm serious." I took another ragged breath. "We barely know each other."

"You've lived next door to me for five years," he pointed out.

"And you never spoke more than a handful of words to me!"

Shane rubbed his chin. "I always liked you. You're a great mom, you're beautiful, but I don't know—I guess I felt like I was lying to you by being there on Iris's orders . . . like some kind of spy. Which I was *not*, by the way. And so, I never did anything. And you never talked to me either."

I thought about my life—the drudgery of work and school and the bright moments with my kids. I shrugged. "I liked you, too, I guess. But I don't have time for men."

He scowled. "Don't call me *men*—like I'm a nameless guy who tried to flirt with you at the grocery store. I'm Shane."

I stared at him, noting his narrowed eyes and his lips, which were swollen from our kiss. Why had I never tried to talk to him before? I wasn't a nun. I dated . . . sort of.

I'd been hyper aware of Shane since the start of this whole adventure, but I didn't trust my instincts. Was I taking my sexual frustration out on him because he was my nearest target? I'd spent the past six months ogling a sexy goblin, knowing nothing could ever happen. Was Shane just convenient? I didn't think so. But how could I be sure?

I frowned at him. He'd never expressed any kind of interest in me before. I worried I was only a handy body to him, the way I'd been with Paul, and that thought made me scooch away.

"I'm not interested," I lied.

"Baby, you *are* interested. My boar can smell it. You flood my senses—the softness of your skin, the curve of your hip. I ache to touch you. And I see the way you watch me."

My mouth fell open.

"You dominate my thoughts, even at the expense of my duty. And we're going to see where this leads."

Shane loomed into my personal space again. I shook my head. This was a bad idea. Men didn't stay—they didn't stick. I was never enough for them. Look at my father; look at Paul. Kalo . . .

A flash of inspiration hit. "And that's another reason we can't get involved! I need to be able to count on you to guard the children."

Shane recoiled and rubbed the back of his neck. "You think I won't protect the kids if this"—he gestured between us—"doesn't work out?"

I crossed my arms, not liking his tone. "My first responsibility is to my children. I can't do anything to jeopardize their safety."

"Jeez, Willa." Shane stood up. "Who do you think I am? Some deadbeat like their dad? I won't ever stop protecting them, even when they're old enough to protect themselves. I swore an oath, and I'm a man of my word."

He turned and stalked to the other side of the fire, facing out across the meadow. I frowned at his back. I hadn't meant to hurt his feelings or question his *honor*, but I was right to halt things before they could get out of hand. A romance between us would only complicate matters, and all our focus needed to be on Finn and Dara. It was as simple as that.

I crawled into the tent and zipped the door.

He'd get over it, I reassured myself. Once his libido calmed down, he'd realize I was right, and we'd return to the way things were before we kissed.

I shivered, reliving the memory of his strong arms wrapped around me and the movement of his lips on mine. I'd get over it too, I resolved.

Kalo, Shane, Paul, and my father appeared in my fitful dreams, all swirling together in my mind and filling me with doubt and fear. Each of them walked away from me while I watched, all alone. And when I woke, it was with renewed determination to unlock my dragon form, no matter what anyone said. I trusted myself *first*, and that included all of me. And all my magic.

***

Mab watched the two humans by the campfire. They were too far from her reach to hear, but she could see, and she was troubled. They'd gotten deep into the Green Lands—these two unknowns. What was their purpose in her kingdom?

With an elegant swipe of her hand, the scene vanished from the wall. She sat on her throne, her spine straight and her brow clear despite the questions circling her brain.

The female looked familiar.

"Send for Paul," she ordered in an even voice.

Footsteps hurried away. While she waited, she considered the choices before her. Human servants were always amusing, and the winter solstice approached. She'd been perhaps a little too greedy last year, she judiciously admitted. The blood had flowed too freely, and she'd gorged. And now she sometimes noticed dust motes floating through her throne room. She needed more staff to fill the holes she'd created.

If she binged again this year, she'd regret not nabbing these two humans. Her magic had been urging her to prepare, to gather her strength, but for what purpose she didn't yet know. It rankled.

The sound of a throat clearing focused her attention. The half-fae stood before her, his shoulders back but his eyes wary. In his sensual, cunning features, she saw a trace of her old friend. Iris had been a fool to sacrifice herself for her son, and Mab had never forgiven her for begging to take his punishment on herself. Still, Paul's gift had gone a long way to assuaging her temper about the subject. And now Iris was dead, murdered by this ambitious son. Maybe the fates had been right. Still, it would be wise to watch him closely.

Mab's blood-red lips parted as she drummed the arms of her throne with long fingernails topped with sharp, silver spikes. "Paul, tell me more about the children you brought me. Tell me about their human mother."

CHAPTER 16

In the depths of the purple forest, my skin prickled, and not only from the sweaty strands of hair tickling my nape. Already perturbed by the scent of old decay and the way the thick canopy of branches dangled like gnarled fingers and reached for the mossy forest floor, I shivered and shifted my hand to rest on my sword.

Unlike the toadstool forest, this one teemed with life, and birdsong and the rustles of small animals in the undergrowth had accompanied us for hours. But now everything had gone quiet.

"Do—"

"Shhhh." Shane crouched and lifted a leafy bough. In the shadowed space underneath, a dead animal lay on its side—its eyes had gone to bugs long ago, but dirty fur still draped across thin bones.

I stepped back, my stomach churning as a maggot tumbled from its mouth.

"A fox, I think," Shane said. "Or something like a fox. It's been dead a while. Desiccated."

"Natural causes?" I asked.

Shane stood and shrugged. "How would I know? I don't see an obvious wound, but I'm not going to pick it up and check."

I nodded and resumed walking, picking up my pace. I didn't know how far this forest stretched, but we needed to reach the far side before nightfall. Shane fell into step beside me, his urgency echoing mine.

"I've been smelling decay like that for the past hour," he said in a quiet voice. "There are a lot of dead things hidden around."

"Drows?" I asked.

"Why would drows hide the bodies?"

Adjusting the weight of my pack on my shoulders, I tried to think of a predator from our world that would hide the skin and bones of its prey. "Food caches?"

"Maybe, I guess. Or it could be something with some level of intelligence, and it doesn't want others to know it's here and killing."

"A wildfae," I whispered.

A bird lit from the undergrowth to fly into the canopy and the explosion of wings stopped my heart in my chest. After a moment, I released a wheeze and a coughing giggle at my fright. I turned wide laughing eyes to Shane, and my smile vanished. He frowned, his eyes tracking the path the bird had taken.

"I should change to my boar. My nose works better in that shape." His frown deepened. "But I don't know what happened last time to make me go from my boar to the berserker."

"Don't transform," I warned. "I can't carry you

out of here if you fall asleep on me."

He drew his knife, and I copied his movement with my sword.

We started walking again.

A trunk popped and creaked. I leaned away from a slight breeze that brought a deeper scent of decay to my nose, and I scrubbed a hand over my face. The wyrm squirmed in my pack, and through our bond, I got the sense it didn't like the odor any more than I did.

"Should we go back? Find a different way around the forest?" I asked.

"And lose another day? No, we keep going."

Shane took the lead, and I hurried after him, scanning the roots and limbs underfoot and the open spaces between the surrounding trees. The sweat at my nape and brow cooled as a chill filled the air.

A whisper of sound broke the stillness. Another bird burst from a low branch to fly directly at us. Shane batted his hands in the air, and it veered off, the sound of its frantically beating wings fading quickly.

My magic reacted to my spiking fear, and I pushed back against the burning sensation in my fingertips. *Don't shoot flames at the innocent wildlife. You'll set the whole forest on fire.* Still, the hilt in my hand grew warm, and I realized I couldn't completely vanish my flames—I was too wired. Taking deep breaths, I focused on calming thoughts.

I veered wide around a thicket and stumbled

over the uneven ground. Ahead, a mound loomed above the forest floor, grassy and wide—easily the size of a bus.

Shane and I stopped simultaneously, both eyeing the barrow with wary eyes.

"I don't think that's natural," I said, licking my lips. My skin prickled again.

Something nearby shrieked a keening wail, and I jumped.

"Go around it," Shane ordered. He turned and jogged back the way we came.

The forest darkened around us, like a sudden storm approached, and the wind picked up to whistle through the trees. I moved faster and caught up to Shane. He pivoted, heading toward an opening in the center of the dense forest.

We staggered into the clearing, and a gust of wind lifted my hair and twisted it around my head. The wyrm in my pack chimed a warning tone, and I dropped to a crouch and flung a jet of fire at a bush. It caught with a whoosh, and another scream sounded, raising goosebumps along my arms. The bush vanished into a swirl of black ash. Sharp needles of pain drilled into my temples. Something scraped at my arm, and I spun in place, my sword high, but I found nothing there.

"Shane!" I shouted and froze when my voice vanished as soon as it left my throat. I clawed at my skin and jabbed my elbow into Shane's side, getting his attention. *Something's here with us,* I mouthed, my eyes wide as saucers.

He nodded and scanned the dim clearing.

A thin line of blood appeared on his forearm. Another mark licked down his neck. His cheek. He gawked at me.

I glanced down at my own body. Trails of blood appeared along my thighs and wrists.

The wyrm scrambled from my pack and curled around my neck. Its purr centered me, and I opened my mouth and soundlessly shouted, *Something's happening!*

Shane stared at the wyrm and reached for it, but I backed away with a shake of my head and hovered a protective hand over it. Shane's brow furrowed.

A keening voice ripped through the tension-thick air for the third time, but this time the voice screamed my name.

The cuts on Shane's body spattered blood onto my arms, and my vision wavered as my own blood spilled. I felt no pain, but the rivulets tickled, and the eeriness of having no voice made me slam my teeth together to hold in my scream.

My sword felt heavy in my hand, but with effort I lifted it and waved it around. What was this invisible attacker?

Pushing me forward, Shane pointed to the far side of the clearing and ran. I followed, the darkness closing in around us. The wind churned up a small tornado of leaves and dirt, and Shane dove into a shallow rocky depression and turned to face the clearing, shoving me behind him. I nudged him aside and reached desperately for my coal of magic. Fingers steady, I grasped it, and golden scales instantly snapped into place. The wyrm purred, still wrapped around my neck like a scarf.

The scales covered the blood on my skin. The invisible lashes continued, but they were unable to break through the barrier. More thin red lines appeared on Shane's body. I needed to stop whatever caused them before he bled to death. Before I ran out of magic and followed his demise.

I jabbed my fingers into his side and pointed at my armor. With a nod, Shane fell back, letting me take the lead. A heady feeling moved through me as I assumed the protective position between him and the clearing. I would save us. *As soon as I figure out how to fight an invisible whip.* I shook off my doubts.

Squinting through the murky light, I searched for an opponent, but the clearing was empty. A cool nose nudged against the scales on my neck and the wyrm lit up with a blue glow, illuminating the space in front of me and breaking through the unnatural shadows. The blue beams solidified and the radiance illuminated a shape.

Cloaked and tall, it stood a few feet in front of me, and I resisted the urge to jump back. Shane's heavy breaths stirred the hairs at my nape. There was nowhere to run.

Under the hood of the cloak, eerie purple eyes flashed open. The flare revealed a gaunt face, haggard and pale. It was a woman. *Or something like a woman*, I amended as her mouth gaped and flashed sickle-shaped teeth. The teeth gnashed. I flinched but remembered to lift my sword.

Once more, a keening wail carried on the wind. It didn't come from the creature in front of us. Something else was out here.

A heavy lash hit my chest, but the force didn't penetrate my armor. My scales were stronger than her magic, and the realization made me feel powerful and bold. My muscles loosened and warmed, and I twirled my sword in the air. *She can't hurt me, but oh, I can hurt her*. I stalked forward, a feral smile on my face.

The creature's confusion lasted only a moment. Her hissing voice filled the clearing. "Human. Mab has ordered your capture, but she did not say anything about the state of you. Your blood will feed me for days." Clawed hands emerged from under the folds of her cloak and reached for me.

Instinct took over, honed from my months belowground, and I slashed at her talons. She moved preternaturally quick and I missed, but I finished my lunge with a backswing that caught her in the side.

Violet eyes widened, then narrowed. She grabbed my wrist, holding me in place. Her mouth gaped, far too wide for a normal jaw, revealing two rows of those nasty teeth. Her head lowered toward my neck.

My heart exploded with adrenaline, and fire erupted across my scaled skin. She shrieked and released me, batting at the flames licking at her cloak.

Without thought, I swung my sword and struck the head from her shoulders. Her cry was replaced with a gurgle, and the wind and darkness vanished.

I stood blinking at the sunlit clearing. A rasping noise behind me made me turn.

Shane lay in a pool of blood, his skin chalk white and his eyes rolling in their sockets.

Leaping to his side, I dropped to my knees and scrambled to put pressure on the myriad cuts covering his body. My scaled fingers slipped and slid over his blood-soaked skin, and the armor vanished without thought. His skin was cold under my fingertips.

“Shane, Shane,” I chanted. “Wake up.” Scrambling for my pack, I pulled out a fur I’d taken from the caves and used a knife to tear it into strips, binding the pieces around his wounds. He groaned, and the noise spurred me on.

The wyrm slipped from my shoulders and lapped at the blood. I stared in horror for a moment before pushing it away. “No,” I said, my tone stern. Its blue glow paled at my rebuke.

“I’m not mad.” I bound another deep cut on Shane’s forearm. “But you shouldn’t drink the blood of my friends.”

The wyrm chimed. Curling up in the shadow of my pack, it closed its row of eyes.

I shook my head and lifted Shane’s shirt to check his skin underneath. The cuts there were shallower, like the shirt had offered him moderate protection from the creature's whips. What kind of wildfae *was* that?

My scalp prickled and I spun to face the clearing. Nothing moved in the open space, but I sensed something out there. The creature's bloody head, its eyes open and staring at the sky, lay perfectly still beside the body. Still, something gnawed at my gut.

Mab had sent the creature. Maybe she'd sent more.

Flames grew at my fingertips as I stepped in front of Shane's prone form and faced the trees. In a blink, another cloaked figure appeared at the edge of the shadowed woods.

Exhaling, I reached for my armor again, and the figure vanished. I stared at the empty spot for several seconds, wondering if it had turned invisible like the other. No lashes whipped at my skin, so it probably wasn't the same type of wildfae as the purple-eyed one.

Fingers wrapped around my ankle, and I let out a startled yell, but my voice was gone again. I gasped as I realized this new figure had to be responsible for both the keening wails and our vanished voices. With a pat on Shane's arm, he released me, and I paced forward, scanning the woods around us.

My ears popped and a cacophony of sound hit me—chirping birds, blood rushing in my ears, and the wyrm's purrs.

Shane limped to my side. "It's a bean sídhe."

"What?" I rubbed my ears and gaped at the crimson drops on my fingertips.

"Bean sídhe." The word sounded like *banshee,* but he added a slight Irish accent. "It's manipulating the sound. It gains power when it witnesses death. It was probably working with the Dearg-Dur."

"The what?" *Why is that name familiar?*

"The vampire."

I swallowed as I remembered the image in the book Kalo and I had found in the dragon hoard —the pale-faced fae with the bloody mouth and sharp claws. With effort, I straightened my hunched shoulders and eyed the headless body laying a few feet away.

"Not a bloodsucking vampire like in fiction books. A bloodletting one."

With the adrenaline draining from my body, my thoughts were sluggish. Finally, I understood. "The cuts. It was bleeding us to death."

Reaching up, I flicked a trickle of red from Shane's neck. "You lost a lot of blood."

His face still colorless, Shane nodded. "It's clotting now though. I'm a little dizzy, but that's it."

"What do we do about the bean sídhe?"

In answer to my question, a wail rose from the woods and echoed across the clearing, pounding against my eardrums before fading away.

"I think we leave it," Shane said. "I don't think it can affect us directly, more than hurting our ears."

I shook my head. "I don't like the idea of it behind us."

"We can't kill it if it doesn't take a physical form." Shane gestured at the empty clearing.

Reluctantly agreeing, I bent to grab my pack, careful to tuck the sleeping wyrm inside, and walked toward the tree line. Shane fell into step beside me, and I counted down in my head, *Three, two, one . . .*

"When were you going to tell me about the creepy glowing salamander in your bag?"

"It's a cave wyrm," I corrected as we stepped back under the dim canopy.

Shane stopped in his tracks and inhaled a deep breath. After a minute, he pointed, and we hiked in the direction he'd indicated.

"It's venomous," I warned. "So don't try to touch it."

"Why are you touching it?"

"It likes me. Kalo said it's something to do with my dragon nature."

Shane's silent disgruntled thoughts were written on his face. It was also obvious he was still in pain.

I tugged him to a stop and traced my finger along the tight lines bracketing his mouth. "You're hurt. We should set up camp and rest."

His eyes warmed as he leaned into my touch, and his lips brushed the skin of my wrist. He shook his head. "We need to get out of these woods. I can keep going."

As if to echo Shane's worry, another bean sídhe shriek broke the silence, startling a squirrel to dart across our path. The wail sounded a little more distant, and I hoped it meant the wildfae wasn't tracking us.

Shane set a brisk pace and I followed; my hand heavy on my sword hilt as images from the brief fight with the Dearg-Dur circled in my anxious brain. It had moved fast, but I'd been faster. I sent a mental thank you to Kalo, wherever he was. He'd prepared me well.

Still, we were both hurt. If the wyrm hadn't revealed the vampire's invisible presence, I didn't know what I would have done. And the ramifications of that didn't sit well. The High Fae would be far more formidable opponents than a lone wildfae.

Mab had sent the Dearg-Dur to capture us. That meant she knew we were coming. What would she send next?

CHAPTER 17

A week passed, and each step through the Green Lands was fraught with more danger and worry than the last. The bean sídhe appeared to follow us, though its wail never grew closer than a distant train whistle. The steady keening accompaniment to our strides raised my blood pressure every day.

This morning, as the shriek dissipated into the dawning sky, Shane had to restrain me from storming down our trail and demanding the wildfae face us so I could silence its mournful cries.

"It's not harming us," he said, cupping the back of my neck in what I assumed was an attempt to soothe me. "As far as I know, a bean sídhe can't do more than scream."

"Says you, with only meager information," I mumbled and shook off his hand, stuffing my sleeping bag into my pack with sharp jabs. "I say she's murdering me slowly with anxiety, so I should just go and kill her." My teeth ground together. "Didn't you say it feeds on death? I bet it's trying to call the wildfae to eat us," I reasoned.

His mouth opening to argue more, Shane's

forehead wrinkled, and he stared at me, his eyes widening. "Uh, that's actually a good point."

I nodded, smug. "So let's go kill it."

"We don't know how."

I stomped toward the last echo of the sound, determination giving me new energy, but Shane slung an arm around my shoulders and spun me back toward camp. Aggravated, I struggled in his hold, pressing against him and then bending over to flip him, like Kalo had taught me. But his hips twitched, suddenly cradling mine, and a blast of heat swept over me. I gasped and lost all sense of purpose. Grinding against him, I dropped my head on his shoulder, the wave of sensation overwhelming me. My restless need for action had found a new target.

Shane's grip on my arm tensed, and he tugged me to face him. He crushed me against his chest, and my body responded with roaring desperation. I devoured his mouth, ignoring how our teeth clacked together—I needed to feel something other than fear, and Shane's steady presence soothed me like nothing else. His body curved around mine, forcing heat to push aside my cold worries.

We'd been dancing around this for days. Maybe it had been weeks—or even years. Each night, I lay in my tent, unable to stop myself from thinking about the night by the fire. Each night, it grew more difficult to step away from him and zip the tent door with him on the other side. He was warmth and constancy, and my body hungered for both.

I slipped my hands under his shirt and scraped my fingernails across the skin of his muscular chest, and he gave a gratifying groan in response. I nipped at his lower lip.

"Willa—"

I pressed my mouth harder against his. I didn't want to talk. I wanted to *feel.*

"I—" he tried again, and I shoved him, sweeping his leg so he dropped to the tall, sweet-smelling grass. I fell on top of him and ground my core into his lower half.

"Shane," I murmured, trailing kisses along his jaw. "I want—"

He broke free of my hold. "Willa! Listen. And this kills me, please believe me, but we don't have time for this."

I sat back and my lips twisted into a frown. Crossing my arms over my chest, I gripped my elbows and fought the blush now moving across my neck and face.

Shane sat up, gripping my hips hard. I peered into his bright blue eyes, and my embarrassment eased. He nuzzled his nose across my cheek. "We're close. I smell the children. One day out, maybe."

My pulse beat in a hard rhythm as I ripped myself from his lap and jumped to my feet. My voice squeaked. "You're sure? This is it?"

He rose to his feet beside me and grabbed my pack. "I caught their scent just now, plus a pile of other unfamiliar scents, and something smells like cultivated fields and orchards. I think the castle is ahead of us."

A beaming smile stretched across my face, and my heart grew lighter in my chest. I could almost feel the warm, small bodies of my kids in my arms.

"Then let's go," I rasped.

We'd camped in a small copse of trees. As we approached the edge, the landscape dropped away, and I realized we'd been on a plateau. Below lay an expanse of fields arranged in a grid of various shades of green and gold. A straight gray road stretched through the center, seeming to originate somewhere below us, and at the end of the road, a medieval-looking castle presided over it all, its turrets and spires slim, graceful, and pearly white in the sun.

Behind the palace, a massive shimmering lake stretched to the horizon.

After scraping a hand through my hair and tucking it out of the way, I gripped Shane's forearm. "How do we approach it? It's too exposed."

Shane pointed at small distant figures moving slowly through the fields and along the road. "We impersonate whoever those workers are. Maybe slip into some farmer's wagon and get a ride straight into the bailey."

Swallowing hard, I nodded. "We need disguises."

"We need to get off this ridge first."

The steep slope leading to the fields below looked impassable from a distance, but as we approached the edge of the cliff, the narrow paths leading down became visible.

My skin prickled. "We're too exposed," I muttered. "If anyone looks up, they'll see us climbing down. Or if anyone else is using the path, we won't have any place to hide."

"You're right. We should wait for nightfall."

I chafed at the delay—we were so close to our goal—but getting caught when we were this close would be worse than waiting.

We settled behind a rocky outcrop and took turns watching the paths and the fields, trying to detect any patterns of movement.

On the closest edge of the fields, tiny figures scampered up and down ladders along rows of trees. Straining my eyes, I searched for blond curls, but we were too high to make out details.

I shifted my gaze to the cleared tracts, trying to count the number of workers. It had to be hundreds.

When I caught sight of a pair of particularly small fieldworkers, I couldn't contain my gasp. "What if those little ones are Dara and Finn? We could snatch them right now."

Shane pointed to a pair of armed guards at the edge of the field. "We'd never sneak past them. There's no way to creep into those fields without being seen." He leaned forward, squinting. "And those aren't the kids. See, they have green skin."

"Goblin children." A band of sorrow tightened around my chest. Were Kalo's armies nearby even now, readying their attack? I wished I could tell those children their people were coming, and soon.

I sat back, my fingers itching to reach for my sword and charge down the slope.

MANY hours later, I was ready to jump out of my skin. The sun had barely set, bathing the lands and palace in hues of mauve and pink, and the fields were now empty of workers and guards.

Shane led the way to the nearest path, his footsteps careful in the gathering dusk, and I followed, my heart galloping in my chest. I warned the wyrm to be silent, and it vibrated its purr of agreement from where it nestled in my pack.

The steep winding trail crisscrossed the slope. The slow pace grated already frayed nerves, but we would alert every guard in the area if we sent rocks skittering down the track.

We couldn't see them, but there had to be guards. The windows of the castle's watchtowers were lit with fires.

The air smelled of dirt and growing things, more so the closer we got to the fields. I had no idea what High Fae ate, but the closest grids looked to be full of wheat, the stalks tall and rippling in the warm breeze off the lake.

The neon glow of the rising moon and circling comets lit the landscape in shades of grayish pastels. How could a place so dangerous be so breathtakingly beautiful?

When we finally reached the base of the

plateau, I was relieved to see a row of small wooden huts. A few windows flickered with candlelight, but the rest were dark. Clotheslines hung behind the homes, the shadowed shapes of shirts and pants visible. The mouthwatering scent of roasted meat lingered in the air, rich and succulent. My stomach rumbled, and I pressed my hand against my abdomen, willing it to silence. We hadn't eaten fresh meat in days, not since the bean sídhe started following us and all the game had vanished.

Tugging on Shane's wrist, I lifted my chin toward the hanging clothes.

He nodded and we crept toward the cottages. Snippets of quiet conversations broke the silence, but nothing in a language I recognized. I wondered who resided here—upper-level servants, given some autonomy to keep their own households? I saw no guards.

My feet scuffed on an exposed root, and I froze, listening intently for any sign someone heard me. Nothing happened and, after a few moments, I crept forward again, my lungs in my throat.

When we reached a laden line, we grabbed clothes from the rope and slipped them on. The material of my robe was coarse, but it smelled clean. I ignored the pang in my chest at the thought of stealing from a servant or slave.

We crept to the road and walked toward the castle, staying in the shadows of the undulating wheat stalks.

The whirling sky illuminated the road in

uneven patches. We crept along, not wanting to risk twisting an ankle or kicking a noisy rock.

It felt like forever before we reached the shadows under the towering castle walls. The road ahead was lit with torchlight from the battlements, so we ducked into the wheat field and crouched. My pack grew heavy on my back, and I itched to discard it so my sword arm would be free.

"We need a door," Shane said.

The main gate in front of us looked to be guarded by at least four soldiers. Their swords and helmets gleamed copper in the dim light. I remembered what Kalo had told me about the High Fae and iron; I had an advantage in a swordfight —not only would my iron sword be stronger than their bronze weapons, but any cuts would likely hurt them more.

Still, we couldn't march through the front door. Archers manned the battlements and there were likely magic wielders among the guards.

Sweat bloomed across my skin. I felt woefully inadequate, an impostor—my sword like a fake plastic weapon at my waist. I was a mom; a paralegal —and what? I thought I could just storm a *castle* and rescue my children? I knew if I confronted anyone inside, I would die. And that would be it. My kids would be trapped forever.

Bile traveled up my throat in a painful gush, and my lungs pushed out an unsteady breath. My hands shook, and I gripped my elbows, huddling lower in the fragrant dirt.

Shane's callused fingers on my chin lifted my face, but my unseeing eyes tracked only the vibrant swirls of the night sky, and the bile burned deeper. I yanked my chin away and quietly retched into the mud, my stomach clenching painfully as sweat trickled from my hairline.

From a distance, I heard Shane murmur something, and a hand stroked through my hair. The wyrm slipped its cool body around my wrist, and the twin sensations grounded me.

I inhaled the warm night air that smelled faintly of stone and water and exhaled again, repeating the actions several times. *I'm not alone.*

I sat back on my heels, my thoughts calmer. The deep pulse of magic throbbed in my core, reassuring me I could call on my fire and armor if I needed them. I would *not* fail.

I met Shane's eyes with a wry twist to my lips. "Sorry."

Although the contours of his face were vague in the shadow of the castle wall, his teeth flashed white when he spoke. "We're going to do it. Don't worry, Willa. I won't let you down."

Nodding, I straightened my shoulders. "I know."

We crept along the wall for several minutes, searching for a way inside. Finally, I caught sight of a small wooden door under a tall turret.

I saw no guards, which probably meant the door was locked. I frowned, staring at it. Like a ninja, Shane slipped between the stalks until he reached the wall, pressing his back to the stones and staring at me. He lifted his chin.

Swallowing hard, I tried to copy his movements until my own back scraped against the castle walls and I stared out across the fields. The plateau we'd descended only a couple of hours earlier was a black blur on the horizon.

Shane fiddled with the door handle. His muffled curse echoed softly, and an idea—either mine or the wyrm's, I wasn't sure—pushed into my brain.

Bumping my lips against the curve of Shane's ear, I breathed, "Let me."

He stepped away as I knelt, and the wyrm slipped from my wrist to walk daintily up the frame of the door. When it reached the top, it wriggled briefly, then vanished through a small crack. Only a few moments passed before the handle twisted and the door swung open.

The wyrm rested on the other side, its sticky padded feet encircling the handle. I scooped it up to coo praises and stroked a finger along its tail. Satisfaction laced our bond, and I smiled triumphantly at Shane.

He hmphed, but I knew he was impressed, and I sent more silent praise to the wyrm as it pranced up my arm to drape itself around my neck. Its quiet purr felt vaguely gloating, and I suppressed another smile and followed Shane into the dark interior.

Given the slight scent of rotting vegetable matter, I assumed this was a place for the field workers to drop off the fruits of their labors. And that meant the kitchens were nearby.

My heart rate increased. A castle would have many uses for human servants—cleaning staff, serving staff, and kitchen staff.

I paused to pull the hood of my robe over my head and to rip a hole in the material at the waist. The cloth separated easily under my fingernails, and I felt steadier when I could slip my hand inside and reach my sword. My pulse fluttered at my throat, and my stomach churned and bubbled, like all the blood in my body had taken up residence there.

"Keep your head bent," Shane warned. "You're much shorter than a High Fae, so you need to impersonate a servant."

"What about you?"

Shane straightened to his full height and the air in front of his face shimmered. When the haze dissipated, his features had hardened into a sort of cold beauty—his lips were thinner, pinched together in an expression displeasure, and the pointed tips of his ears poked through his gleaming dark hair. His skin glowed like the inside of a seashell under a bright sky.

I gasped.

His coarse robe was now a lustrous blue silk and his shoes bore little tassels. I reached out and touched the robe, shocked it felt as smooth as it looked. "How?"

His lips curved into a familiar smirk. But he spoke in a slightly higher pitch, with a musical lilt.

"A glamour. I can maintain it for a short span of time."

"That's pretty neat." I stared at him for another long moment, bemused, then shook out my hands and tucked my braided hair out of sight under my hood.

We walked through a narrow corridor that opened into a large room full of crates and jars. My mouth watered at the scent of honey and spices. The room was dark, lit only by the neon brightness of the night sky streaming through high, narrow windows. We navigated carefully through the stacks until we reached another door at the far side.

This one opened into a massive kitchen. A thick stone table stretched the length of the space, and a wooden shelf underneath contained neatly stacked pots and pans. The walls were lined with shelves of delicate-looking plates and bowls and tall, glimmering stemware.

I followed Shane's confident stride to the far wall, where a row of fireplaces stood, banked and glowing softly in the dim light.

Shane froze and I caught myself before I crashed into his back. Patting his shoulder, I looked around him and sucked in a pained gasp.

In the shadows, I counted six small bodies curled up on blankets in front of the largest of the smoldering fires. Two of the children slept a little apart from the others, their hands twined together. The sight of their curly blond hair ripped my heart from my chest.

Shane's hand moved to my mouth, muffling my cry, and I trembled with the urge to leap forward and snatch them into my arms. We needed to wake them carefully and keep them quiet until we reached the top of the plateau. And then we needed to get all the way back to Iris's gate without getting caught.

My mind stuttered from fear. There was no way we could accomplish all of that. Shane's hand fell from my mouth, and a sharp pain bit into my skull. Everything went black.

CHAPTER 18

Something growled in my face. I blinked awake, only to freeze at the sight of misshapen eyes peering down at me from under a thick brow. I stifled a scream, taking in the wild glare, the prominent nose, and the sharp tusks emerging from beneath a thick upper lip.

Berserker Shane growled again, narrowly missing impaling my eyeball with a tusk. My body jostled, and I clutched at his chest and looked down. He was sprinting with me in his arms.

The night sky whirled above, making my stomach lurch sickeningly as Shane's heavy stomps vibrated in my aching skull. Tree branches passed by in a whip of slim, dark shapes.

Touching the back of my head, I found the source of the pain—by the sting and wetness, I guessed something or someone had struck me on the head in the kitchen. *The kitchen!*

"Stop, Shane," I hissed. "We have to go back!"

The growl deepened and Shane's arms tightened around me, squeezing my ribs and constricting my lungs. I looked back up at his face and noticed blood streaming from a cut on his forehead.

"Was there a fight?" I asked softly, patting the warped chest at my cheek. "Did you transform to save us?"

Shane didn't answer.

We were running through a forest—the thick tree trunks and gnarled roots were familiar. My heart sank. Had we traveled all the way back up to the plateau? I struggled in his vise-like grip but still couldn't wriggle free.

"Shane!" I shouted. "Stop. You're going too far!"

An eerie howl echoed from behind us, and goosebumps popped up all over my skin. Shane ran faster.

Craning my neck, I looked over his shoulder to see the sleek, powerful trio of fae hounds chasing us, their lips pulled away from their razor-edged teeth with silent snarls. Yellow eyes glared at me, and I turned my head and urged Shane to run faster.

His thick thighs bunched and elongated as he barreled forward, but the hounds were gaining. My pulse beat a galloping rhythm in my throat, then seemed to stop altogether when I reached for my sword. Gone. And I didn't have my pack. I felt for my bond with the wyrm. Nothing.

Was it dead? Had I lost it in the kitchen? I was a terrible wyrm parent—or just a terrible parent in general. I was knocked unconscious as soon as I'd caught sight of my kids. My blood ran cold. Had they seen me? Did they witness me getting hurt? Had they screamed for me?

My stomach lurched again, and my eyes lolled in their sockets. My head wound and the jolting motion of Shane running with me in his arms were taking their toll—I didn't care what the romance novels said, this was not a comfortable way to travel. Shane leaped over another bramble and my head slammed against his chest, the force of the impact clacking my teeth together.

Then I was suddenly airborne, my limbs flailing. I hit a tree hard enough to stun my senses, and when I blinked again, Shane faced the trio of hounds, his spear in hand.

He stabbed at the closest one, and it jumped away with a snarl as the other two circled. I watched for the frenzy to claim Shane like it had against the drows, but he seemed to be waiting for the hounds to move closer.

Scrambling to my feet, I yanked at my magic and shimmering armor encased my body. My confidence soared with the protection offered by my scales—now the hounds' teeth wouldn't easily rip through my vulnerable human flesh.

One hound crashed into Shane with a howl, knocking him down before he had a chance to stab it. I reached for my sword, only to remember it was gone. I muttered a curse, then slammed my hand over my mouth when one of the hounds turned to stare at me.

Saliva dripped from its slathering mouth, and I measured the distance between us. Could it leap that far?

The ground shook and a pair of armed warriors burst into sight, breathing heavily. I called my magic to my fingertips and readied a jet of fire.

I opened my mouth to call a warning to Shane, but the sound vanished before it left my lips, and my eyes widened in shock as the bean sídhe stepped from behind the guards to smirk at me. "Caught you," she hissed.

My scales faltered, and I clawed at my throat, trying in vain to warn Shane. He went down with a silent roar as all three hounds leaped on him at once. My heart clutched with an agonizing lurch. A spear flashed in the moonlight. A guard bashed me on the head with her armored gauntlet, and everything went dark for the second time.

I woke up chained to a hard, bitterly cold bench. My vision tunneled to pinpricks of white light and I yanked at the metal links, my brain catapulting me back to the thirst and the hunger, the pitch black, and the despair. My breaths sawed in and out of my lungs and animalistic grunts escaped my clenched teeth as I strained. I had to get away. I wouldn't die here, chained in the dark and starving.

The skin at my wrists broke and bled, and the sight of the crimson flow halted my frantic struggles. Realizing I could see the space around me, I froze—I wasn't in the dark.

Rolling my head on my shoulders, I tried to still my quaking. I took deep breaths and lucidity returned. I'd escaped Renfri's chains. I wasn't there anymore.

Glancing around, I saw I was in a small chamber, the walls made of stone, and across from me, bars blocked a narrow door. I staggered to my feet and took a few steps toward the door, but the chains stopped me. The clank and clatter nearly caused another flashback, so I closed my eyes and centered myself in the here and now. My pulse gradually returned to normal.

The manacles grated against my wrists as my breaths puffed in and out, steaming in the frigid air. My eyes felt gritty. How long had I been out? The bump at the back of my head throbbed with every beat of my heart, now twice the size it had been before the guard struck me. I fingered it gingerly and hissed.

The corridor beyond the barred door was lit with a flickering glow, probably a torch, and the cell around me stood empty except for the stone bench and my chains.

I wore the clothes I'd had on for the past few days, with no sign of the robe I'd stolen, my pack, my sword, or the wyrm.

My voice quavered as I called out, "Shane?"

No one answered. I shouted his name again, louder, but the only sound I heard was a steady drip of water from somewhere nearby.

My hands trembled, rattling the chains, and terror threatened to crush me. I stumbled back to my bench. Had the hounds killed him in the forest?

Or did he lay unconscious somewhere, trapped in his berserker stupor?

Bitter despair flooded my mouth. If I lost him, I would grab my kids and burn this whole world to the ground.

Harder tremors shook me, and I sank onto the bench. The chill immediately seeped through my leather pants. The sensation grounded me.

I need to get free. My thoughts circled. I was likely back in the castle—in the dungeon—and if I escaped, I could find Finn and Dara again. And Shane.

Lifting my chin, I reached for my armor, and when my skin shone with golden scales, I wrenched hard at the chains binding my wrists. They broke with a clatter, and I froze, listening. When I heard nothing, I crept to the door and peered down the Stygian passageway.

The scents of dampness, chalk, and old rot swirled in the empty space.

Some distance away, a torch flickered, casting long shadows across the stone corridor. It seemed like I was in the last cell, and I had no idea if the other barred doors stretching ahead of me hid other occupants.

I tested the bars on my cell with a solid yank, and they didn't budge. What were they made of? Not iron, I knew. Maybe lead? They felt heavy, heavier than the chains on the ground behind me.

My scales were still out, so I wrapped my fingers around one bar and used all my strength to heave against it. The bar didn't move.

I coated the metal with a jet of flames and sustained the blast for as long as I could. When dizziness threatened, I shut off the power and pulled once more. The bar broke to pieces in my glowing hands.

I wedged my leg and hip through the narrow gap, but I couldn't quite get the rest of my body out.

Panting, I stepped back a few feet and tried to summon the energy for more fire. I blasted the next bar, holding it for less time than the previous one, then bucked against the metal with my hands and feet before it finally broke.

Without waiting to see if all the noise had alerted a guard, I started forward, trotting down the dim corridor. I glanced inside each cell I passed, but there was no sign of Shane.

My heart twisted in my chest, but I refused to think of the possibility he lay dead in the forest. He slept somewhere, I reassured myself. I felt again the tight band of his monstrous arms around me, protecting me even as he lost his human self, and I swore I'd find him.

The door at the end of the hall was made of wood, with only a small open square showing the hall beyond. Standing on my tiptoes, I peeked through. The next hallway also stood empty and contained more cells.

Sighing, I rocked back on my heels and debated my options. I wasn't sure I had enough magic in me to burn the door down after my earlier depletions. Already, my tongue sat parched and swollen in my mouth, and my head strummed with a dull throb. I vanished my scales, which helped a little with the headache.

I stared at the door as if I could open it with my brainpower alone. I needed my wyrm. Or a battering ram.

Turning, I jogged to my cell and grabbed a couple of broken bars from the floor, still warm to the touch. Back at the door, I squatted and gouged at the wood near the handle. The scrape of metal on wood was loud in the silence of the corridor, and I worked as quickly as I could.

A pile of shavings and splinters accumulated by my feet, and the handle steadily loosened until it finally dislodged from the door and fell out of sight with a heavy plonk. The hole created by its absence was just wide enough for my hand.

I stuck my arm through and patted around until I found the bar locking the door in place. Grunting with effort, my brow dripping sweat and my mouth filled with the taste of sawdust, I strained until it lifted free. A loud clang sounded when it hit the ground, and a splinter bit into my palm.

The door swung open, and I stepped through, shaking my hand and grinning.

The sound of several people clapping penetrated my euphoria, and I stopped mid-stride, the grin falling from my face.

"We were correct, Captain. She does appear to be dragonkin. How clever of me to let her sneak into the castle and my trap."

"Very clever indeed, my queen."

"She didn't transform, however. Is she too diluted?"

I gaped at the small group standing on the other side of the door. I could have sworn the hall was empty only a moment ago. Two were dressed in silver chainmail—tall, slim warriors with swords at their hips. I recognized one as the soldier who'd struck me in the forest. And the third figure was the most beautiful woman I'd ever seen in my life, with rich coppery skin, deep golden-red hair, and eyes that swirled with a maelstrom of colors.

"I will check," the queen said.

The whirling eyes focused on me, sharpened, and I froze like a mouse before a raptor.

A piercing pain split my skull in half, and I dropped to my knees, swaying as an unknown force pried apart my psyche. My life flashed before my eyes in a series of disjointed images, each lasting only a fraction of a millisecond. My father's vanishment, my mother's death, my interlude with Paul, the twins' birth, my job, Shane, Kalo . . . Each piece of my life a speck of insignificance against the onslaught of the fae queen's disregard.

The pain compounded, and my mouth opened in a soundless scream.

The foreign sensation of fingers inside my mind, ripping me apart and throwing pieces of me into space, splintered my control. I burst into flames.

The power sucked every bit of energy from

my body, and I collapsed. The figures in front of me wavered. Finally, the fingers manipulating my mind disappeared and were replaced by unwavering nothingness.

I woke in chains again, only this time my arms were manacled to the wall behind me. Automatically twisting away from the cold stone, my shoulders wrenched in their sockets, and I rose on my tiptoes to relieve my creaking joints of the weight of my body.

Blinking blearily around me, I took shallow breaths, fighting hard against the panic threatening to erupt. My coal of magic smoldered dimly, nearly spent, and I didn't think I'd be able to form my armor to wrench out of the chains any time soon.

My headache continued to pulse, making the skin at the back of my skull feel tight. I sucked in a deep breath and the scent of old blood and dank air flooded my nostrils.

"Awake?" a smooth, lyrical voice asked. "Excellent. Now we may begin."

"Begin?" I repeated dumbly. My eyes zeroed in on the queen, who stood under the light near the barred door of my cell. Torchlight flashed off her jewels, shooting new arrows of agony into my brain.

"The question of whether or not you can shift has not been answered to my satisfaction. In your memories, I see that you have not. *Yet*. However, I don't know if that means you can't. So, now I will hurt you—a lot—and we will see what happens."

Sweat beaded on my upper lip.

"Why do you care?"

Mab grinned at me, her pointed teeth sparkling white. "A dragonkin woman will bargain with me. A dragon must be chained and enslaved. We will see what you are. And then we will plan."

"Don't do this," I whispered.

"I won't if you can shift to your dragon form and stop me."

"I can't. I don't know how."

"Well, we shall see."

And then the queen hurt me. A lot.

I screamed until I could scream no more. Still, my dragon didn't come.

CHAPTER 19

I lay naked in a bath. Foreign hands touched my body. My thoughts coalesced and I flinched, splashing water at the figure by my side as I shrieked and batted at her arms.

The water spattered harmlessly to the floor as the woman stepped back and chided me. "Careful. You'll split your stitches."

"Stitches?" I repeated stupidly.

My fingers stretched up to touch the back of my skull, and I shivered at the sensation of bare skin and tight threads embedded in my flesh. Tenderness radiated from the wound.

"The bald spot is very small," the woman assured me. I blinked at her, speechless.

I glanced around the sumptuous room, my warm bath in front of the lit fireplace. Tapestries on the walls glowed with jewel tones, and across the room sat a large canopy bed, the blankets turned down. Gilded lights flickered, and the air smelled of milk and honey. My bathwater swirled with bubbles as I shifted position and pulled my knees to my chest.

The woman crept closer and showed me the

washcloth in her hand. “May I continue?”

Shrinking, I shook my head. “Sorry, but I’m not comfortable with that. I can finish up by myself.”

She nodded and placed the cloth on the rim of the tub, then moved behind a screen on the other side of the fire. “I’m not permitted to leave you alone,” she called, “but I’ll wait here until you’re done.”

I hastily scrubbed my body, ridding myself of weeks’ worth of travel grime, sweat, and blood. The water turned gray around me as my skin pinkened and then turned red under my heavy ministrations. I wanted to get out as soon as possible, though I couldn’t deny it felt amazing to be clean. I left my hair alone so I didn’t get the stitches wet, though the strands smelled sweet, like maybe the servant had washed it?

A vision sparked. I was missing something. Memories of swirling luminescent eyes surfaced, along with the tangy smell of blood. My eyes shot to my wrists. There should be deep, jagged cuts along the veins, but my skin was unbroken.

I swallowed. It must have been a dream.

Shivering, I stood and wrapped myself in the voluminous towel that waited for me before moving in front of the fire. “Where are my clothes?” I muttered, glancing around the room again.

“There are clothes on the bed,” the woman said from behind the screen. “Would you like help?”

“No, thank you.” Hurrying to the bed, I found a simple pair of leather pants and a cotton shirt, very similar to what I'd been wearing since my time in the goblin caves. Exhaling with relief, I dressed quickly.

Eyeing the door, I wondered if I could slip out but dismissed the thought. I was likely deep within the castle, and it was safer to play along with whatever the beautiful High Fae queen sought from me if I hoped to find a good opportunity for escape. She'd been toying with me, first with the Dearg-Dur, then with the trap in the kitchen.

I rubbed at my forehead, remembering the torment of her magic as it penetrated my brain—like the tentacles of a squid splitting open a clam to get at the meat inside. Shuddering, I swallowed the bile scalding my throat. She'd seen *everything*.

"I'm ready," I called softly, moving to stand in front of the fire.

The servant came out from behind the curtain and approached me with a brush in her hand. With gentle fingers, she braided my hair, and when she finished, she tilted her head and gave a decisive nod. "You cannot see the spot, dear. I promise."

A small smile touched my lips. "Thanks."

Her gaze skittered away from mine as I stared. I noticed the delicate points at the tips of her ears and frowned. I'd thought she was human, but now I wasn't sure.

"Are you half-fae?"

Her face turned chalk white as she backed away from me. "Please," she whispered, "I have no magic, I swear."

Her fists clutched at her shirt, and I squinted, confused. I reached a hand toward her, and she sucked in a sharp breath and scuttled away from me.

I dropped my hand. "Why are you scared of me?"

Her eyes popped wide. "My blood has no power. Please don't sacrifice me. I have survived two hundred winter solstices, and I swear, my blood is too weak for you."

My brow cleared. "Relax, I'm not a blood witch. You're safe from me."

Her eyes still wide and darting about nervously, she nodded and cleared her throat. "I'm to take you to the queen now."

Straightening my spine, I braced myself. Though my stomach dipped, I resolved to hold onto my meager courage for as long as I could. Everyone was counting on me. Somewhere in this castle, my kids waited for me. And Shane. I needed to find him and guard his berserker sleep.

The servant led the way down a narrow hallway, which opened into a larger carpeted corridor. Richly colored paintings lined the walls, and my feet sank into the plush carpet, muffling my steps. We walked for several minutes before entering an open hall with towering ceilings and a slick marble floor. Our footsteps grew louder as we crossed the space, the servant hurrying her pace as if she didn't like to be here.

On the far side, a tall set of doors stood closed and guarded by two soldiers. They wore the same silver chainmail I'd seen earlier and carried swords at their hips. They were beautiful—their skin different shades of dusky tan and pearly white and their faces composed of perfectly symmetrical, delicate features. They watched us approach with hard eyes; one of them fingered the hilt of his sword.

I wished for my own weapon. Would I ever see it again? Without the iron, I didn't stand a chance in a fight against a seasoned soldier.

The servant pushed the door open. We slipped inside the room, and I froze in my tracks, my eyes and mouth wide open.

It was the largest room I'd ever seen—easily the size of a football stadium—and it glittered under the lights of a thousand flaming chandeliers.

Tugging at my arm, the servant woman pulled me forward. I followed, still craning my neck to track the light reflected from the sparkling shards.

"Mom!" Finn's voice echoed across the cavernous space, and it took a moment for my brain to catch up to my ears. Adrenaline tingled through my body as I spun in place, searching the room. At the far side, at the base of what appeared to be a solid-gold dais, two small figures stood, waving at me.

A small scream fell from my lips, and I ran toward them. My eyes devoured the sight in front of me—their blond hair, their sturdy bodies, their shocked faces—and I ran faster. Although the time felt interminable, seconds passed and I was on my knees before them, squeezing their faces to my chest. Finn's arms went around my neck and Dara's encircled my waist. My shirt dampened under their tears. Whispering their names, I stroked my hands through their hair and down their cheeks.

My heart broke at the sobs racking Dara's tiny body, and I squeezed her tighter. Finn suddenly drew back, and I reached for him, my eyes locked on his face. He flinched, and I dropped my hand.

"My fault," he mumbled, stepping farther away from me.

Still holding tightly to Dara, I lunged and recaptured him in my arms. I shook him a little, and his curls flopped. "Not your fault. None of this is your fault," I rasped. He avoided my gaze, and I made my voice stern. "Finn Overholt, you look at me."

He quaked but raised his eyes to meet mine

"This is not your fault. It's not my fault. I've been chasing you from the moment I lost you again, and I will always find you."

His lips quivered as he gave in and collapsed into my embrace.

I crushed their bodies to mine and looked up at the queen sitting on the throne. Her beauty struck me again, but this time I could easily read the cruelty swirling in the depths of her vivid eyes. Another memory flashed, this one involving a fae male at my back, wrenching my neck into place as the queen dripped something vile into my mouth. I'd tried to spit it out, but she'd covered my mouth and nose with a blanket of magic until I passed out and the liquid slipped down my throat.

Had she poisoned me? I shook my head. No. She'd let it burn and boil in my stomach until I vomited blood, and then she laughed and said I obviously didn't have a dragon's constitution. *When did that happen?*

My gaze narrowed on the queen. When she knew she had my attention, she spoke in her lilting voice. "We have a problem."

I stood and shoved Finn and Dara behind me, keeping hold of their hands. Dara started to speak, but I shushed her.

The queen continued, her gown rustling slightly as she leaned forward. "These children were given to me by their father. Which means I have rights to them."

I shook my head, my mouth opening, but she silenced me with a gesture.

"Yes, as their mother, you also have rights. However, as I am queen, my rights trump yours."

Blood pounded in my ears, and I squeezed the small hands in mine tighter.

"But I'm willing to make a bargain with you."

"I'm listening," I said through clenched teeth. This was it, the culmination of all my training with Kalo. I needed to best the fae queen, but I didn't know how. Her mind magic had crippled me once, and I knew she was cruel and wicked. My stomach twisted; my knees knocked together. I didn't even have my sword.

"As you're aware, I've gone through your

memories. I know where you've been and what you've planned."

I swallowed hard and sent a silent apology to Kalo.

The queen gestured and a lean figure moved to stand beside her. I recognized Paul, though he looked much better than the last time I'd seen him. His skin glowed with health, and he had muscles on his frame again. He sneered, and I growled under my breath.

Finn echoed my growl. Paul's eyes widened.

"I propose a bargain. The news of the goblin plot to invade is not a surprise to me, whatever the king's son might have told you. We've been aware for years of their numbers under the ground."

My stomach roiled, but I kept my face expressionless.

"But I would still like to avoid a battle, of course. It's a lot of work, and the solstice approaches. I would rather direct my energies elsewhere." Her grin turned feral and greedy.

I nodded carefully.

"Paul will return the children to your home and remove the memory spell. He will swear to do it quickly and safely, if he values his restored status in the Green Lands."

The queen sent an icy look at Paul. He paled and bobbed his head. "Yes, Queen Mab. I swear it," he said. His eyes tightened, and he rubbed his chest before straightening his shoulders.

"And in return?" I asked.

The queen smiled, the expression turning her exquisite face to a mask of malicious glee. "You will go to your goblin friend and kill him."

I squeezed my eyes shut and an involuntary whimper was ripped from my throat.

"My spies have informed me the king is ancient, on his deathbed, and Kalonymos already rules in his stead. If you kill him, it will be years before the goblins find a ruler to unite them again to attack the Green Lands."

"It's impossible," I grated, my mind reeling. "He's too strong. I could never kill him, even if I agreed. Which I won't. He's my friend, my teacher—"

"And they're your children," the queen interrupted in a harsh tone. "If you don't agree, they shall remain here as kitchen servants forever. They shall age but not die until centuries pass and the memory of you and your life together are forgotten. Then I shall devour what remains of their magic and kill them."

Agony burst in my chest, and I fell to my knees at the vision of such a future. "Please," I whispered.

Dara tugged on my hand, and I mindlessly bent my head to her.

"Don't kill anyone for us, Mama."

I blinked and nuzzled a kiss into her hair. "I won't, baby."

Racking my brain, I tried to think of other options, but the queen's words circled in my mind —an unending litany of doom. I couldn't separate logic from my emotions. There was no price I wasn't willing to pay for my children, even if it cost me my soul. But Kalo—my stomach twisted. I couldn't do it.

"How will I even get to the goblin caves again?" I asked, hoping to buy myself more time. Hoping she would reconsider. "No one trusts me but Kalo. I'd never get near him."

Mab waved her hand and the far wall vanished. In its place, the plateau above the castle came into view, and on it teemed thousands of green-skinned warriors.

I gasped.

"They arrived just this morning while you slept in my dungeon."

"Then it's too late," I argued. "The army is here. The battle will happen even if I kill him."

Shaking her head, the queen tsked. "I will send an emissary under the white flag. You will accompany her. Kalonymos will let you get close to him, and you will kill him. The army will collapse and vanish back below the ground."

"He won't let me get close to him. He'll have no reason to trust me if I'm with your emissary."

"You forget I've been in your memories. I think you will have no problem getting close enough to slip a knife between his ribs. I've seen the way he looks at you."

I blinked, rocking on my heels. She was wrong, but I didn't know what to say to convince her.

Snapping her fingers, Mab summoned a soldier from where she stood against the wall, and I watched her stride forward. My knees trembled.

The soldier carried a white flag, and as she knotted it onto the end of her spear, my legs gave way entirely. Sitting on the cold marble floor, I cradled first Finn's face, then Dara's in my hands, memorizing their features. I knew what I had to do.

Locking eyes with the queen, I spoke from my position on the floor. "Swear to me on your life that Paul will take them home immediately and they will arrive safely. That he'll call the human police and turn them over so they can be cared for while they wait for me."

Mab smiled again, her eyes gleaming with satisfaction. "I swear it."

"Then I will bargain. I will kill him."

A sharp tug on the coal of my magic startled me, and I rubbed at my chest. The queen mimicked my movement, her fingernails rasping against the jewels lining the bodice of her dress. "We are bound."

Dara began to cry again, and I kissed her eyelids. Although Finn's chin wobbled, his gaze was steady when he looked up at me, and he leaned forward and pressed his warm cheek to mine.

"I will see you soon," I lied. I was unlikely to survive this, and the falsehood curdled on my tongue. Dara's wails grew louder, and the servant woman who'd escorted me to the throne room bustled forward to lift Dara to her hip. Tugging on Finn's hand, she pulled him away and followed Paul out of the opulent room.

I watched them go; the sight of Dara

screaming and thrashing in the woman's arms as she reached for me nearly broke my resolve. But Finn reached up to hold his sister's hand, and my heartache eased. They would take care of each other.

Climbing to my feet, I straightened my spine and locked eyes with the queen. "I need the pack I was wearing in the kitchen. And I'll need my sword." I swallowed hard. "And what about the man I was with in the forest? What happened to him?"

Confusion marred Mab's perfectly arched brow. The soldier next to me answered my question. "Killed by the hounds."

I staggered, my knees going weak again. The queen's voice barely broke through the whoosh of blood in my ears. "Oh yes, the berserker. I'd forgotten about him. A pity. I always wanted one. Leave it to Iris to have found one in the human world."

My vision tunneled and I focused on the heat rising in my fingertips. I couldn't react. I could do nothing to jeopardize the deal I'd made. But oh, how I ached to douse the queen with fire and dance on her ashes. My despair enveloped me, violent and unreasoning.

Shane was dead. I couldn't imagine it. My friend; my protector. Fire flared in my core as my coal burst into a black flame and scales hardened on my skin. I hadn't meant to call them, but the armor soothed me, making me feel like the queen could scratch no more pain out of me.

Shane would have been happy the kids were safe, I told myself. That was all he wanted.

I closed my eyes. *Not all,* I acknowledged, and the ache in my chest grew. I saw his face, stoic but ready to smile at me, and I imagined stretching up on my toes to kiss his warm lips. But I was too late. I would never again touch my lips to his; never again feel the weight of his strong arms around me.

My brain battled between mute and dazed, fierce and cold.

Concentrating on slowing my frantic breathing, I clenched my hands until I had myself under control. My heart numbed as the pain leached away, until only one thought remained—*Mab will die*.

When I reopened my eyes, I was alone in the throne room with the female soldier. She watched me, her narrowed green eyes tilted at the corners and locked on my face, the tips of her sharp ears peeking from her tight braid.

"You may call me Captain Helarth. We go now," she stated, gesturing to the tall doors.

"Not without my pack and my sword," I said, planting my fists on my hips and lifting an eyebrow.

"We will go see if they're still in the kitchen."

I followed her from the room, my steps determined despite my wounded soul. A litany of forthcoming tasks circled my brain like water around a drain—*kill Mab, save the kids, kill Mab . . .*

In the hallway beyond, Paul stepped out from a shadowed alcove. I paused. He gestured imperiously at Helarth, and she moved a few steps away.

"What do you want?" I asked, working hard not to give into the desire to punch him in the nose. Or yank Helarth's spear from her hands and stab him in the gut.

"I heard you screaming in the dungeon."

I flinched.

Paul smirked, and his eyes traveled up my pants to linger on my breasts before locking on my face. My mouth filled with acid. His expression warmed. "Why didn't you tell me you were dragonkin? It would have changed everything between us."

My jaw tightened, and I narrowed my eyes. "I didn't know. And I'm glad I didn't know. If you'd stuck around, you would have destroyed my life even sooner than you did when you stole my children."

Ignoring me, he stepped closer and purred, "Our children, Willa. And it was good between us, wasn't it? After you kill the goblin, you should stick around. I have—"

Disgust curled my lip. I backed away from him. "I don't think so, Paul. You're a murderer and a sociopath. Once you return the kids, I never want to see or hear from you again."

In the flickering light, his lean figure morphed to add height and a new layer of muscles, and my mouth dropped as his face changed. Shane's face stared back at me. I sucked in a breath. His blue eyes softened, and he held out his hand.

For a moment, I wavered. I wanted so

desperately to touch that hand. But my heart shattered in my chest at the memory of the guard's words. Shane was dead.

"Are you sure, Willa?" Shane's deep voice rasped. "I can help you get your revenge on the queen. And with my power restored, there are certain benefits—"

My magic exploded out of me, and Paul slammed against the wall, barely dodging my fireball. He dropped the glamour, and his expression hardened. "You'll regret that choice." He spun and stalked down the hall.

"Won't be the first decision I've regretted about you!" I called to his retreating back.

My all-encompassing rage drowned out my grief and worry as I followed Helarth to the kitchens. A new litany circled—*kill Mab, save the kids, kill Paul . . .*

CHAPTER 20

In the quiet kitchen, empty of servants or any signs of food preparation, I found my pack and my sword resting on the massive center table.

Peeking inside the bag, I sighed—no sign of the wyrm. I couldn't deal with anymore loss at the moment, so I chose to believe it had deserted me. I strapped on my sword and gestured around the room. "Where is everyone?"

Helarth eyed me with suspicion.

"Just wondering." I shrugged.

"In the times between meals, the servants sleep. The queen ate this morning, so she will not eat again for several days."

Cocking my head, I wondered at that but quickly dismissed it from my thoughts. I didn't care about the dietary habits of the High Fae.

We strode through another set of doors and into an open hall. Muted sounds echoed from outside. Helarth threw open the doors to the courtyard in front of the castle, and my mouth dropped open.

Assembled in dozens of rows, with swords, axes, and bows at the ready, stood thousands of fae warriors. Some wore armor and some chainmail, and others looked to be almost naked in the bright sunlight. Their skin and hair were every color combination imaginable, but nothing disguised the pinched, hungry expressions on their faces.

Multitudes turned to look at me and growls rose in the air. I stepped behind Helarth, keeping her body between us. Their hate pierced my skin like hundreds of poisoned darts. My hand crept to my sword and the cold iron steadied me.

Helarth strode for the massive gates enclosing the bailey, and at the last minute opened a smaller door beside them. We stepped on the gray road outside of the castle, and as the door shut behind us, the sounds of Mab's army faded. I sucked in a deep breath, scenting the green crops in the fields.

Without Mab's magic, we were too far from the cliff to see Kalo's army, but I felt an invisible force ahead of us. The air was still and expectant.

I shivered. How did I come to stand between two such unearthly armies?

Jogging to keep up with Helarth's long legs, I asked, "What's the plan?"

Ignoring me, she lifted her spear with the white flag at the end and walked down the road. I followed her. When we reached a halfway point between the castle and the plateau, we stopped. And we waited.

SEVERAL hours later, I paced the road, kicking small stones out of the way as worry chewed at me.

"This isn't my fault," I said to Helarth. "Mab still has to complete her end of the deal."

Helarth, still standing with her spear in the air, ignored me.

"How will I even know if Mab does it?"

She sighed. "You are both of you bound. Your magic has been tied to the bargain. If either of you fails, your magic will kill you."

Blinking, I rubbed a fist against my sternum. "If I don't kill Kalo, I'll die?" I asked. "And Mab will be free of her vow?"

Helarth nodded.

My blood turned to ice. I'd been planning to betray Mab, to confess everything to Kalo and get his help to ensure Paul followed through with his promise. After all, he still owed me a boon. But this new information changed everything. If I broke the bargain, I'd die. And Mab could do what she wished with my children.

I shouldn't have agreed. Or I should have asked more questions. Regret filled my mouth with ash.

I couldn't kill Kalo. I swallowed hard. I had to kill him, or the kids would return to Mab. And it was almost the winter solstice. Everything I'd struggled for—everything I'd fought for and killed for would be lost. But how could I value my life more than Kalo's? Killing in self-defense wasn't the same as murder, and I didn't think I was capable of the latter. How could I ever meet my children's eyes with the weight of such an act on my soul? Dizzy, I almost missed Helarth's next words.

"They're coming."

Straightening, I scanned the road and caught sight of two approaching figures. One carried a white flag on a spear like Helarth's, and the other was achingly familiar.

Tears filled my eyes, and I rapidly blinked them away. I didn't know what to do—no, that wasn't right. I knew what I had to do, but I also knew I couldn't.

I'm sorry, babies. I was condemning them to a life of servitude. I tried to reassure myself with what Paul had said when he'd stolen them—that Mab would keep them as servants and not kill them at the solstice; that they'd live a long time with no human illnesses, but the absurdity of his promise carried no power to soothe me. I was sacrificing their freedom and my life. No platitudes could erase that fact. Maybe one day they'd forgive me . . .

After scraping a shaky hand through my hair, I reached into my pack and withdrew one of Shane's long knives. While Helarth watched the approaching figures, I sidled closer to her side and pressed the knife against her ribcage.

Her eyes widened, then narrowed. She snarled. "What are you doing?"

"Be still," I said. "Keep your mouth shut if you want to live through this."

She stopped protesting, her dark eyes searching my face. If she wanted, she could shake me loose, but I was hoping she thought this was part of my master plan to kill Kalo and she'd play along until it was too late.

My gaze traced Kalo's features as he strode closer, and my chest tightened in shock as I realized how much older he'd gotten. His dark hair bore shocks of white at his temples beside his horns, and lines creased the skin around his mouth and eyes. He looked like he'd aged twenty years. I thought of the time he'd spent in his capital city, readying his army for war. He must have lingered for years, perhaps to give me as much time as he could.

He stopped a few feet away from us, and a sad, wistful look crossed his face. "Lady," he said, his voice husky. "You look well."

I sent him a tremulous smile. Sparing a glance at his companion, I saw a goblin who bore nearly identical features, only he was much younger. My breath caught.

"My son," Kalo affirmed. "Folmon."

The goblin lifted his chin at me. "Lady."

My brow furrowed. "How can you have a fully grown son? You planned to march at once on the king's command?" I was focused on the wrong questions, but my curiosity over what had happened with Kalo and Syfa in the goblin city was too great to ignore.

Small lines of grief flashed at the corners of Kalo's eyes. "The king fell ill. There was infighting among the army commanders." He released a heavy breath and turned to look at Folmon. His expression brightened. "In the end, my father's will triumphed and we marched. We fight this battle in his honor."

Folmon nodded sharply, his young face keen.

I swallowed hard and pushed my knife a little deeper into Helarth's side, ignoring her faint growl.

Was Mab watching us through her magic window? If so, she was about to get an eyeful. But nothing about to happen would break our deal, I hoped. *Yet.*

"I'm here to kill you," I said.

Helarth squirmed, and I jabbed the knife at her again.

"I made a bargain with Mab. If I kill you, she returns the children to my home."

Kalo nodded, watching me carefully. Folmon stiffened and swore.

"Obviously, I'm not going to do it."

This time Helarth broke free of my hold. "Oathbreaker," she spat, her spear positioned in front of my chest.

I backed up a step, eyeing the sharp tip of her blade.

Before I could reach for my armor, Folmon lunged and drove his spear through Helarth's chest. I fell away, her blood spattering across my face, and the white flag poked through her back with a crunch.

Helarth's body slackened. Folmon casually pushed her off the end of the spear, the blade scraping audibly across her ribs, and pointed it at me.

I held up my hands and turned beseeching eyes to Kalo. "I said I wasn't going to do it!"

"Folmon, hold." Kalo's broad shoulders slumped and he closed his eyes for a long moment. He looked even older than before. Old and tired. His gaze refocused, his eyes dulling to the color of rust with his grief. "You will die if you do not."

Exhaling a puff of air, I nodded. "I know. But I can't kill you. Not even to save my kids. I'm not a murderer. I'm not a blood witch out to steal a life that doesn't belong to me. You know me."

Kalo's eyes narrowed on my hands, which trembled in front of me. I felt a pinch in my chest. Was it my magic? Preparing to destroy me for breaking my bargain with Mab?

"Mab knew you were coming," I said quickly, not sure how much time I had left. "She has an army waiting in the bailey."

Folmon waved his bloody spear at me. "We outnumber the fae by thousands."

I ignored him, speaking instead to Kalo. "Shane was killed in the woods near your army. If you see his body, please bury it for me." I grew cold, and goosebumps erupted on my skin. A harder tremor shook me. I searched my core, and my coal of magic appeared to dim. It flickered, and I doubted my choice. But it was too late.

The chill reached for my lungs as I rasped, "If you can—if you win, please save the children. And I'll consider your promise to me fulfilled."

Kalo's chin dipped, and I swayed on my feet.

My ears popped and a roar grew in my head. Instinctively, I reached for my armor, but my fingers slid through the coal without gripping it. It was almost burned out. My power was deserting me. Like everyone deserted me. Starting with my father.

As I stared at the barely flickering light, something woke in my memory. A deep voice, my father's voice, warned, "Never, ever pick it up, Willa. Promise me." My fingers spasmed.

In a flash of green, Paul appeared beside Helarth's lifeless form, Finn's and Dara's hands held tight in his grip. I staggered back, and he stepped over Helarth's body, his expression incendiary. "You're choosing the goblin over your children?"

Rage filled me, and I shook off my doubts to stand taller. "I will not murder for your barbarous queen! My life, my children's lives"—I met the wide eyes of my kids watching me and tightened my jaw—"will not be weighed more than any other person's life!" Black spots appeared in my vision, and I staggered.

Dara's lips moved, the muscles in her neck straining as though she shouted for me, but I couldn't hear her over the ringing in my ears.

Paul sneered, dropping the children's hands to draw a short sword. From the darkening corner of my eye, I saw Kalo move. Paul braced and leveled his sword.

Dara raced forward and stood between the men, throwing her hands up. The air rippled.

"Stop!" she called, and everyone froze.

"Mama." She turned to face me. "Remember your promise."

I nodded to her, my head heavy and wobbling on my neck. *No killing.* Acid rose in my throat. Weakness and exhaustion threatened to pull me under.

"Finn," she whispered.

My son moved to stand beside her, and his glowing eyes hooked mine. "Mom," he said. "Pick it up. I will help you." A warm sensation of peace and calm swirled through me.

I stared at him, and his voice merged with the deep one of my memories. Finn's features swam, aging. I stretched my fingers toward the dimming coal in my chest, its dying glow barely penetrating the dark.

Kalo shouted for me to stop, but he was too late.

The coal burst into flames as I grabbed it, and my thoughts went blank. Gone.

Icy golden fire cascaded along my skin. It took a moment for the pain to hit.

A great wave of agony ripped through me, and I screamed. My magic exploded out of every cell. My body broke and warped, and I thrashed my head, trying to shake loose the pain. My scales formed, then grew, and I grew with them.

Great wings erupted from my back and claws appeared on my hands and feet—giant claws, each gilded tip as long as a machete. My scream transformed into a bellow and flames dripped from my open mouth, landing in the dirt around me.

I whirled in place, my brain roiling and my senses overflowing with new sensations. I wanted to leap into the sky, to fly, but my mind couldn't translate the message to my wings. My long, sinuous neck twisted as another coil of pain whipped through me.

I felt like I was on fire, or my body enclosed a fire—I couldn't tell the difference. Flames licked through my veins and ancient knowledge churned in my head. My pain vanished, and I filled with a terrible purpose.

I wanted to rend, to burn, to set the world aflame. My human psyche shrank, and it was all I could do to hold onto a small kernel of my spirit. My human self curled into a ball,watching as my dragon took control. And she was angry.

Writhing, my body grew even larger, then I was airborne and spinning in place. Looking down, I saw the figures on the ground and wanted to eat them. No. I wanted to burn them. No. I wanted to fly.

The man who stood a little apart stared at me with a stricken expression. I snapped my teeth at him, and he vanished in a swirl of green.

Rage took over, its unstoppable force building in my veins. My head whipped back, and I roared my anguish into the sky. I'd wanted something. I'd wanted to do something to that man. I'd wanted to hurt him.

My mind burning with purpose, I needed to find a new target. Spinning in the air, I turned to the castle, then to the field lined with armored forms. A hole scraped at my chest. Something was missing. I'd lost someone.

No, I'd never had anyone. I was empty. My parents were gone—dead and lost. My lovers left. Two souls called to me, but I forgot the remnants of them in a blast of brilliant fury. My throat opened and an orange flame shot from it, arcing across the sky like a rocket.

I had no one, and I didn't care. Bugling my wrath, I bent my neck to launch another dart of flame at the closest ranks of soldiers. The line shuddered but didn't break. Spears and arrows clanged against my scales before falling to the earth.

Someone screamed, the small, high-pitched scream of a young creature. A child. I tilted my head to look more closely at the ground, my heavy wings beating the air behind me.

Arrows lined the road, encircling the people who watched me with shocked faces. My breath rasped in my lungs as I prepared a jet of flames.

One of the small figures screamed again, and my massive heart stuttered in my chest. A ball of air hit me, and my wings faltered for a moment. I fell a few feet.

The two smallest forms, the children, raced toward me, and I didn't see the spear launched by one of the green-skinned ones. It pierced my wing and I bellowed, pulling the wing closer to my body. I spiraled and slammed to the earth with a great plume of dirt. I thrashed. I needed to get to my feet, then I could devour them all.

A small hand pressed into my clawed foot and the pulse of magic that accompanied the faint sensation penetrated my red haze. A faint trickle that grew into a stream of pain and compulsion.

"Mom," the boy cried. "I'm calling my blood. Do you hear me?"

My mouth opened in a soundless scream. My bones broke and shrunk, and my scales fell at my feet. I collapsed, my skin burning.

"Finn," I coughed, my throat full of smoke. I rolled onto my back and stared up at the bright sky. "Dara."

I felt hands on my arms before small bodies pressed against mine.

"Mama," Dara sobbed. "You were a dragon."

Managing a nod, I stroked a trembling hand through the blond curls of my kids' beautiful heads. Uncontrollable rage still burned in the back of my brain. My skin flushed and chilled in alternating waves, and my heart stuttered in my chest. If Finn hadn't forced my shift, I would have killed them. Would have killed everyone. *I'm a monster.*

Tears filled my eyes as my head hit the dirt underneath me. The dragon wouldn't help me defeat Mab. If I shifted again, I wouldn't know family from foe. The curse was real. A lick of pain signaled Finn's blood burning to ash in my veins.

"I don't have any more, Mom," Finn whispered against my throat.

I nodded. "I know, baby." I pressed my hand

into his cheek and met his eyes. "You saved me. Now I need you to help your sister. I need you to be strong for each other."

Finn paled, but his chin firmed, and he nodded.

I sat up and looked past my kids to where Kalo watched me with fathomless eyes. Folmon's empty spear hand mocked me, and I pushed back against the madness. He'd knocked me from the sky so Finn could reach me. I should be thankful. My arm burned with the remembered pain of his strike.

I stood. My knees were like jelly, and I staggered.

"Remember your promise," I warned Kalo. The coal in my chest was now black and cold. My magic was gone, suborned by my burst of madness and my broken bargain with Mab. I kept my eyes on him, knowing I'd falter if I turned to look at Finn and Dara again.

Through my darkening gaze, I watched Kalo say something to Folmon. His son appeared to argue at first, but then bent his forehead to rest it briefly against his father's.

"I missed you," I whispered inaudibly, flashing back to our time in the caves, before he'd left me. When he'd spoken of duty while I dreamed of love. I should have known then that my path was doomed. The love I felt for Kalo was a shining thread between us, made of loyalty and trust. From the woods, miles away, another thread tied me to Shane, that one born from devotion and passion. Except the thread to Shane had frayed and snapped, and he was dead. My grief loomed, cold and endless.

I readied myself for the end, reassuring my faltering heart that my kids would forgive me if Kalo failed to get them out. Dara had told me not to kill anyone . . .

I sank to my knees and squinted at the sky—it was so blue here.

A shadow dropped in front of me. I blinked hazily as Kalo picked up my knife from the dirt of the road. A swirl of dust rose into the air, and I watched the motes without seeing them. Kalo wrapped my hand around the knife's hilt and guided it to his neck. "I missed you, too," he said.

I flinched and tried to pull away, but his grip was too strong. "No," I wheezed. "Don't."

"It'll be okay, lady. Transform again. Save them. For love of a dragon," Kalo murmured as he kissed my brow, then he plunged my knife into the skin of his neck and tore it across. Blood spurted in a crimson wave.

I screamed as he fell backward, and magic punched to life inside me once more.

From a great distance, Folmon shouted something at me, but a pitch-black flame unfurled in my core, and all I heard was the roar of its growing conflagration.

I curled my fingers to touch the coal, the glow burning bright with renewed magic, and I lifted it.

Scales covered me in an instant and my wings ripped from my back in a single excruciating burst.

I used my tail to turn in the air, my wings beating and my heart pounding. In the distance, the castle gates opened and the fae warriors resumed their forward march. Glee rippled through me.

Trumpeting a warning, I flew higher and blasted them with a jet of flames. Panic rippled through the ranks as the first few lines of soldiers turned to ash in moments.

From behind me, the enormous goblin army roared and stampeded down the cliff toward the battle. I wanted to turn, to flame them too—but no, I shouldn't. *Shouldn't . . .*

Rational thought seeped into my raving dragon brain and my rage settled, becoming a deep compulsion rather than an unstoppable force. I could think. I could reason. I knew myself. I bugled at the sky, spinning in the air and feeling the joy of the movement in my soul.

The curse was broken. *How?*

I looked down to see my kids watching me, their faces calm. Beside them, Kalo's body sprawled, and I faltered, my heart screaming in pain. The children vanished. My dragon eyes frantically searched for their shapes, then I remembered the bargain. Mab's promise. Kalo was dead by my hand.

They're home, I told myself. *I did it*. I thought of Shane—*we did it*. Sorrow filled me anew.

Pumping my heavy wings, I flew for the castle. Swirling through the air, I flipped my body and blasted another flaming torrent, but this one halted before it struck the soldiers, like an invisible wall held it back. The fire vanished, and I swooped lower, screeching my fury as the wind blew past my wings in a cold caress.

A glowing figure appeared amid the ranks of soldiers and gestured imperiously for me to descend. I ignored the request, calling my flames forth again for them to fail me a second time. I circled lower to land in a wheat field a little apart from the armies. My claws furrowed into the earth with an explosion of dirt and green stems, and I stretched my wings to catch my balance.

Admiring my iridescent, resplendent gold scales, I preened.

Without me circling between them, the armies met with a great screaming clash of weapons and armor, and my keen dragon ears rotated in place. I relished the echoed cries and groans of battle. What great fun.

I moved to join the revelry but stopped at the sight of Mab striding toward me, appearing to float through the green stalks. My rage coalesced into a determined thought, stronger than my slowly melting madness.

Bending my head, I met her sneer with a dragon's toothy smirk. My forked tongue flicked out, tasting the air. She smelled of roses. My human self remembered someone else who'd smelled like roses once. *Iris*. This was the creature who'd caused the murder of my children's grandmother, who intended to enslave or murder Finn and Dara. The one who bargained with me to murder my friend. The person responsible for killing the one man who'd stuck with me through the brutal task pressed on him by a sense of duty. A duty that had turned to love. A love that perished at her hands.

I inhaled again, and memories crashed into my mind in an avalanche of torment and terror. I parsed through them, feeling the agonies of my human self, and with a shocked inhale, I remembered everything. I remembered the dungeon and the chains. The blood. The final red haze of my madness vanished.

"You broke the deal," the queen accused me.

No, I said, though no words left my mouth. ***I fulfilled it. I killed the goblin.***

"Kalonymos killed himself," she argued.

The magic knows my bargain was met. Are the children home?

I turned to scan the field and saw only the clashing armies.

Mab's pretty face twisted into a scowl. She appeared to focus elsewhere for a moment, her gaze distant, before she nodded at me. "My oath is fulfilled as well. The children are home. Dragon, you must—"

No. I dropped my head and bit her in half. The crunch of her bones and the spurt of her blood in my mouth made me gag, and I immediately dropped her again. She didn't taste like roses. Her broken body stained the verdant green grass around her with crimson rivulets, and her wide, shocked eyes stared sightlessly at the sky.

Satisfaction moved through me. ***For Kalo***, I told her dead body. ***And for Shane***.

My heart burned in my chest. I hoped wherever they were, they knew I'd avenged them.

A groan echoed from Mab's army, and I turned to a sea of faces watching me, their expressions ranging between rage, chagrin, and relief.

Queen Mab is dead, I informed the fae soldiers. ***Surrender***.

Then my body convulsed and shrank, and the agony of bones breaking and reforming sucked me into a black abyss.

CHAPTER 21

I woke with a whimper. Blinking at the canvas ceiling above me, I tracked the sounds of people moving nearby and moans of pain. Pressing a hand to my head, I sat up gingerly to look around.

Pallets lined the ground, most full of sleeping or writhing goblins, and a few figures moved around them, offering water and whispering words of comfort.

A hospital tent, I realized. Or the goblin equivalent. Clearing my throat, I croaked, "Hello?"

A figure beside me stirred, and I muffled a shocked scream. The goblin male leaned forward, and the light highlighted his weary features.

"Folmon?"

My chest pinched, and tears welled in my eyes. "I'm so sorry. I didn't mean for him to do that."

He gave me a tight smile. "He talked of you often. He worried for you and your children, and what role this battle would take in helping or hindering your attempt to rescue them. And he wanted you to know he translated the curse."

I rubbed my eyes. "Curse?"

Folmon handed me a familiar book, a scrap

of paper poking out of it. "Diaevan's curse," he affirmed. "He translated it. 'For her mother vowed until another died for love of a dragon, none of her line would transform without madness again.'"

"For love of a dragon," I muttered.

"My mother spoke of you, too." Folmon's voice turned soft. "She knew she did not have my father's love. Respect and admiration, yes, but not love."

"And he killed himself for me?" My voice rose. "He knew if he died, I would transform into a dragon? Who does that!" I cried harder. "I didn't want to be a dragon! I was trying to save *him*!"

Folmon ignored my tears. "And now his people are safe, and his vow to you is fulfilled." He stood and turned away but hesitated and said, "I don't blame you. He made his choice, but you should not linger in the Green Lands. My people will grow apart until I can unite them under my rule. And some may wish to harm you."

Swallowing, I gave him a small nod and rose from the bed. The clothes on my body were different from the ones I'd worn before my—I gulped—*transformation*, but they were still stained and dirty. My pack lay on the floor next to my sword. I slipped them both on and, without another word, stepped into the late afternoon light.

My heart sat like lead in my chest as I walked toward the plateau and the forest beyond. Tents and small cooking fires littered the fields around me. I shot a glance over my shoulder at the smoldering castle, its walls bent and broken. I hoped the servants inside had escaped, but I couldn't seem to scrounge up much worry for them.

Numbness enveloped me. I'd won—my kids were home and waiting for me—but I'd lost so much.

A flash of Kalo's face, young and smirking at me in the caves while I waved my sword at him, made tears prick at my eyes again. I hurt for Syfa too, and Folmon, and all the goblins who'd lost a strong, fair ruler so I could fly in the sky and chomp on the crazy fae queen.

A snort of laughter bubbled.

Had the events of the previous weeks and months made me hysterical?

I trudged on and started the slow climb up the steep cliff to the forest above. The darkening sky announced the coming evening. I needed to stop and set up a camp for the night, but my tired stupor kept me going upward and onward.

When I finally reached the top of the plateau, I paused and looked at the valley behind me. Smoke from thousands of goblin campfires hung heavy in the air like a fog across the landscape. I could barely glimpse the shining lake beyond, and the castle was no longer in sight.

I smiled a little and turned to the forest.

Signs of the army's passing—broken and trampled bushes, churned mud—marred the woods, and I wondered where they'd surfaced from the goblin caves. But then I stopped wondering. I didn't care. My hollow chest made it impossible to care about anything.

I meandered in what I thought was the correct direction and let the sounds of the night forest soothe me—the squeak of a mouse or bat, and the rustle of leaves in the cool breeze.

After a little while, I altered my course, still wandering aimlessly, until a sour smell permeated the air. I stepped into a clearing and found the bodies of the Slaugh hounds that had chased Shane and me, stacked and rotting next to a fallen log. This was the clearing where the fae had caught us. Which meant this was the clearing where Shane died.

I fell to my knees, ignoring the sharp stones digging into my bones, and looked at the bodies with sightless eyes. The breeze swirled harder, and I flinched, blinking to release the piece of dust that had flown into my eye.

I staggered to my feet and approached the funky-smelling corpses. My ears rang.

No, not my ears. Something tangible made the ringing sound.

I jumped to my feet and ran to the other side of the clearing, where a pale blue glow illuminated the sleeping forms of Shane and my wyrm.

A silent scream fell from my lips, and I dropped to my knees beside them. The wyrm woke and chimed a greeting, blinking its numerous eyes at me, and I stroked my finger along its spine.

"Oh, you sweet thing," I breathed. "Were you keeping him company?"

It chimed again and purred, wriggling a little, its body rising and falling slowly with Shane's sonorous breaths.

I curled up beside them, tucking Shane's arm around my shoulders and stretching my arm across his chest, my leg draped across his thighs. Tremulous but eager hope unfurled in my heart.

"You didn't leave me," I whispered, knowing he couldn't hear me.

My finger rasped along the wyrm's scales, and its humming grew louder. "I'm going to keep you, too," I told it. "And I'm naming you Lucky."

Then I listened to the combination of purrs and Shane's light snores for a long time before my eyes finally drifted shut.

THE sunlight woke me, and I hurried to move the hound corpses far away from Shane's still-sleeping body. After burning them to ash to get rid of the smell, I set up the tent and dragged Shane inside. Lucky seemed content to stay with him, so I wandered the woods, searching for food ideas.

I had no success until I found a narrow creek. I flipped over some rocks, uncovered a handful of crayfish, and stuffed them in my bag.

Back in the clearing, I made a small fire and roasted them, hoping the scent would wake Shane. It didn't, so I ate them and went back for more.

A few hours later, while roasting the second batch of crustaceans, I nearly fell into the fire at the sound of Shane's scratchy voice emerging from the tent. Catching the skewer before it fell into the flames, I set it aside and scrambled for the tent. I burst through the flap, tripped, and sprawled across Shane's warm body. He grunted and banded his arms around me. Snuggling into his chest, I breathed in his citrus and pine scent and fought to swallow the knot burning in my throat.

"You're alive," I said, my voice breaking. "I thought—" My nose ran, and I ducked my head to wipe it on my sleeve. I cleared my throat and tried again. "They told me—"

I burst into tears and wailed, releasing days of pent-up anguish against his neck. I vaguely registered his hands in my hair, stroking my back. I was lost in a maelstrom of emotion. I sobbed out my relief that Shane was okay and my deep grief that Kalo was not. Those feelings, combined with the overwhelming relaxation of my worry for Finn and Dara, broke me to pieces, and it felt like I would never stop weeping.

Eventually, my tears slowed, and after a few embarrassing hiccups, I lay silently on Shane's chest, absently tracing a finger along the hair curling there.

I sniffed and exhaled, then propped my chin on my fist to face him. Aside from the worry in his blue eyes, his face looked the same—handsome and steady, with the slight trace of a scar on his cheek, presumably earned during the fight against the hounds.

I stroked the mark with my fingertip. "What happened in the kitchen? Do you remember?"

His lips twisting into a frown, Shane's gaze

went distant. “I don’t quite remember. I think you fell, and someone was standing over you. One of the kids screamed. And I transformed. I think it was instantaneous.”

I sighed. “That’s what I figured. I woke up and you were running with me in the woods, and we were being chased by the hounds.” I dropped my finger to his lips. “You saved me. You fought off the hounds.”

Shane shook his head. “I remember that part. My strength was waning. I had two of them down, but the third was staying just out of my spear’s reach. Your salamander dropped on top of it from a tree and bit it.”

I grinned. “Wyrm, not salamander.”

Shane smiled back, his lips shifting under my fingertips, and deep longing curled in my stomach. I met his eyes and left my hand in place. Driven to touch as much of him as possible, I settled more firmly across his body.

His eyes darkened.

“Then I was out, I guess,” he finished. “What happened to you?”

I told him everything—waking in the castle, the bargain, Kalo’s death, and my transformation . . .

When I finished, I furiously blinked away the tears pooling in my eyes.

“I’m so mad at him,” I confessed, my voice small. “I didn’t even get a chance to say goodbye. And his son”—I exhaled noisily—“he watched the whole thing.”

The tight band encircling my heart grew more rigid, and I pressed my hand over it, as though it would stop the ache.

Shane gripped my hand, holding it to his chest. "He was old, you said." His voice was soft. Gentle.

I nodded.

"He lived his life. He raised his son. He prepared his people for war. And he chose to help you. He knew your ability to control your dragon gave his people their best hope at winning the battle. He made a difficult but ultimately understandable choice."

Sitting back, I stared into Shane's eyes and shook my head. "Maybe I'm not explaining it correctly. I was holding the knife. I *cut* his *throat*." I made a slashing motion with my hand and then stared down at it, horrified. "I *killed* him," I repeated, and the leash around my heart tightened until it snapped. A keening noise rose in my throat, but I held my breath until it subsided. As if holding my breath somehow made up for my actions.

I'd let Kalo sacrifice himself for me. And I despised the large part of me that overflowed with relief that he'd done it. I couldn't even begin to process the complex web of misery, regret, and gratitude in my soul. And love—unending love for my friend who sacrificed everything for the love he had for me—love he couldn't name.

My lungs emptied with a whoosh when Shane pulled me down again. I lay flat on top of him, our chests pressed together and our breaths mingling. He held my head in place so I was forced to stare into his eyes or close my own. I stared.

"He made his choice," Shane said again, the force in his tone shaking me. "And you need to respect it."

His irises contracted and expanded, blowing out the cobalt blue of his eyes. His lips were so close to mine.

Lowering my head slowly, giving him time to move away, I brushed my lips once, twice across his.

A feral noise tore from Shane's throat, and he wrapped a hand around the back of my head and clasped me to him.

His mouth was hot, and I reveled in the fire it built in my core. I wriggled my legs to straddle him, a low moan slipping free as my senses swam.

With a groan, Shane abruptly pulled away and I sprawled sideways on the tent floor, squinting at the ceiling while my senses worked to come back online. My skin flushed; my lips burned.

Shane cleared his throat, a deep growly sound, and I turned to look at him.

"This is grief, Willa," he said to the ceiling, "and I want to help you process it, but not like this. Not when it means more to me."

I blinked at him, a smile spreading across my face. "You're protecting me from myself?"

When Shane sat up, it was his turn to blink at my smile.

"I am grieving," I said slowly. "But you're

not just a distraction. When I thought you were dead"—my breath hitched, and I looked down at my clenched hands—"I felt such grief as you can't imagine."

I reached over and stroked my fingers through his, feeling our calluses scrape together. "I thought you'd left me behind again, to where I couldn't follow."

I met his eyes. "I don't want to wait anymore and make safe choices. I don't want to think about all the things that could go wrong. I want to celebrate that you're alive and I'm with you. I want to think about all the things that could go right. I want to show you how much I love you, Shane. Will you let me?"

With a sigh, Shane pulled me back into his arms and rested his chin on top of my head, indecision weighing his shoulders down.

I shifted and traced my lips across his neck, sucking gently. His skin tasted like sunshine and sweat. I licked along his collarbone and found myself airborne again as Shane flipped us and braced himself on top of me. His lips found mine once more, and this time they were wet and soft.

Relaxing into the dreamy warmth of his embrace, I explored the hollows of his mouth until my head filled with the scent of citrus and pine. Shane's languid kisses traveled from my lips to my collarbone and back again until my legs shifted restlessly. His mouth grew harder and full of demands.

I arched under him, meeting those demands with my own. I stroked my fingers across his golden chest until, slipping a hand between us, I pulled at the laces on my pants.

Pushing my hand aside, Shane whispered, “Let me, baby.” A thrill moved through me as his mouth trailed across my chest, his lips leaving hot, wet marks on my shirt before he tore it off with a muffled groan. His lips on my skin were heaven. I sighed, lifting my hips as he tugged my pants down and tossed them away.

My fingernails traced the muscles of his back, and the heat in my core tightened to a kernel of need. He stopped to nuzzle along the skin of my abdomen. I let out a low whimper.

He cupped me and stared into my eyes. “Do you want me here?”

I moaned in response, reaching down to grab his fingers and slide them where I needed them most. He grinned against my thigh and caressed me with his thumb. His touch was both rough and gentle, and my breath shook as I dug my nails into his thick wrist to urge him on.

Delicious warmth spread from his touch, traveling through my body in a steady strum. My back arched, my hips rolling in time to his strokes. Shane whispered something too low for me to hear. I detonated, my body curling into his hand as I bit back a shriek. My nipples tightened, and a wave of pleasure spread from the tips of my toes to the roots of my hair.

When I recovered, I looked down to meet Shane's gaze and grinned at the satisfaction on his face. "Don't get cocky," I warned. "It's been a while."

His eyes turned predatory. "Then let's go again," he growled.

What felt like hours later, as he slowly pushed his hot length inside me and began to rock, his hands gripping my hips with feverish strength, my moans turned to breathless screams. My heart opened as wide as the night sky above us, and we climaxed together to the sound of his triumphant laughter.

LUCKY had eaten the crayfish at the fire, so I returned to the creek for a third time and finally fed Shane his dinner.

Later, we lay by the smoldering coals, and I watched the smoke drift into the vivid sky while reflecting on everything that had happened. It felt like a lifetime ago that I'd taken Finn and Dara to the playground, beginning the whole chain of events leading to Iris's death. And then Kalo's. I knew their deaths weren't my fault, but I felt the weight of my decisions like an albatross around my neck.

Shane's warm presence at my back helped a little. I knew now he wouldn't leave me— he would fight for me and for my kids to his dying breath. And I knew I wanted to be with him, not just for those reasons, but because he lifted me up; he made me soar. He made my pulse race and my blood sing, and the pain of my wounded heart lessened in his arms.

I felt selfish for keeping him, but I wouldn't let him go. He was mine now. As I was his.

I laid my head against his shoulder and smiled at the fire.

"What's that smile for?" he asked.

"You. Thanks for waiting for me to catch up."

CHAPTER 22

In the morning, I ate the bean sídhe. Well, I didn't eat her *exactly*.

She woke us with her scream, and I startled so hard I slammed my forehead into Shane's chin and saw stars.

Recognizing the wail, I leaped from the tent, rage rampaging through me like fire. The bean sídhe had led the hounds to Shane after we fled the castle. She deserved to die.

She stood at the edge of our camp, and I could tell she felt emboldened after her earlier actions. Her unearthly eyes gleamed with malice. Her mouth gaped impossibly wide, preparing another shriek, likely to call another nasty wildfae toward our camp, and I dipped my fingers into my chest and lifted the smoldering coal of my magic.

Unlike the first and second times I transformed and my mind had spun with disorientation, my body knew what to do, even without Finn's blood to jumpstart me. I stretched and snapped into my new shape, thrusting my wings out wide enough to brush the trees at the far sides of the clearing.

The bean sídhe gaped, then shimmered as if she'd turned invisible, but my dragon eyes could see her sidling backward, away from the clearing.

I bent my head and bit her in half. She struggled briefly, caught in my teeth, and the sensation made me gag. I spat out her torn body with a large gob of saliva.

Eyeing the mess distastefully, Lucky climbed up my neck to chime in my ear, and I bobbed my head in agreement. Maybe no more biting the bad guys.

A noise from the tent made me turn my massive head. In the pink morning light, Shane watched me, his eyes bulging wide. My gaze fell to his nude form, and I licked my lips with a sibilant hiss.

He paled and moved his hands to shield himself. My dragon body shook with laughter, and I dropped the coal, falling back into my human form. Strolling forward, I grabbed hold of what his hands sought to protect.

"I promise it won't hurt when I gobble you down," I purred.

Shane's eyes rolled back in his head, and he followed my tight grip into the tent.

AFTER a morning spent learning each other's bodies all over again, we packed up and made haste toward home. I didn't know if it were because the creatures of the Green Lands still reeled from Mab's death or if they were hiding from their new goblin overlords, but we encountered no more wildfae as we hiked and camped across the landscape.

The new dragon piece of my soul preened, telling me it was because we'd eaten the bean sídhe. I didn't disagree with her.

When the familiar narrow river came into view, the tension in my body deflated. Shane picked up the pace and I followed toward the site of his key. The glowing green symbols he sketched on the ground were familiar now, and I traced one of them on my hand. Could I learn this language? I still had the book Folmon had given me with the curse's translation.

We crossed realms, the dreadful sensation only slightly twisting my stomach, and then we stood in the woods behind Iris's house. My knees weakened with both relief and new worries.

With a deep breath, I tugged Shane's hand and jogged through the trees. "What if the magic failed? Or Mab cheated the vow?" My voice caught. "W-What if they're not here?"

Shane yanked me to a stop and pulled me close for a hard kiss. I relaxed into his grip, my stress ebbing from my limbs at his touch. He was really good at that.

He released me and brushed my hair back from my face. "With Mab dead, all the mind magic and guises she wrought will have vanished. The kids' records, their stuff—everything will be as it was. We just need to get to a police station and identify you, then find where the foster system placed them."

The reality of the situation hit home, and the saliva in my mouth dried up. "I have to go to court now to get them back, right? I've been gone for a month, at least. And they returned without me. This is a mess." My hands gripped my elbows and my shoulders hunched.

Shane's hand at my back steadied me. "It may take some time, yes, but the important thing is they're free and you're home. They're safe, wherever they are, and they're waiting for you."

I nodded briskly, blinking away tears. I knew he was right.

TWO months later, the four of us stepped through the doorway of Shane's house, and the jagged pieces of my heart seemed to come together. It had taken so long to sort out the details of our disappearance, the fire, and the fact the kids had reappeared days before me . . . but finally, we were together again. My joy knew no bounds, but it still seemed surreal.

Every day, I'd visited the kids at their foster home, yet the wait had been agonizing for all of us. Shane's steady presence had grounded me—like always—and I loved the life we were building together. This moment was the one I'd dreamed of when it felt I couldn't continue.

I held each kid's hand in my own. Would I ever manage to let go? The time apart had hardened my babies, and my soul wrenched at the wariness painted across their sweet faces.

With time, I believed we would figure it out. Together.

Inside Shane's familiar living room, the kids sat on the couch. Shane and I faced them, our fingers linked. Finn eyed our hands with a scowl on his face, but Dara only had eyes for me.

"We have to make some choices now, guys," I said, studying their faces. "We have magic in our blood, less here than in the Green Lands, yes, but enough that we may be in danger from the fae again."

"From our father," Finn corrected, his sharp shoulders hunched forward.

My fingers itched to smooth the hair from his brow and reassure him nothing would hurt him again, but I'd learned such promises were naive and unwise. Instead, I swallowed and continued. "Yes, from Paul, and from any other fae who may sense us here."

"What are we going to do?" Dara asked.

I straightened my spine. "We're going west, like we originally planned. We'll go to California; to the beach." Finn perked up, his expression brightening with enthusiasm. "And we'll begin to learn about our magic."

Finn narrowed his eyes. "Uncle Shane's going too?"

Shane squeezed my fingers. "Yes. I am going to teach you and keep protecting you, like I promised."

"And Mama too?" Dara asked.

Shane blushed and glanced at me out of the corner of his eye. I grinned, and he nodded, returning his attention to Dara. “And your mom.”

“Good,” she said, then launched her small body off the couch in our direction. Shane caught her like they’d practiced the move a million times.

He swung her up over his shoulder and offered a hand to Finn. “Want to help me get the RV rental this time?”

Finn’s answering grin settled my nerves, and I waved them off. Humming a little, I stepped into the kitchen to start a grocery list. I wanted us on the road as soon as possible. Lucky crept from my shirt pocket where it liked to snooze and draped around my neck with a heavy purr. I stroked its spine as I grabbed a pen.

The door opened, and a small green goblin child stepped inside. It took a long moment for my brain to catch up to my magic, but when it did, I banked the fire I held in my hands.

I studied him. He eyed me back, his shoulders straight and his black hair shaved into a mohawk behind the stubs of two small horns.

“Willa Overholt?” His strange pronunciation held a musical lilt.

“Hello,” I said, lifting my eyebrows.

“I am Connak, son of Folmon, son of Kalonymos. You killed my grandfather.”

My lungs compressed, but I dropped my chin in acknowledgment of his accusation.

“My father sends me to you and requests a

boon." He handed me a letter, his crimson eyes tight with worry, and I resisted the urge to hug him. He looked so much like that goblin child I'd rescued a lifetime ago. I wondered at Folmon's decision to send his son so far from home. Years must have passed underground since Kalo died on that battlefield.

I swallowed and read the note. I'd been practicing with Shane.

Lady Willa,

Dark deeds occur in the Green Lands in the aftermath of the death of Queen Mab. The father of your children, Paul, has gained a place of power at the new Court with the sacrifice of many half-fae and goblins. I send to you my son for safekeeping, as I feel in my heart you will protect him as one of your own.

My head spun, but I kept reading.

Let him grow slowly and with care, and I will send for him when my people are ready once again to war. In return, he will guard you from the fae who search for the dragon's children. Beware.

The letter fell from my numb fingers, and I looked up. The boy placed a hand at the hilt of the small sword sheathed at his hip. "Yes. They are coming for you. Again."

ABOUT THE AUTHOR

K. Panikian

K. Panikian lives in Massachusetts with her partner and three children. Aside from reading and writing, she enjoys golf and snowboarding.

Check out her website at www.kpanikian.com

BOOKS BY THIS AUTHOR

Yellowstone Shifters

The world is divided into territories and every shifter, from the elk to the wolves and big cats, belongs to a pack, subject to the dominance hierarchy and the whims of its alpha. But pack life isn't for everyone—there are some shifters who just don't belong. In the neutral national parks, the exiles make their home.

From Book 1:
"My name is Sienna Wilder and up until about age twelve, I thought I was human."

From a young age, Sienna learned to control the savage creature that raged in her heart. Swearing never to unleash the puma again, she kept her head down, her emotions level, and she survived.

Inside though, she yearned to find a place where she could roam free. Landing her dream job as a park ranger at Yellowstone, Sienna thinks she's finally found it, only to discover that she's not the only one with a secret beast. Now, women are disappearing and no one is paying attention. Sienna must discover the truth or she may be next. Can she learn to trust her wild side in time to save herself and the others?

Varangian Descendants

A thousand years ago, a Varangian cohort deployed to the steppe disappeared without a trace, banished to a parallel world. On that parallel world, the soldiers and their families fought monsters and learned magic. Now, in the present day, the realms are colliding once more and the Varangian descendants must work together to stop a demonic horde from invading the modern world.

Summoned from grad school, Verena must learn to master her new magic and lead her family to war. Torn from everything she once knew, Astrid must find the portal; find the dragon. Suddenly on a journey that leads to a place she never imagined, Callie must face her fears and choose her destiny.

From the snowy Urals, to the vast, arid steppe, to the mysterious Bermuda Triangle, and to the parallel world full of gods and monsters and magic, the Varangian descendants will confront their greatest enemy and forge a new future together.